The Fiery Spiral Trilogy

— BOOK ONE —

The Thousand Steps

BY HELEN BRAIN

CATALYST PRESS
San Bruno, California

Catalyst Press

California, USA

The Thousand Steps, Book 1, The Fiery Spiral trilogy

For further information,
email info@catalystpress.org.

Originally published in 2016 in South Africa
by Human & Rousseau, an imprint of NB Publishing.

FIRST EDITION 10 9 8 7 6 5 4 3 2 1
Library of Congress Cataloguing-In-Publication
Number: 2019944738

Cover design and illustrations by
Karen Vermeulen, Cape Town, South Africa

For Denise Ackermann

who knows about the Goddess.

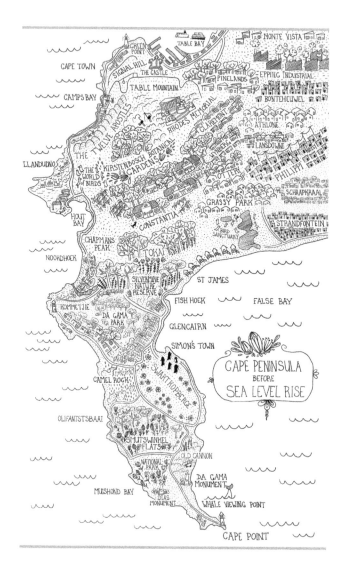

CAPE PENINSULA
BEFORE
SEA LEVEL RISE

MILITARY POST
ENTRANCE TO THE COLONY
TABLE MOUNTAIN
-THE COLONY-
THE SHRINE
THE ORPHANAGE
THE TWELVE APOSTLES
RHODES MEMORIAL
LYNBERG HILL
GREENHAVEN
HARBOUR
BOAT BAY
CHAPMANS PEAK
ARMY BARRACKS
SILVERMINE SOUND
CAVES
SILVERMINE ISLAND
SWARTHOPBERGE
CAPE PENINSULA
AFTER
THE FLOOD
CAPE POINT ISLAND

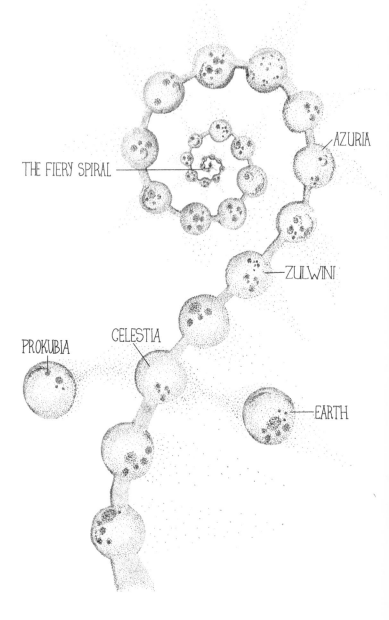

THE FIERY SPIRAL

AZURIA

ZULWINI

PROKUBIA

CELESTIA

EARTH

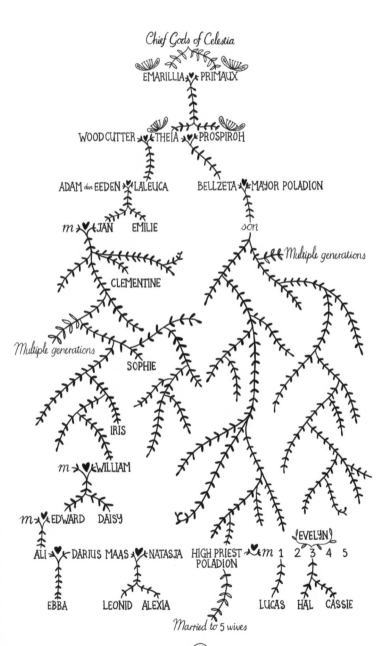

Prologue

Long ago, before Earth was created, all living creatures journeyed through numerous worlds during numerous lifetimes. God or mortal, they faced trials that proved them worthy to move onwards, closer to the Fiery Spiral that burns with love and is the heart of all that is.

But not every living being wanted to face their trials. Those who lacked the courage to look in the eye the thing that frightened them most stayed in their world, coming up against the same weakness again and again, until they had confronted and conquered it. Then, strengthened and purified, they were ready to move on.

It was such a weakness that caused a conflict between the gods of Celestia. A conflict that lasted millenia and resonated far beyond their own world. The cause of the conflict was a powerful necklace. Their battleground was Earth.

Myths of Celestia:
The birth of Theia and Prospiroh.

Under the branches of a spreading Ficus tree, the great goddess Emarillia and her husband Primaux awaited visitors. The queen, belly swollen, was embroidering a pattern of fern fronds on a tiny vest. For many years they had longed for a baby, and soon their child would be born.

"The elemental gods," a herald announced.

Four shimmering figures emerged from the forest. The first was a woman dressed in fiery red that vibrated against her ebony skin.

The second woman was so pale she was almost translucent. Her robe was grey-white and a spray of mist surrounded her.

Behind her the two men were as striking as the women. One had hair the color of soft earth and a beard as thick as lichen. His robe was a rich loamy brown. The last man was tall, with long hair that rippled like water. His robe was aquamarine with a border that curled like the crest of a wave.

"Your majesties, we are here to pay homage to your child," the Earth god said with a bow. "In time, you will leave this world and move upwards to the next. This necklace gives your child the power to rule over each of our elements, earth, fire, wind and sea."

"Used well, it will bring balance and harmony to Celestia, and all the worlds below us." The water god's voice rippled like a mountain stream.

The queen's robes fluttered as the wind goddess's words blew across the clearing. "But used badly, it will cause untold pain and destruction."

The four gods stepped forward and knelt at Emarillia's feet. The fire goddess presented the necklace to the queen. But instead of moving back like the other gods, she rested her hands on the queen's swollen belly. "You carry two children, your majesty."

The queen laughed. "There's only one baby, of that I am certain."

"There are two, my queen." The fire goddess flared up, making the amulets sparkle in the sudden light. "I feel them in your womb."

"We have consulted the oracles." Primaux's rich voice echoed through the trees. "There is one child. We thank you for your gifts."

It was time for them to leave, but the four gods had gathered together, whispering.

"My queen," the water god said at last. "We request that the amulets be divided between the two children. The boy, Prospiroh, must have dominion over fire and air. The girl, Theia, will govern earth and water."

"There is only one child," the queen insisted. "Such a beautiful necklace will never be split."

That night the queen went into labor. She delivered a baby girl, a healthy child with hair like flame.

"She's a bonny, strong baby," the midwife said. "You rest now, your majesty."

Suddenly the queen arched her back and screamed. There was a flurry among the women. The midwife felt her belly. "There's another baby."

For hours the queen battled. The first baby was lying backwards, and she was tired. Finally, the baby emerged, bottom first, screaming, streaked with blood. The queen collapsed, exhausted.

The women whispered to each other as they washed the baby in the stone basin. He was healthy and strong, but a birthmark covered the left half of his face like black velvet. They wrapped him in a blanket and put him on her breast. The queen was too tired to open her eyes.

He seized her nipple in his mouth and fed hungrily. They brought the little girl and lay her in the crook of the queen's other arm.

When the queen finally opened her eyes, she took one look at her son's face and shrieked. "He's damaged. The king will never accept a child so ugly." She pushed the child off her breast. "Get rid of him," she cried. "Take him into the forest and leave him for the wolves. The king must never know he was born."

She sobbed bitterly, rocking her red-haired daughter as the nurse wrapped the screaming baby boy in a sheep-skin and called the queen's most trusted guard. "This baby is deformed," the nurse whispered. "Take it into the forest and leave it there. Never tell anybody or I will have you killed."

A horse was already waiting, and the guard rode away. But instead of going into the forest, he turned towards the distant mountains. Beyond them lay a small town where his wife waited; his sad eyed wife with the barren womb.

Chapter One

I jolt awake, drenched in sweat. I dreamed the walls were crushing me as the roof and floor pushed together, squeezing the air from my lungs. No matter how long I stare at the ceiling—tracing the pattern of speckles in the rock, waiting for my heart rate to slow—the sense of foreboding doesn't leave.

I roll over. Is Jasmine awake? Her bed is empty. Letti's in the bed below me, mouth open, snoring gently. She stirs as her twin Fezile coughs in his bunk across the aisle. She murmurs something, a frown tugs her eyebrows, and then she's asleep again.

I swing my legs over the edge and find the rungs of the ladder in the semi-darkness, trying not to wake Letti. She and Fezile need to sleep. They must look as strong as possible today.

I pad quietly down our sleeping chamber—fifty sabenzi groups, a hundred double bunks, one hundred ninety-eight sleeping sixteen-year-olds. How many beds will stand empty tonight?

At the end of the last bunk are the small cells where our housemothers sleep. I check Ma Goodson's door, closest to the entrance. It's firmly closed, and the light is off. I tiptoe past—she's a light sleeper and has a sixth sense about her three sabenzi groups. At the slightest sound, she comes to check on us.

Jasmine must be in the bathroom. But the fifty toilet stalls are empty, the stainless steel showers and basins gleaming against the rock. She's gone.

I sink against the wall as a thought hits me like a falling rock. What if they've come in the night and taken her? Keep calm, I tell myself. Why would they take Jaz? She's healthy as an ox and strong. It's not her we have to worry about.

I creep back through the sleeping cell and out into the wide corridor that runs in a circle around the ventilation shaft. It's a little lighter here—the year threes have started their treadmill shift, generating the electricity we'll need to get going for the day. I peer into their two sleeping cells. Both empty. Those who aren't running on the treadmills are preparing breakfast and tending to the animals.

My heart starts pounding as I near the last of the ten sleeping cells. I'm almost back to where I started, and there's no sign of her. An armed guard sits in front of the metal door to the stairwell. He's staring into space, half asleep, and barely registers my presence.

I'm about to go and wake Ma Goodson when I hear a sob.

Of course. She's in the cupboard, under the stairs. It's where the memory boxes are stored—all 1,999 of them, deep square metal cases issued to each set of parents to fill with memories for their child to know where they came from. And one non-standard, non-issue cardboard shoebox with a necklace and a baby blanket inside it. Jasmine knows so much about her family—she knows the names of the Indonesian ancestors who were brought to the Cape as slaves by the Dutch hundreds of years ago. She knows what her family ate and drank, how they celebrated birthdays and weddings. I envy her.

I don't have a proper memory box like everyone else. Ma Goodson found me a empty shoebox so I wouldn't feel left out. It was small, but that didn't matter, because all I had to put inside it was a necklace and a baby blanket.

The memory cupboard was our secret hideout when we were small. I should have guessed Jaz would be here.

I open the door a crack. There she is, huddled under the shelves. I crawl in next to her. "Tight fit, huh? We used to all fit in easily, remember?"

In the half light from the ceiling bulb, I catch a glint of tears in her eyes. She brushes them away, and the mask of "I'm feisty, don't mess with me" is back in place. It's become almost part of her lately, and I don't often see the laughing, mischievous girl who has been my best friend for sixteen years.

"Couldn't sleep?" I ask.

She shakes her head, her corkscrew curls bouncing.

"Me neither. Too many nightmares."

She bites her lip. "You know this is just the start, hey."

"What do you mean?"

"Last time the High Priest chose three of us to be sacrificed. Today he'll take double that. He won't stop there. He'll be back soon, picking off the weak and sickly. And there are going to be more and more of us becoming too weak to work."

"It's the growing medium, isn't it?" Our sabenzi group works in the plant nursery, preparing the seedlings for transplanting into the revolving planters. They have to be fed regularly with a liquid growing medium that gives them the nutrients they need. It's that liquid that is running short.

"Mrs. Pascoe has started watering it down. Haven't you noticed how pale it is?"

"And the seedlings are spindly. None of us are getting the nutrients we need anymore." I don't want to think about where this is going, but I must. "And when it's all used up?"

Jasmine's hair falls across her face, but not before I've caught the shine of rising tears. "They'll shut the ventilation shaft and bury us alive."

"What if we—if someone like Mr. Dermond or Ma Goodson, or all the mentors even—what if they spoke to the High Priest and got him to change his mind?"

She rolls her eyes. "Ebba, you think he cares what we think? He's been down here once—maybe twice in the sixteen years we've been shut inside. He doesn't even consider us human. We're just machines to feed him and the army. No, we have to find a way to escape."

"And then what? Everything is destroyed out there. The nuclear fallout killed every living thing, remember? How are we supposed to survive with no food, and water that's probably still contaminated?"

"We've only got the High Priest's word for it. Who's to know if he is telling the truth? It might be perfectly safe—it's been sixteen years. Surely the contamination is long gone? Things must be growing again by now. I would rather take my chances out there than die in a rock tomb. Just once I want to see what the world is like. Even if it's destroyed, which I don't believe."

We lean against each other, lost in our thoughts. It's the sky I long to see. I've seen it in Kinetika movies, of course, and in the reference books Mrs. Pascoe has in her office, but I want to see the real thing—does it really go pink at sunset? Do the clouds really change from bits of fluff like the feathers from a plucked chicken, to massive brooding mounds of grey and black? And rainbows—do they really exist? Or were they imaginary, like unicorns?

Jaz pulls her knees up to her chest and hugs them. "If I got out of here, I'd cross to the Mainland. I'd travel through every valley, climb every hill, search every cave, every scrap of land around Riebeek Kasteel to see if anyone in my family survived. My mom was a scientist. She must have made a plan. I'm sure she found some-where to hide."

"Then why haven't they come to find you?" It's too late to stop the words from coming out of my mouth, and her mask cracks. I see the real Jaz, the vulnerable, gifted, sensitive girl who feels too much and has to pretend to be tough to hide it. Because down here in the Colony, any sign of weakness is jumped on and attacked. We year fives are easy targets for the year ones. They're twenty-one soon, and they like to pull rank as much as the guards who watch us every waking minute.

"We've got to get out," she mutters. "There has to be more than one way out."

She's talking about the ventilation shaft that runs down the center of the mountain, through all the layers of the Colony from the High Priest's quarters, the army barracks, and right down to the sanitation and composting department at the bottom. Not that we've ever seen the shaft—the doors are heavily guarded.

"They'd never make a bunker with just one entrance," she continues. "It's common sense to have an escape route in case something blocks the main entrance."

"Jaz..." I take her hand and hold it tight in mine. "Remember what happened to Micah. Please don't go asking questions and causing trouble. What will Fez and Letti and I do if you aren't around anymore?"

She looks at me sideways from under her curly hair, and the tough mask that hardens her delicate features is back. "They probably won't be around much longer."

The sirens go off then, and we race to fetch our towels and soap and get to the bathroom before the morning rush. Letti is already there in the last cubicle, along with seven other girls. There's room for two more next to her, so we strip, hang up our clothes, and push our way through to the two last shower heads. Then there's the moment when we wait, holding our breaths, for the tap to be turned on and the water to hit us. We're so deep in the mountain that it's always freezing cold. Usually we're all still half asleep, trying to remain in that half-conscious space where we haven't remembered that the coming day will be as tedious and tiring as every other day. But today we wait, shivering, filled with unspoken tension, and instead of ignoring the naked bodies we've seen every day for the last sixteen years, we're glancing surreptitiously at each other, checking for signs of weakness or illness that might make us a soft target for the High Priest.

I'm shocked to see that everyone has lost weight lately. Ribs, once lightly covered, are emerging as bony ridges, and even Letti, who is naturally short and plump—cuddly, Ma Goodson calls her—has sharp collar bones and a deep hollow at the base of her throat. Her full name is Lithalethu. It means our ray of light, and it suits her perfectly. Always hopeful, always cheerful. Everybody likes her—but today her luck has changed.

The water blasts suddenly, and I gasp for air. Thirty seconds and it switches off. In unison, we grab our washcloths and soap and lather ourselves. Then Letti drops her soap. It slides across the smooth metal floor and lands at the feet of Greta Taylor, a tall, athletic girl with blond hair and a tongue like a blade. I tense up as Letti squints at the floor, her eyes scrunched up. She bends down and starts feeling for it against the floor. Quickly I step forward and retrieve it as the water comes on again. The thunder of fifty showers hammering rock is loud, but not so loud that we miss Greta's high pitched voice. "I hope he picks you, Letti. You're blind as a bat."

Jaz is in her face straight away, glaring up at her, fists clenched at chest level like a boxer. "Just watch it, you hear me? Watch it. If you cause any shit for Letti in the meeting, I swear I will hunt you down and cut you."

The water switches off, and the next group of year fives are waiting with their soap and washcloths in hand. I pass

Letti her towel, and we wrap ourselves up—as well as we can in towels that have been mended so often, they're as thin as rags.

Greta glares at Jaz, but when Jaz shoves her finger in her face and scowls, Greta turns away. Although she's the shortest girl in the Colony, everyone is wary of Jasmine. She's not afraid of a fight, she says it like it is, and she always keeps her word.

We're among the first at the refectory for breakfast. I take my tray and join the end of the nearest queue. The noise is usually overwhelming, with chattering, joking, always gossiping. We're endlessly fascinated by our quarrels, our rivalries, and the budding romances that must remain secret from our mentors and the guards. We discuss the mentors and how they relate to each other. There are two hundred of them, and just like us workers, they have their cliques, their goody two-shoes, their manipulators and bullies. Then there are the guards who are so mysterious to us because they barely speak, appearing every morning at the same time to watch over us, revolvers tucked in their holsters, their dark blue uniforms spotless; they disappear into the ventilation shaft at bedtime through the doors marked "Out of Bounds," and we speculate about what they get up to in their barracks on the higher level.

But today nobody is passing the time with gossip or jokes. Instead, we wait in uneasy quietness for the bowls of porridge that will keep us going until tonight.

The boy at the front of the queue, Primod—a long skinny Indian boy with sticking out ears—is arguing with the year three girl behind the service hatch who is adding protein milk to the bowls. He says it's been watered down. She says he's talking rubbish. The guard watching over the queue paces towards them, hand on his holster.

I'm wondering if causing a scene and having sticking

out ears is enough to make the High Priest choose you when the last group of boys troop in and join the end the queue. My heart drops as Fez enters and I compare him to the boys in the rest of our year. Although he's the smartest boy in our year, and is as popular as Letti, years of wheezing have taken their toll on him. He's a full head shorter than the other boys, and his chest is sunken. He gets his bowl at last and comes over to join us at our table. His full name, Fezile, means "I have accomplished it," and it is perfect for him because he's never let his asthma hold him back. He's just used his intelligence to work out smarter ways to do things.

Jasmine has kept a seat for him and she squeezes his shoulder as he sits down. We have ten minutes left to eat before the year fours arrive for their meal. None of us have much appetite, even Letti who never says no to food. I'm tempted to push our hardly touched plates across to Fez, but what good will three helpings of porridge do at this point? He's going to be chosen. I see it in the way Jasmine sits close to him, as though she's his body guard; in the way Letti stares at him with big, half-blind eyes; and in the way the other year fives whisper when he finally gets up to take his half eaten bowl to the sinks.

He's the cleverest person in the Colony, and that's something in a group of two thousand people chosen for the contribution their parents made to society. Everyone in the Colony is smart, but there are no lessons, almost no books. Yet Fez taught himself to read using Ma Goodson's first aid manual and the reference books in the plant nursery. Still, cleverness means nothing in a world where the ability to keep standing through twelve-hour shifts and to run fast enough and long enough on the treadmills to generate enough electricity to sustain us are the only things that matter.

Ma Goodson meets us in the sleeping cell when we go

back to brush our teeth and make our beds. She calls us into her room. We don't often go inside—it's her private space, and she's a private person who doesn't talk about herself much. Today her lip is giving that tiny twitch that means she's anxious, although she tries to hide it behind a jolly voice. She closes the door behind us, and I lean against the wall, breathing in the smell of her that fills this space, the sense of safety and love and warmth I always feel around her. Photos of a man and two children smile from frames on the wall. I asked her about them once, but she refused to answer, and I could tell from the tone of her voice that I shouldn't ask again.

Her room is the only colorful spot in the bleak grey rooms we live and work in. Her bedspread is a rich tomato red, although its got holes in it and the fringe is long gone. She's hung deep blue curtains on the wall behind her bed, and the green and gold cushions are like the jewels in the ring she wears on her wedding finger.

Fezile's whole chest shakes from a hacking, wheezing cough. Ma Goodson frowns as she rubs his back. She opens a drawer and takes out a small brown bottle, unscrews it, and hands it to him. "Here. Drink half now. It's buchu and aloe. It will stop you coughing for a while. Drink the other half just before the High Priest enters. Don't let the guards see you."

"We'll hide him in the middle of the row," Jaz says. "They won't see a thing."

"And Jasmine." Ma Goodson grabs Fez's cheeks between her thumb and fingers and squeezes until color runs into his ashy skin. "Pinch his face too. We need the authorities to think he's in peak health."

Letti squints at his face and Ma Goodson takes a second, smaller bottle from her drawer. "I don't know if it's still good," she says. "It's very old, but put a few drops into each eye before the meeting to take away the redness.

And whatever you do, don't scrunch up your eyes to help you see better. Look at the ground throughout."

She hugs her, cradling Letti's dark head against her shoulder. She's always had a soft spot for the twins, and for me of course—the one she called her laatlammetjie—the baby who arrived after all the rest, when they thought the Colony was complete.

Next she turns Jasmine around and tugs her hair out of her face, tying it back with a length of stretched out elastic. "Let them see this strong, handsome face," she murmurs, giving her pony tail a twist. "My girl. As true and hardy as the plant you're named for." Jasmine's mask drops for a second, but then she shakes her head and puts back her shoulders. She's the strong one, who keeps us going.

Her expression softens as she turns to me. "My gentle Ebba. What are we going to do with your hair?"

Letti gasps. "Ebba's not in danger, is she? Say she's not."

"We can never be too careful. People are suspicious about redheads. When my grandmother was a girl, she said redheads were common, but nowadays—I mean by the time of the Purification—there were almost no red-heads left." Her fingers are pulling and twisting, working my tangle of tight curls into two plaits. Then she pulls them around my head, weaving them together until it feels as though nothing will ever get them loose again. Lastly she takes a bottle of oil from her cupboard, pours a little into the palm of her hand, and works it into my hairline so that not even a tendril of hair can escape.

A pile of clean tunics and pants lie on the bed as well as four of the caps that we wear when we go to Shrine. "Put these on," she says. "I've been saving them for a time like this."

Like us, the mentors wear v-neck tunics and loose pants, but theirs are striped green and blue, whereas ours are plain undyed, and worn thin. Soon they'll wear through completely, and then we'll have to wear the thick, prickly sackcloth the weavers make for the storage bags.

But today we're in luck. The clothing Ma Goodson has put aside for us is virtually undarned, with no frayed edges. Ma Goodson takes care to pick the biggest cap for me. It comes down to my forehead, and as long as the High Priest doesn't get too close, hopefully he won't notice the color of my hair at all.

She takes us by the shoulders, one by one, and kisses us, her voice firm and sure. "I love you all. Stay positive, stick together, and I'm certain you'll be all right."

It's time to go. The bell is ringing, calling everyone to the meeting chamber, the only space in the bunker big enough to hold all 2,220 of us at once.

I look back as we join the throng. She's standing in the doorway, and she's not looking firm or certain of anything. She looks worried to death.

Chapter Two

The meeting hall crawls with guards brought down from the barracks on level two. I scan the benches looking for the best place to be invisible. The hall is massive, a round room with rock pillars in rows holding up the roof, which is double the height of the ceilings in the rest of the bunker. Wooden benches are arranged in rows around the central altar.

When we were younger we fit into the meeting hall easily, but now that we're all adult size, it's a real squash to get everybody seated. But today we can use that to our advantage by going into the middle of a row. So we're less visible for inspection by the High Priest.

We look for a bench near the back, where the rows are longer. But everyone's had the same idea and we're forced into a row about a third of the way from the front.

We push Fez right to the middle. His cheeks are still glowing, and he looks a bit healthier than usual. For now.

Letti is next to him. Then me and lastly Jasmine. Another sabenzi group fills the remaining four places.

Soon the hall is full, all five hundred sabenzi groups, plus two hundred twenty teachers, mentors and cell parents, all waiting in silence for the High Priest to descend from the top of the bunker. At last footsteps ring in the corridor outside. We keep our heads down, trying to be invisible, as the guards open the doors and the High Priest and a team of worship leaders march up the aisle. Letti shivers as the most feared man in the Colony, General de Groot, marches in, his medals glinting against his dark blue uniform with gold trim. I slip my hand into hers and give it a squeeze.

"Praise Prospiroh," the High Priest calls when he reaches the front. His golden robe glitters in the bright light ball above the altar.

"Praise Prospiroh," we respond in one voice.

I watch him carefully as he walks slowly around the altar with his hands in the air, followed by the six worship leaders, their long robes of rich purples, reds, and emerald greens—the most majestic garments I've ever seen. I watch him, trying to read his face. His eyes are dark and large, his jaw and shoulders square, and his hands long fingered and expressive. He lights the big brass burner and the worship leaders pull on the chain that raises it to the roof. Fragrant smoke pours out as they swing it across the expanse of the meeting hall.

"We are gathered here for the Sacrifice," the High Priest calls. "Prospiroh, the Source of our Abundance. He blesses us with strength and prosperity, but those who do not please him do not thrive. Their weaknesses, and diseases infects each one of us. Prospiroh desires that only the best, the strongest, abide in his Colony, preparing for the day when it is once more safe to return Above."

Am I really at risk of being chosen? I look different to everyone in the Colony with my red hair, green eyes, and olive skin. And then there's my birthmark. I pull my cap lower down over my forehead, and keep my left hand hidden.

General de Groot salutes the High Priest, then swaggers down the aisles, inspecting us row by row. He's a short stocky man with ruddy skin the color of aramanth seed, a jutting chin, and ice blue eyes that cut through the crowd, zooming in on us one by one. Behind him walks the High Priest, chin in the air as he looks down his nose, scanning us for imperfections.

Don't cough, Fez, I think. Just don't cough.

The General calls Shameema in year three—she broke her elbow falling off her bunk and it's bandaged up. He pulls out Jaco, the guy who lost an eye when Major Zungu hit him for backchatting. He picks Thandeka, Flora, and Elton, three year ones who are sneezing and coughing.

He's walking away from us.

Thank you. Thank you.

But then suddenly he turns and strides down our aisle, straight towards our row. I bend my knees deeper, keep my head bent down. My thighs are burning. I dare not look but I can feel his stare drilling into me. Sweat beads on my forehead but I can't wipe it away.

He's going to see how pale and thin Fez is. He's going to pick him.

He comes closer, closer. My heart is racing. He's next to Jasmine, looking down our row, but...but...oh...he moves on to the next row. "You," he says to the person behind me.

When I hear her scream I know who it is. It's Tanaka, the girl from the weaving gallery with the crooked back. "No, no, no," she screeches. "Not me. Don't take me."

We're frozen. Nobody argues with the General.

"Fetch her," he snaps, and a guard pushes into the row behind me.

"Not me, not me," Tanaka screams. "Ebba's got a birth-mark. Take her."

I shrink. Letti and Jasmine close in, packing me tight, gripping my hands. The General is examining me, assessing my value to him.

"A birthmark is nothing," he snaps. "She's strong. She can work."

The guard drags Tanaka out of the row. "No," she screams. "Not me, not me. Take Ebba. She's got witch's hair."

She grabs my cap. My hands fly up to save it, but it's too late. The cap comes away, it's in her hands, and the High Priest swoops our row, shoving the General aside. I don't move, I can barely barely breathe, Letti's hand shaking in mine.

He points straight at me. "You—you with the red hair."

I look directly at the High Priest for the first time. His face is hard and full of contempt. Without dropping his gaze, he jerks his head towards the altar.

I've been chosen? They've taken me, and left Tanaka behind? It's impossible. Her back is so twisted that she can barely work the looms. And I'm the best gardener in the plant nursery. I'm getting confused by the smoke swirling above our heads. It can't be me.

But he jabs me in the chest with his forefinger. "Do not waste my time."

Letti and Jasmine grip my hands like we're grafted together. But I've got to let go. I've got to leave them.

I want to throw myself at the High Priest's feet, beg for mercy—but I've seen his face. The sneer on his full lips. The hooded eyes burning with disgust. I stumble up the aisle and dare not look back.

The worship team steps forward and takes our arms. They lead us into the small room off the meeting hall where they keep supplies. It's been set up today with six chairs, and the worship leader—he's the one in the deep red robe—gestures to them and says, "Sit."

I'm dumb with shock. A strange woman unplaits my hair and brushes it, letting it flow down my shoulders in red curls. "I'm humbled to be working with you today," she says, as she paints my lips with a red salve. "You are so blessed. Everyone dreams of being chosen for the Sacrifice."

Is she crazy? Why would we dream of being killed? "What blessing can there possibly be in being picked out for not being perfect?" I want to shout. But there's no point in protesting. Not when there are guards with rifles at the door, and she obviously has absolutely no idea what it's like to live like ants crowded into the lower levels where we spend our lives. When she's finished painting my face, she opens a basket and brings out a white shift, pulls it over my head, covering my tunic and trousers. Then she takes a wreath of silk leaves, and places it on my head, clipping it into my curls with a pin. I look in the mirror, and don't even recognize myself. As though Ebba is dead already.

We're all ready now. The six of us, scared and pale, looking unfamiliar in the ghostly white shifts that float around us as we walk. The worship leader rings a bell and calls, "It is now time to bid farewell to your sabenzis and houseparents. Praying that Prospiroh will strengthen them, and all of us, by your sacrifice."

I look over at Fez. The Adam's apple is going up and down in his throat as he tries to think of something clever or funny to say and for once he can't think of anything clever or witty to say.

Jasmine's face is ashen. She twists her fingers in the hem of her tunic. This is one battle she can't win.

"We can make a run for it," she whispers, leaning into my ear. "I'll distract the guards, and you run for the door to the ventilation shaft."

I take her hands. Squeeze them. "There's no point in both of us dying. You have to look after these two."

"I hate these bastards," she hisses. "If I get a chance, I promise you, I'm getting us all out of here. We'll find a way to survive up there."

"Jazzy, no. Promise me you won't do anything dangerous...I don't have a choice but you do. You stay alive. You keep Fez and Letti alive. If I escape, I'll come and get you out too, I promise."

She holds out her pinkie finger like we did when we were little girls. "Deal. I promise to keep our Sabenzi team safe until you come for us.""

Ma Goodson comes in then, trying to look brave. "This is wrong..." she begins, but instantly, at the hint of anger in her voice, the guard lifts his rifle.

Jasmine tugs on her arm. "Don't do anything stupid," she hisses. "We need you."

Ma Goodson sighs, reaches in her pocket and takes out my necklace. "You need to take this with you, wherever you're going," she says, her voice cracking as she lifts my hair to tie the clasp.

"Please, Ma, don't you want to keep it?" My throat is so tight I can barely get the words out. "It's not going to be much use to me now."

"You arrived with it, you should leave with it." She's finished clipping the clasp, and the necklace falls into place, the silver charm with the brown stone hanging just above my breasts. The chain is heavy, formed from multiple strands of carved gold twisted into an ornate rope. It's tarnished after so many years in the memory box, and she polishes it on her handkerchief. She can't look at me as the tears run down her cheeks.

I want to hug her, to thank her for everything, but the worship leader announces, "It is time for the procession," and they usher everyone out of the room, force us into a line, and give each of us a lighted candle to hold. They throw open the doors and we're led out, followed by the worship team, who are chanting The Processional for The Long Night. Billows of smoke from sacred herbs loom up around us, and the tinkle of bells on the worship team's ankles and wrists gets inside my head until I think I'm going mad.

Back in the meeting room, the High Priest stands in front of the altar, chanting in his sonorous voice that resonates around the room. His hands are elevated as though he's pointing towards the world above.

When I'm two steps away from him, his chant falters. He's staring at me, at my necklace. Then his eyes flicker to my red hair and down to my hand, clutching the candle. He sees the birthmark and a strange, indecipherable look ripples over his face. I brace myself, thinking he's going to order a guard to shoot me right there and then, but his voice picks up the chant again, and we move on, down the aisle. My head swirls in the smoke and noise and heat. My knees wobble, and I'm going to fall. The faces of everyone I know, everyone I love, come in and out of focus as I stagger up the aisle.

Ma Goodson reaches out as I pass her in the front row. "Be strong. I love you."

The guard lifts his gun and hisses, and she drops back in line. I can't look when I reach the row where Jasmine, Letti, and Fez stand rigid with misery....I can't lose them. They are all I have.

"Open up," the General shouts.

The back doors open, and we step into the passage that leads to the ventilation shaft, the only access to the world above.

Chapter Three

Major Zungu struts towards us, the toxic mix of anger and power apparent in every swing of his arms and stride of his barrel legs. He assesses our size. He's relishing our fear as he pokes his sturdy forefinger right into our faces. "Useless scum," he snarls, and his too-close-together eyes bore right through me.

He gives a signal and six guards fall in line next to us. They march us down the gloomy tunnel while the worship team dances ahead, their bells jingling as they wave their arms, thanking Prospiroh for giving us the chance to sacrifice ourselves for the greater good.

I search the walls and roof for a way to escape, but I'm wasting my time. Like the rest of the bunker, this passage is carved out of solid grey rock, and armed guards stand in all the doorways. They're not going to kill us down here, in the Colony, or our bodies will bring diseases as they... as they...I can hardly think of it...as we rot. They are taking us somewhere where they can throw us out.

I'm going to have to cooperate for now. It's my only chance at surviving. But how will I know the moment to stop cooperating? What can I do to stay alive when I don't even know what's coming? Will I be able to survive the fall? I don't even know what the world is like above; if by chance I'm not killed, will I die of starvation? The High Priest and the General come bustling past, the guards gesture with their rifles, and we press ourselves against the walls. The High Priest looks straight ahead, chin in the air, but as he passes me, he stops midstride, looks back at my necklace, frowns briefly and is gone.

How did they kill Micah? I wonder as we reach the end of one corridor and turn down another. Did they bring him along this route? One day he asked the wrong question. The next day he was gone, taking part of my heart with him.

Maybe I'll meet up with him again, if there's an afterlife. They've always taught us that this world is all we have, but I've always wondered if it's true. I focus on imagining seeing him again, that golden brown body, the chipped front tooth, and the lock of straight black hair that fell across his forehead.

We reach the end of the passage. The High Priest and General have disappeared into the wooden Elevator and three guards shove the huge wheel, their shoulders taut, grunting with effort. We turn down a short passage to the left and stop at a grey metal door.

The worship leaders end their hymn. Major Zungu opens the door and gestures to us with his rifle. "Go."

And we're in the ventilation shaft. A metal staircase runs around and around the inside, clinging to the rock like a bean plant on a growing frame. A tiny circle of blue, the size of my fingernail, rests at the very top, so high I can barely make it out.

The sky.

The sky.

The sky!

I've finally seen it.

My guard nudges me with his gun. "Hurry up!"

I follow the others up the stairs. Fourteen steps then a sharp turn and up the next fourteen. A turn, another flight. I trudge on, holding up the hem of the white robe that threatens to trip me up.

"Where are you taking us?" I ask the guard keeping

pace with me, step by step.

Not a flicker crosses his face.

Did he even hear me? "Where are we going?" I repeat, louder. Still nothing.

I've got to try to work it out. What did they teach us about the Colony? That it's buried deep inside Table Mountain, on an Island that was once part of the continent of Africa. The top part of the mountain is sandstone. The lower half, where they built the bunker, is granite. Hard, impenetrable granite, where we'd be completely safe.

We've climbed six flights so far. By my reckoning we've passed the workshops, the weaving galleries, the plant rooms, the levels where the animals are kept. That's as high as we're allowed to go. Above that are the out-of-bound areas—the storage galleries, then the army barracks and the High Priest's chambers. Above that is nothing but six hundred meters of solid sandstone, with a web of ventilation tunnels running through them, like a termite's nest.

"That's the storage gallery through there, right?" I ask the guard as we reach another metal door opening onto a landing. Maybe there's a way out I haven't discovered yet.

"Shut up."

Shameema, the girl with the broken elbow, is in front of me. "What are you going to do with us?" she says, cradling her arm. "Are you going to shoot us?"

"They wouldn't waste their bullets," Jaco says wryly, looking over his shoulder as he turns up the next flight. "They're probably going to throw us over the edge of the mountain."

"I said shuddup," my guard snaps. "Get in there."

Major Zungu opens a door. We step into a low, narrow corridor, flooded at the far end with light. Bright, hard light, not the softer light refracted through mirrors and skylights.

A gust of wind hits us so hard, we have to grab each other to keep upright.

"We're in a side passage," Jaco exclaims.

"They're going to open the end and shove us out," Shameema says. Her voice cracks.

"But we're not at the top yet," Thandeka says. "Maybe we won't fall far."

I can hear the hope in her voice, but she's forgotten how high Table Mountain is. We haven't got a chance of surviving if they push us out.

What if, by some chance, I do come out of the fall alive? Everything is dead out there. No plants, no people, no animals. Even the water is irradiated and dangerous. Unless by some miniscule chance Jasmine is right, and the world has begun to recover. All I can see from here is bright blue. The bluest, most intense color I've ever seen. The sky...the sky...

We reach the end, and two guards undo the bolts that hold the thick metal grille over the opening. Shameema is sobbing, and I put my arm around her. Jaco hugs us both and sweat pours off him. Flora and Thandeka huddle together too, clutching each other. Elton stands stiffly alone, trying to look as though he doesn't care.

It comes undone suddenly, and the grille clangs to the floor. A blast of dust and dried leaves swirl inside. Major Zungu grabs Thandeka and shoves her towards the opening. She gives a sharp scream as she drops out of sight. I catch a glimpse of mauve mountains, across an expanse of vivid sea. "The Indian Ocean," Fez's voice says in my head. "Where it meets the Atlantic." But Shameema's deafening wail makes me turn away. I'm going to vomit, my mouth filling with saliva.

Now Major Zungu has Flora. Tears stream down her face as she wrestles with him. I look away too late. He's bashed her head against the wall, then tosses her out.

I try not to see the mess of blood and hair left on the wall.

"Save me, Prospiroh," Elton screams as the Major seizes him by the shoulders and pushes him towards the opening. "Saaaaave..." His voice ends abruptly.

"The witch next," Major Zungu snaps. He pulls me away from Jaco and Shameema.

"No!" I dig my heels into the floor, leaning backwards, but he shoves me to the edge of the tunnel. I cling onto the metal rim, teetering, half blinded by the light. Below are three blood-splattered bodies splayed on a rock ledge. Flora hangs half over the edge, her feet caught in a bundle of roots. Is she still alive? Waiting to fall even further to her death? I draw my elbow in and dig the Captain sharply in the gut.

He gasps and loosens his grip. I hit back again, but a guard catches my arms and twists them behind my back until I double over.

"Throw her out," Major Zungu pants.

I squeeze my eyes shut, struggling to kick the guard in the knee cap, but it's no use. I'm going over. They're too strong for me.

Suddenly footsteps ring in the passage. "Change of orders," a man bellows. "High Priest wants the redhead."

"She's all yours, Captain Atherton," the Major snaps, and the guard jerks me back inside so quickly, I hit the wall. I bend over, groaning, half pretending I'm going to be sick. Is this my opportunity?

I surreptitiously inspect the Captain as he gestures for me to start walking. He's lighter than the Major, but he's taller and fitter although his face isn't as hardened. But there's a revolver in his holster. Now is not the time to be uncooperative. Jaco and Shameema watch with huge eyes. They think something worse is waiting for me. Or is that hope that they'll also get a reprieve? I reach out to hug them, but the Captain shoves my shoulder and mutters, "Get moving."

As we reach the end of the passage, Shameema screams, her voice fading as she falls. The Captain doesn't flinch.

At the stairwell, he points with his thumb and we start climbing again.

Soon my thigh muscles are shaking with exhaustion and sweat drenches my clothing. But the circle of sky is getting bigger, light creeps into the stairwell, and I focus on the single puffy cloud. At least I got to see the sky, though it's little consolation. What's going to happen to me now?

We reach the last flight of stairs, and I look through the transparent dome at the vibrant, astonishing circle of sky, even bluer than the photographs in Mrs. Pascoe's books. Captain Atherton bashes on a door, and it opens from outside.

He pushes me through it, and I falter, expecting a cliff to open up at my feet, or an enraged General to greet me with a firing squad, but instead I'm in a room with one wall made of glass. I don't care if Captain Atherton shoots me. I have to see it. I dash across the room and press my face against the window.

The sky sweeps down to meet purple grey mountains rising from the blue green sea. I lean forward, peering down past the cliff face, expecting nothing but sand and ash. There are bushes, scrubby plants, but still living plants. A few dashes of yellow and pink splotches lie scattered between the rocks.

The world is alive. The world is alive!

Jasmine was right.

A hand drops on my shoulder.

This is it. The end.

I refuse to turn around. I need to see everything. Everything.

"You're a lucky girl, aren't you!" It's not Captain Atherton. The voice that speaks is soft and unfamiliar. He turns me towards him, a middle aged man, smiling broadly, as he sweeps me into his arms.

"My dear Ebba," he says. "We found you in the nick of time. I'm here to take you home."

Chapter Four

"Home?" This must be a joke. Any moment he's going to open the window and push me out.

But he squeezes me against him, saying again and again, "I can't believe we've found you. I simply cannot believe it."

"I'm not going to die?"

The man chuckles. "Certainly not. I am Fergus Frye, your lawyer, and we've been looking for you for sixteen years. You disappeared when you were a few hours old. And here you were all along, under our noses. In the *Colony*."

I pull out of his embrace and examine his face, trying to read his expression. They've been searching for me, and they didn't think to look in the Colony? Is he part of some elaborate trick by the High Priest to torture me psychologically? He isn't dressed like a soldier. His hair is pulled into a small knot on the top of his head, and he wears a flowing pale blue robe that reaches just above his ankles, with matching pants underneath.

I have so many questions to ask, but he opens a door and gestures to me to go ahead. "This way. I'm taking you home to Greenhaven."

Somewhere the High Priest and General de Groot are hidden away, watching my hope rising as all my dreams of going home come true. They must be laughing already, waiting for me to step out onto the mountainside so this strange smooth talking man can push me over the edge.

"Come along, dear."

A flight of stairs is carved into the rockface, with nothing but a flimsy railing to cling to.

The heat, the wind racing across the mountainside, even the air that smells so fresh—it's all making me dizzy. I cling to the doorframe, looking for a way to escape. But there's only the metal door leading back to the Colony. Captain Atherton stands in front of it. He salutes. "Congratulations, miss." Then he's gone, back into the stairwell.

"Come on, dear, don't be afraid," Mr. Frye says gently. "Take a moment if you need to."

There's nowhere else to run; staying here is not an option. I may as well do as he says. I take hold of the railing and take my first step into the outside world. A grey bird swoops past, its wings rising and falling so smoothly it seems to float. My eyes tear up as I watch it. Such a small creature, traveling fearlessly across that huge, huge sky.

"Ah, a pale chanting goshawk," Mr. Frye says. "Very rare. Now come along. We have a long drive ahead."

I focus on the pinch of yellow a few meters down, between two rocks. Just ten, fifteen steps and I'll be able to see it close up.

Mr. Frye's voice comes over my shoulder. "Good job, Ebba. Keep going."

I reach the yellow patch, and my heart jumps. It's a flower, growing close to the ground like it's scared to let go. Letti would love it.

If Fez was here, he would know its name. He wouldn't have trouble breathing in this clean air.

What are my sabenzis doing right now? Are they already back in the plant nursery, next to my empty work station? What if Jasmine has lost her cool? The guards will drag her out and throw her over the edge if she gives any trouble. The image of Thandeka, Flora, and Elton splattered on the rocks is too real still.

"Sir." I stop and look back at him. "Please can't we go back and fetch my sabenzis? They don't know I'm safe. They don't know the world is alive out here. Why—?" I start to form a question in my mind and then stop. I'm so confused by what is happening, I don't even know what question to ask.

"No dear, not today. Now come along, just a few more steps."

There's a bush further down—just past the big boulder that protrudes onto the stairs. It's got huge pink flowers and silvery leaves. I know these from Mrs. Pascoe's book. They're proteas. I'm going to keep looking at them, not at the mountain side below me, at how far I'd fall if he pushed me over. I'm not going to think of Jaz, Letti, and Fez broken hearted, thinking I'm dead.

We reach the bottom, and he pats me on the back. "Well done. Now where's my carriage?"

I look up at the mountain. A white cloud flows over the flat top—the tablecloth Ma Goodson told us about, the reason it was called Table Mountain. I've spent my life inside it, scuttling around the tunnels and galleries in the semi-dark, and I had no idea it was this huge, this impenetrable. No wonder they chose to put the bunker here when they knew the Purification was close. It's like a fortress.

"Come now...in you get." Mr. Frye holds out his hand to help me as the carriage drives up. I climb inside, eyeing the horses warily. The driver closes the door, the horses whinny and snort, just like they do in the Kinetika movies—they even smell the same, and off we go, in a strange, rocking, jolting movement that makes me feel a little nauseous.

"This is just marvelous. I can't wait to introduce you

to everyone," Mr. Frye says as we drive down the mountainside. "They're going to be so excited when they know you've been found."

"My mom? My family?" Please, please, let me have a mom and a dad, and sisters and brothers.

His voice is short, matter-of-fact. "I'm afraid not. Your mother died when you were just a few hours old."

"And my father?"

"Ahem." He rubs the back of his neck as though he's embarrassed. "I'm afraid we never knew who your father was."

I stare out of the window while it sinks in. After all, what did I expect? Almost everyone died in the Purification. That's why they sent us to the Colony, to keep us alive. Correction—that's why they sent the other two thousand Colonists. I was a last minute, unplanned entry.

"But I must have sisters and brothers." I turn back to him, almost pleading. "Aunts, cousins, a grandfather—anyone? Someone?"

"I'm afraid you're the very last den Eeden. It makes you a very wealthy girl, which is actually rather marvelous."

"So I'm alone?" No family, no sabenzis. It can't be true.

He squeezes my hand. "You're never alone, Ebba. You're a Citizen now. You're one of us."

I stare at him blankly.

He gives a little chuckle. "It must be so confusing! The Citizens are the people who live on Table Island. It's where you belong."

"But...but we were told that everything was dead. They told us that nobody survived the Purification except us, because we were underground, in the Colony."

"Ah. Yes. Well, you see, the Citizens built brand new houses especially designed for the absolute worst nature could throw at us, and they came with fully equipped bunkers and store rooms beneath them, so we could survive for as long as it took. And, surprise, surprise, it didn't take that long—two, maybe three years tops, and we were able to move into our spanking new homes with all the modcons. Isn't that marvelous?" He seems so delighted, with his white toothed smile, inviting me to be as happy as he is, but I'm not. Not yet.

"Two years? It's been sixteen and we're still living in the Colony. Why didn't they let us out?"

"My dear, you will have to ask the High Priest that. I'm just a simple lawyer, not a theologian. Maybe it's got something to do with food supplies and land. Two thousand plus people is a lot to suddenly accommodate into a city the size of Table Island."

I peer through the window as we reach the bottom of the mountain and turn along a winding road. The land is dry—he's not lying about that. Almost nothing is growing but scrub. Ruined buildings and rusted old motor cars lie abandoned in the shadow of a huge stone wall that towers over the road, extending as far as I can see.

I haven't seen a single tree so far. I used to dream about a place filled with trees. It was cool, and the trees rose so high, their branches spreading so close you could barely see the sky. There was a pool of water in the middle, and everything was calm and serene, and made me feel safe, like my mother was holding me. The third time I dreamed it, I told Ma Goodson.

"That's very strange," she said, looking up from the sheet she was mending. "It's not like you've seen a tree. When I was a child, there were forests halfway up the mountain, but the developers cut them down, and by the time we entered the bunker, there were almost none left. There was an elderly woman—an artist. They called her The Tree Lady. Now what was her name? Daisy someone. Anyway, she was fanatical about them. When everyone else was chopping down trees, she kept buying up land

and planting it with tree seedlings. I wish you could have seen it."

The horses have slowed down as they climb a hill, and I try to imagine what this khaki expanse looked like once, when families lived here, when there were houses and gardens, and people walking on the roads. At the top of the hill, I can finally see over the wall. The ocean lies just beyond it. The wind ripples the surface, waves crash onto the black sand, and breaking through the surf are the ruins of the City where my family lived, the City that was flooded in the Purification.

As the road turns, the range of mountains we've been driving next to opens up into a half circle like the sides of a bowl. The sea fills most of it in a deep bay that ends with the wall, leaving just a narrow strip of land squashed up in the foothills of the mountains. The section closest to us is sand and scrub like everything else we've passed, but suddenly it changes into a stripe of vibrant green, stretching from the wall right up the mountainside.

I sit forward, craning my neck. "What's that? Why is that section so—so..." I struggle for the right word. "So alive." That's it. Everything out here is half dead except for this one area that bursts with life and growth.

"That's Greenhaven," Mr. Frye says. "Isn't it marvelous? And it's all yours. Most of it is the forest your great aunt planted. That wood is worth a fortune. I always told her, 'Cut down the trees.' Grow more food. But she'd say, and I can hear her still, 'Fergus, the planet cannot survive without trees.' And then she'd go and plant a couple of hundred thousand more. Remarkable woman. Remarkable."

He looks me over as though he's assessing me. "You're going to be more sensible, aren't you, Ebba?"

I gulp. That huge piece of land is mine? I'm used to overseeing ten rotating planters.

"Don't look so worried," he chuckles. "You'll have Leonid to help you. See that lighter green section in the middle? That's the farm. Your house is there—it's white. Do you see it? Remarkable old house. The last of its kind. There's the farmyard, orchard, vineyards, and over there, behind the house, are the fields for vegetables and live-stock. It's a lot of work, but as time goes on, we'll find you more staff to do the heavy work. You'll make a marvelous success of it. After all, you're a den Eeden. Farming is in your blood."

I doze off. It's late afternoon when the carriage slows and I wake up. We're driving along a narrow road lined on the left side with a thick wall the height of my shoulders, which must once have been white. It's the other side of the road that captures my attention. It's lined with trees —thick trunks, gnarled, with twisting branches and so, so many leaves, forming a blanket that floats above the Earth. I want to get out of the carriage and run to them, feel their bark, break open a leaf and smell it, but we've reached a pair of white gateposts, and the carriage turns down between them.

"Welcome! Welcome to Greenhaven," Mr. Frye beams. "The home of the den Eeden family since 1697, and it all belongs to you! You lucky, lucky girl." And he pats my knee, delighted with himself.

The buggy jolts along a road and I try to take it all in. "That's the orchard," Mr. Frye says, pointing to the rows of trees on the right.

They don't look like the trees we just passed. These are planted in tidy rows, with space between them where the last rays of sun still flicker.

"And on this side are the grape vines. They're looking a bit neglected. With your great aunt so ill, we'd gone down to the bare minimum of staff." He leans over and points to another white wall running along the far edge of the orchard. "The fields are beyond that wall. There's a wind pump so there's plenty of water. You're very lucky."

I'm not really listening. We've turned off into a narrow road, lined with two rows of enormous trees, and I can't take my eyes off them. They're like the giants in the fairy tales Ma Goodson used to tell us. Mr. Frye sees me gaping. "One of your ancestors planted those oaks. Some of them are three hundred years old. But look. There's your house."

"Very typical Cape Dutch homestead," Mr. Frye says, beaming. "Isn't it marvelous that it's still standing? There used to be so many—all with the curly gable, thatched roof, and green shutters. They've all been destroyed. This is the very last one."

The carriage stops, and I clutch the seat as a big white dog runs towards the carriage, barking and showing its teeth.

"Here we are," says Mr. Frye brightly. "I bet you can't wait to go inside. Prospiroh has blessed you so abundantly. Just be quiet, Isi," he orders the dog. "This is your new mistress."

The dog belongs to me? It's got its front legs on the carriage, leering through the window at me.

"Come on, Ebba," Mr. Frye says, opening the door. "Isi won't hurt you."

The dog jumps up at me as I gingerly climb down the step.

"See? Gentle as the proverbial lamb. Now where's Leonid? He will show you where everything is. I'll be back tomorrow and we can chat then."

He's going? Just leaving me with this dangerous beast and driving off? And who exactly is Leonid?

The front door opens, and a dark haired guy of about twenty runs down the steps. "Morning, Mr. Frye," he says.

"Got the message. Prepared the front bedroom. Good afternoon, miss." He gives me a broad smile. "Welcome to Greenhaven. Do you have luggage? Let me get it for you."

"She doesn't have anything," Mr. Frye chuckles. "She comes from the Colony. Find her the essentials, will you? I'll be back tomorrow."

"Of course, miss..." Leonid says. "Miss..."

"Den Eeden," Mr. Frye grins. "We've found Ebba den Eeden. The baby who disappeared."

Leonid's smile fades. His eyelids lower until he's glaring at me from under heavy eyebrows. He takes a step back.

"How extraordinary is that?" Mr. Frye continues. He doesn't seem to notice Leonid's reaction. "It's a miracle. Praise be to Prospiroh!"

Leonid glowers. What in the world have I done to him?

"Ebba, this is Leonid Markgraaf," Mr. Frye continues. "He and Aunty Figgy work for you. Leonid is in charge of the gardens and the horses. Aren't you, Leonid?"

Leonid scowls.

"People work for me?" I stutter. "I thought we all worked together, for the common good. For Prospiroh."

"Oh, we do," Mr. Frye says cheerfully. "You're right, you're right. Aunty Figgy is away at the moment?" he says, turning to Leonid. "She's in the Longkloof with your people? Send a message to tell her to come home at once."

"Yes sir," Leonid growls.

Mr. Frye pats my shoulder. "I'm so sorry, my dear, but I have to run." He makes a mock pout. "You don't mind, do you? The High Priest is expecting me back for a Council meeting. So much paper work to sort out. Not that I'm complaining, mind you. I'm thrilled to meet you. Thrilled. I'll be back first thing tomorrow, and I'll bring my godson, Haldus Poladion. You'll like him—I know you will. He's the High Priest's son. And he's very handsome!" He winks, climbs into the buggy, knocks on the side, and the horses clip clop off down the driveway. The dog runs after them barking.

"Get here, Isidingo," Leonid shouts. "Heel."

She keeps chasing the buggy until it's halfway down the drive. At last she turns and runs back to him, her tongue lolling out of her mouth, grinning.

"You're a bad dog," Leonid says, fondling her ears. "Chasing Mr. Frye." She wags her tail. When she comes over to me and licks my hand, I freeze. Is she going to bite me?

Leonid could call her off, but he chooses not to. "Your face is bright red," he says instead. "Go inside."

I know I'm flushed from the heat, but I wish he hadn't pointed it out. And I can't follow him up the steps because the dog is blocking my way and I'm too scared to move.

"I told you already. Isi won't hurt you," he says.

I don't want him to think I'm pathetic, so I take a breath and sidle past the dog and follow him up the stairs. He's a jerk. He'd also be scared of dogs too if he'd never seen one before.

The front door is open, and I step through into a long, wide room that seems to stretch the length of the building. I pause, taking it all in. A gleaming wooden dining table with high backed chairs runs down the center of the room. Doors open off to the sides, and between them stand carved wooden dressers and glass fronted cupboards holding crystal glasses and beautiful bowls and dishes. It looks like the museum we once saw in a Kinetika. It's cooler inside, the light is gentler, and a sweet Earthy smell greets me.

Leonid points to the first doorway on the left. "Your room. En suite."

"Thanks." I don't know what en suite is, but I don't want to ask. He already thinks I'm an idiot. I open the door and go inside. It's huge. Maybe that's what en suite means. There's a large carved bed in the middle and two massive wooden wardrobes against one wall.

"Do you also sleep in here?" I ask.

His face darkens and he folds his arms across his chest. "Not part of my job." He spits out the words.

When I realize what he's thinking, I go even redder. "I didn't mean that." What must he think of me? "It's just that..." Forget it, I think.

He's already turned away. He doesn't want to hear that in my world we're never, ever alone, and fifty of us would have had to sleep in a room this size.

"I'm off soon," he says. "What you want for supper?"

"I'll eat anything," I say gruffly. "Whatever's easiest."

"I'll make cream cheese sandwiches and tea." He gives a curt nod and goes off.

The dog has followed him, thank Prospiroh. Why won't she leave me alone? Always nuzzling my left hand. I close the bedroom door, kick off my shoes, and savor the warmth of the wood floor, the deep blue bedspread that matches the curtains, the braided rug next to the bed. I go into the bathroom. The light in this room is soft—the window is small and set deep into the thick walls.

It takes me a second to work out how to open the glass door to the shower. What time will the water come on? I fiddle with the tap, and cold water spurts out, drenching my arm. I can shower any time of the day? There is a bar of soap in a dish, and a half-used bottle of shampoo on the floor. I wish I knew more about the mysterious great aunt who has left me a house, a private bathroom, and a bottle of shampoo that smells of pelargonium and buchu.

Chapter Five

The raucous cry of a rooster wakes me and I sit up, bleary eyed, wondering what I'm doing on the poultry level. But a ray of sun—actual sun—falls across my duvet, Isi is snoring quietly at my feet, and I'm in the softest bed in the grandest room I could ever have imagined, wearing a pair of unfamiliar pink pajamas decorated with rosebuds.

Back in the bunker, we used to play a game called Imagination. The four of us would picture our perfect bedroom in our dream house. We only knew what we'd seen in Kinetika, and from the photos some of the kids had in their memory boxes. We girls wanted connecting bedrooms so we could still talk to each other at night. We would have king size beds with lots of pillows, not the one flat pillow we slept on now. We'd have a whole wall of cupboards filled with clothes and we'd wear a different outfit every day. There were paintings on the walls—that was Letti's idea. Jaz wanted a machine to play music, and a TV. I dreamed of a telephone so I could talk to them even when they weren't around. And Fez—he didn't care about how big the bed was or what he wore—he just wanted books, books and more books.

I always imagined that my mom and dad slept in the room next door, and there were sisters and brothers and grandparents who loved me.

Everyone else had their memory boxes with photos of their families and lists of all their names and where they fit in. The twins had a photo of their grandmother on the beach in the Eastern Cape, her head wrapped in an elaborate, red cloth while spotted cattle wandered on the edge of the surf; and another of their parents in academic gowns on the day they received their doctorates, their mother wearing a beautiful beaded Xhosa necklace.

I loved one particular photo Jasmine had of her family gathered in the garden. They're sitting around a table laden with food while her dad and uncle braai meat over a fire. Her mom wrote down the family recipes for her in a notebook. Fez read them out to us—there was pickled fish, mango atjar, and lamb bredies, something called chicken breyani and small ovals of spicy dough fried in oil and drenched in syrup and coconut that were called koeksisters. We used to peer at the food in the photo and try and work out which recipe was which dish.

But I had no photos, no names, no family recipes, no identity. So I had to dream them up—a huge extended family, waiting to welcome me home.

I never imagined that I would find myself waking in a house with empty rooms and nobody to fill them except me.

I get up and open the curtains. Sun rushes in, soft gold light with a golden pink edge to it. I touch the dark green leaves of the bush growing outside the half opened window. Red trumpet shaped flowers are scattered across it, and a small bird with a shiny green chest and a beak like a needle feasts on a flower, lifting its head every now and then to go chip chip chip, so its throat bobs up and down like a pair of bellows.

I have to find a way to get Letti, Fezile and Jasmine out of the Colony so they can see this miraculous world.

Isi scratches at the door and I open the door. She runs to the front door, looking back at me with hopeful eyes. She wants me to open it.

I'm not used to addressing dogs. What do I say? How do I say it?

"Come on then, girl." My voice sounds overly loud in the silent house. But outside it isn't quiet. Yes, there are no human noises, but there's the breeze rustling the leaves, the horses whinnying in the distance, hens clucking, and a repetitive soft rush that I work out must be the sound of waves breaking on the beach.

I follow Isi towards the trees that surround the meadow opposite the house. The grass is so soft—almost as velvety as the cushions on Ma Goodson's bed. Drops of silver dew sparkle as the sun catches them. In the shade of the gigantic Ficus tree that leans over the meadow, I find a clump of ferns just like the ones I used to pore over in Mrs. Pascoe's books. They remind me of Mr. Dermond—rigid and unbending, the leaves all in a row, until you reach the top, where it turns into Ma Goodson, and curls in on itself in an artistic spiral.

A hen wriggles and squirms in the sand, covering her feathers with dust. This is a fat, happy hen, not like the miserable creatures squashed into cages in the Colony. This part of the farm is flat, but the orchards and fields slope uphill to the road that runs along the mountainside. That's the road we came in on yesterday, I'm sure. And somewhere, embedded deep inside one of these mountains, are all the people I love. The only people I ever knew. Until now.

I still can't believe there's an entire world out here, a world full of people. Did Fez and Letti's grandparents survive when the sea level rose? Are their parents safe somewhere, growing food, raising animals, cooking, eating, cutting trees for fuel? And Jasmine's big laughing family—how many of them survived the fallout from the nuclear warheads and the sea level rising suddenly? Did they come asking the Council for their children back, when it was safe to come out of hiding? Maybe they were told to go away, that their children were dead, just like we were told it was a barren wasteland up here. And while most of the land we passed yesterday was dry and rocky, there were still plants growing, and Greenhaven is a paradise. Why would they lie?

Following the road around the side of the house, I come to a big yard, lined on both sides with buildings. Behind them a cow and a few sheep and goats graze in a field. And beyond that is thick forest, running downhill to the sea. An astonishing fragrance wafts towards me. I track it down to a tall shrub covered in purple, white and mauve flowers. I bury my face in it, inhaling the perfume deep into my lungs. Who created this astonishing world? Was it really Prospiroh?

At the back of the house, I find a water pump and rain tank, and beyond that a walled vegetable garden. I open the gate and wander down rows and rows of to-mato bushes tied to sticks, beans tangling around tripods, fat purple brinjals hanging from thick hairy stems, and every kind of herb—rosemary, rocket, lavender, basil—and many more I can't name. There are beds of onions, carrots, Swiss chard, broad beans, even corn that I haven't seen for five years since our last feeble seedlings caught a disease and died out.

These plants are wonderfully healthy and strong. It must be because they're growing in the ground. I drop onto my hands and knees, and dig into the ground, feeling the cool crumbs of rich soil. I pick up a fistful and watch it crumble between my fingers and fall in a triangular mound. An ant scurries away, disappearing into a tiny hole. A white butterfly flitters between the pea pods. With the sun on my back, soil in my fingers, and a mouthful of the sweetest tomato imaginable, I think I might be in heaven.

When Isi barks and I look up, I know I'm definitely in heaven. The most perfect human being is watching me scrabble in the dirt, his red robe like fire against his mahogany skin. He's got the square jaw and the muscular build of a Kinetika star.

"I couldn't wait for Uncle Fergus any longer," he says. "I just had to meet you. I'm Hal."

I scramble up, brushing my hands on my tunic. What must I look like? "Ebba," I say as he takes my hand and gives it a triple shake.

"I know that." A dimple forms in each cheek as he chuckles. "You're famous. Everyone is desperate to meet you. But I wanted to be first. What are you doing grubbing around in the dirt in your pajamas? You've got servants to do that for you."

"It's so wonderful—to see plants growing in soil..."

He chuckles. "I suppose it is. And all this belongs to you. I bet it hasn't sunk in yet, has it? It must have been such a shock to come up here after being underground for so long. We were lucky. We only had to stay in our bunker for a short while, but I can still remember how dark it was. Have you even explored your farm yet? Have you seen how rich you are?"

I'm reeling from the questions. Which one should I answer first? Fortunately he keeps going. Apparently, this guy can talk! But those dimples!

"You're going to love it here, especially when you get to know everyone. Let's go and see what else you've got."

He opens the gate for me, and I have to pass close to him. I blush. He's so confident, so perfect, and I haven't even brushed my teeth. But he doesn't seem to notice. He's looking across the yard to a long, low building with deep windows that almost reach the floor, and three doors. "These look like offices," he says as we reach the first door. "And this last room is a store room. That big building over there must be a barn. All the old farms had them—you can tell by the massive doors. And behind it must be the stables and the coach house."

I watch him trying every door, peering through windows, simply entering buildings without thinking of asking permission. I wish I could have some of his attitude—he doesn't seem afraid to try anything, go anywhere.

"Amazing," he says when we've inspected the stables and coach house and even gone into what I think must be Leonid's room. "There's everything here—even a blacksmith forge, a dairy, packing sheds. It's just like the history books said. Anyway, I'm starving. What have you got to eat?"

"Um…" I bite my lip. I know from watching Kinetika movies, you are supposed to offer visitors a snack, but I haven't seen Leonid yet and I don't want to tread on his toes.

He stares at me then bursts out laughing. "You don't know what you've got? Have you had breakfast?"

My blush deepens. "Leonid told me I'm not allowed in the kitchen."

"Leonid? Your servant Leonid? And you listened to him? Ebba, you're his boss. This all belongs to you. You can go anywhere you like. Come on, I see the back door, just past the vegetable garden."

The kitchen is bigger than I expected, but still cozy. There's a stove at one end, a sink for washing dishes, and a table in the center, covered with a pretty cloth. He opens the cupboard doors, one by one. "Where's the food? Ah." He's noticed a white door at the far end and opens it. "The pantry. Yay."

He's peering into tins and bottles, trying a bit here, a bit there. There's a confidence about him that I haven't seen in a guy before—maybe it's because he hasn't grown up with guards watching everything he does? He's not scared to open every single cupboard and tin as though they all belong to him.

"Nice, yogurt," he says finally, handing me a bowl covered with a white cloth. "Put that on the table. And honey, and..." He's scrabbling on the shelves, lifting bottles and putting them back. "And...some shelled pecan nuts. Let the feast begin."

He grabs two blue and white striped bowls from the shelf and fills them to the top with yogurt, adds a table-spoon of honey to each, and a handful of nuts. "This is awesome," he grins. "Enjoy."

I nibble a little from the edge of my spoon. He laughs as I wrinkle my nose at the sourness. "You're missing the best bit, silly." And he takes my spoon and scoops up some more, making sure he gets a dollop of honey. "Try this now. Open wide."

The spoonful he puts in my mouth is sweet, smooth, crunchy, sour...I close my eyes, trying not to miss a sec-ond of the flavor burst. When I open them, he's watching me with a huge grin, dimples showing. "You're so cute, Ebba. I can't believe what fun we're going to have. I'm going to show you everything."

He's so extraordinary...so—I can't think of the word. It's not just that he's so much better looking than any of the boys in the Colony. It's not just the rich red robe he's wearing, or his dimples. He's...he's happy. He loves life. I watch him scarfing his yogurt, listen as he tells me all about his family, his horse, the fastest on the Island, how he raced against his friend Oliver and beat him by a mile...and his happiness is infectious. I find myself smil-ing too, as I scrape out the last of my bowl.

He looks up, eyes twinkling, and then grins. "Excuse me. Terrible manners, I know." And he tips the bowl over his face and licks it clean. When he looks up, I burst out laughing. "What's so funny?"

"Your nose. You've got yogurt on it."

"Have I?" He laughs and wipes his sleeve across it, and I flinch, waiting for one of the mentors to shout at him for dirtying his clothes unnecessarily. But of course there's no one here but us, and he doesn't look like anyone has ever shouted at him in his life.

"So what are you going to do today?"

I've been wondering the same thing. "Um, I'm not sure. I'm hoping Mr. Frye will tell me what my work is. "

"Your work? You don't have to work, Ebba. You're a Citizen."

I get up and gather the bowls. This idea makes my stomach knot. I put them in the sink and open the tap to wash them.

"That's a servant's job," he says. "Leave them for Leonid."

I stare at him, checking if he's making another one of his jokes. But he's not. "So what is my job?"

"You don't have one. You're the richest person on Table Island. You don't need to work."

"I don't understand," I mutter, as the heat rises to my face. "What am I supposed to do all day?"

"Enjoy yourself and have a good time, until you get married and have babies. Shame, you're looking all confused. Sit down and I'll explain to you."

I slip back into my chair and he takes the cloth from the yogurt bowl and lays it on the table. "Imagine this cloth is Table Island, and this yogurt bowl is us, the Citizens. We live on the Island, right? We own it all." He plonks the bowl in the center of the cloth. "The wall keeps out everyone who isn't one of us. It runs right around the Island." His hand sweeps around the edges of the cloth. "You with me so far?"

"'Yes, but..."

"The Colony is inside Table Mountain, right? So I'm going to put the bottle of nuts here, on the floor under the table. The Colonists are there to work. That's what you did, right? It was like your own little country?"

I nod, trying to make sense of it. "Why don't they let the Colonists out though? They told us it wasn't safe to leave—why did they lie?"

He shrugs. "I dunno. Maybe it's safer for them inside. Anyway..." And he picks up the jar of honey and puts it just outside the cloth. "Anyway, pretend this honey represents the Boat People."

"Who are they?"

"The people who live in Boat Bay—outside the wall. They're fishermen, and servants, of course, and they transport cargo to the Mainland. They're only allowed onto the Island if they've got a permit and a job to go to."

"So Leonid is from Boat Bay?"

"Yes, and you're a Citizen, although you spent all your life as a Colonist by mistake. So you're one of us." He grins so his dimples dance, pushes back his chair and says, "See? You don't have to wash the dishes. You're the boss of everything here. Let's go and see what else you've got."

A while later we're in the dining room and Hal is opening the cupboards and checking out the glassware when Leonid goes past the front of the house, pushing a wheelbarrow. Hal marches out and yells from the top of the steps. "Where have you been? My horse needs water. Attend to it immediately."

Leonid glares under his eyebrows, and mutters, "Yes sir."

"And don't give me that attitude. Show a little respect. Miss Ebba had to get her own breakfast. It's unacceptable."

"That's how you speak to him," he says to me, turning his back on Leonid. "You have to show him who is the boss, right from the start."

That can't be right. Leonid is not only older than me, he's also run the farm single handed since my great aunt died. I may own the farm, but without his expertise I'd be completely lost. "Can't we get the horse water?" I ask as Leonid shoves the barrow onto the grass and disappears around the side of the house. "He's got a lot to do."

"It's his job. He should have done it already."

I follow Hal back into the house. I'm not surprised Leonid looked so angry. We hated it in the Colony when the guards spoke to us rudely. But I'm not going to say anything. Hal's my only friend up here, and if there's one thing the Colony taught me it is that it's dangerous to be alone.

"To us," Hal grins, as he hands me a long narrow glass and pretends to toast me with his. "To a beautiful friendship."

A short while later, a carriage comes rattling down the road and stops in front of the house. Mr. Frye climbs down, beaming. "Good morning, Ebba," he calls. "I see you've already got a visitor?"

"Hello, Uncle Fergus," Hal says. "We've been checking out everything she owns. It's unbelievable. And she's got no family so she doesn't have to share any of it with anyone."

Mr. Frye kisses me on each cheek. "Settling in, my dear? Isn't this house absolutely marvelous? So quaint. Can you imagine your ancestors built it four hundred years ago? They were some of the first people to settle at the Cape. There used to be nothing here, just empty land. Imagine that. Empty land."

Was this land really empty when my ancestors came?

I wondered. Or was it hunting lands for the first people, the Khoisan, who roamed these lands?

His purple robe shimmers as the sun catches it. He pauses at the front door and turns. "Such an opportunity Prospiroh gifted the den Eeden family. And they seized that opportunity, they seized it with both hands. Do you realize you own everything you can see?" His arm sweeps across the landscape. "You own all this land, from the top of those mountains right down to the sea? You're a lucky girl. A very lucky girl."

He sweeps into the house, pauses in the hallway and bellows, "Leonid! Leonid!"

A moment later, Leonid appears in the passage and Mr. Frye snaps, "Don't just stand there. Bring refreshments." He turns his electric grin onto me. "Let's go into the sitting room and have a chat."

His hand is on my back as he guides me through the door, like I'm an animal he has to herd into a pen.

"Have a seat, Ebba," he says, gesturing to a deep sofa. I sink into it and try to follow as Mr. Frye starts talking about wills and bequests and legal principles and things I have never heard of. My eyes follow Hal, who is wandering around, peering at the paintings. There are so many, lining the faded green walls. One on the far wall catches my eye. It's a long painting of trees, as long as the red sofa below it. Why is it so familiar?

Leonid comes in then and puts a tray on the coffee table in front of Mr. Frye. He keeps his head low, keeping his eyes down like we did when Mr. Dermond was in a bad mood and we didn't want to set him off.

"We have a lot to discuss," Mr. Frye says. He pours the tea and pushes a cup towards me. "We need to reach a decision about the best way forward for you. I quite understand that this sudden windfall may in fact be something of a burden, and I wouldn't be surprised if you decided

that it were a little too onerous for one of your tender
years and you wished to relinquish it. And of course, one
must consider not only one's personal preferences but the
community as a whole, and how one can best contribute
to the general wellbeing...."

It's all too complicated. My eye falls again on the
painting. Where have I seen it before? Suddenly I realize
—it's the forest I walk to in my recurring dream.

"Who painted that?" I blurt out.

"Try to follow, dear, this is important." He's irritated at
first, then he smiles and pats my hand. "I suppose this information is just so overwhelming to you. You're so young,
and you're a girl, of course, so you don't have much pro-
clivity for business. Let me see now." He turns and peers
at it. "Ah, yes. That is one of your great aunt Daisy's works.
She was a famous painter, before the Purification."

How did she paint what's in my head? I keep staring at
it, looking for places where she might have gone wrong,
but it's all there—the tree trunks stretching upwards like
the legs of a fairy tale giant, the tangle of shrubs below,
the three big rocks as high as my shoulder, sprinkled with
moss, that the path winds around....They look like an old
man lying down. She hasn't forgotten anything.

He's babbling on about art and investments and
income and how he will look after my money for me, and
pay the wages, and anything I want, I just have to ask him.
I'm half listening, torn between the painting and the sight
of Hal, who is the most handsome guy I've ever seen, not
just his cute dimple and cheeky smile, but also his phy-
sique which makes all the guys in the Colony look like
straggling weeds.

"You can't live here alone," Mr. Frye says. "Hopefully
it won't be long before you can move to the City, nearer
to us—to the rest of the Citizens. This farm is so far away
from everything, you'll be lonely here with no neighbors.

It was all right for an old lady, but you're a young girl with your whole life open before you, and you'll want to go to parties and entertainments and mix with young people your own age. I hope you'll be all right with Leonid here for a day or two. Although, on second thoughts, these people are very rough, you know, not like us at all. Perhaps I should send over a maid from my house until Aunty Figgy gets back. Anyway, I'm going to need you to sign these papers please."

He snaps open a case and takes out a sheaf of papers. He spreads them on the table as Leonid comes in to fetch the tray.

"Hurry up, boy," Mr. Frye snaps. "Just get it done."

Leonid's shoulders tense and he picks up the tray in a rush. I try to help—reaching over to put my cup on the tray—but I bump the milk jug and it tips over. I try to turn it upright but my elbow knocks the tray and although he tries to save it, it slides out of his hand and lands upside down on the table. There's milk and tea and china scattered everywhere.

"You idiot." Mr. Frye grabs his documents and shakes them. The ink runs down the page and drops in black splodges on the carpet. "Do you know how long it took for my scribe to write these out? You're a complete and utter moron."

Leonid glowers. "Sorry sir." His hands shake as he picks up the cups, but it's not from fear, it's anger.

I can't let him take the blame. "It...it was my fault," I say.

"No, it wasn't," Hal says. "That idiot dropped the tray."

"No, I bumped—" I start but Mr. Frye interrupts.

"I swear to god, Leonid," he says, scrunching his papers into a soggy ball. "Now the old girl's gone, there's no reason to keep you on here. I'm getting very tired of your incompetence. Now get out of my sight."

I don't want to catch Leonid's eye as he piles the crockery on the tray and storms off.

Mr. Frye tosses the papers into the empty fireplace "I'll have to come back. Idiot. Between him and your great aunt's crazy old lover, you just aren't safe here. Who knows what might happen to you here, alone with them. Your great aunt was a different matter. One, she was geriatric; two, she was stubborn as all hell; and three, she'd lived here all her life. I'll come back tomorrow and tell them to be out by the end of the day." He pats my shoulder as he gets up. "But now I have to run. And Ebba, just a word of warning. You can't run around all day in your pajamas. Not in front of the servants. Find something to wear, dear. Something more modest."

"Shall I come and visit again?" Hal asks, as Mr. Frye climbs into his carriage. "You must be missing your old friends." He gives me a quick hug and his kindness brings a lump to my throat.

"I'd like that."

"See you soon then," Hal says as he unties his horse and vaults into the saddle. "I'm so glad you're here." With a quick wave he turns the horse and rides off down the road. His robe shines against the glossy black coat of his horse and he looks like a king.

How do I speak to Leonid after the morning's debacle? What do I say? If I knew why he was so angry with me, it would be easier. It can't just be the tea tray. I can't have offended him. He was friendly until he heard my name.

I go into my room and take a shower, scrubbing myself from top to toe with the brush hanging next to the taps. I wish I could scrub off my skin and take on a new one—to be the person I'm expected to be up here. The clothes I wore yesterday are covered in dust and sweat, and anyway I can't bear to put them on again. They remind me too much of the Sacrifice, of Jaz and the twins, and I'm missing them so much I want to lie on the bed and cry. "No good feeling sorry for yourself!" I can hear Ma Goodson's firm voice in my head. "There's plenty of people worse off than you."

Instead I pull on the blue dressing gown hanging behind the bathroom door, wrap my hair in a towel, and go in search of something to wear. The next bedroom is smaller than mine, but the cupboards are packed with clothes and I find a pair of pants and a loose green shirt that reminds me of my Colony clothes, but are so soft they slide over my skin. Did they belong to my great aunt? It feels good to wear her clothes. She painted the landscape of my recurring dream as though she was walking through it. We must be kindred spirits. Maybe she'll help me negotiate this overwhelming new world.

First thing I'm going to do is explore the forest and see if it's as mysterious in real life as it is in the dream world. What lives among those thick trunks and branches that create a world as gloomy as the Colony, but made of living plants and creatures, not dead rock? Mrs. Pascoe had a book about trees of Southern Africa, and I used to pore over it, begging Fez to read me the names. He loved the baobab that looked as though it was planted upside down, but I loved the ficus, with its thick twisted trunk and roots that crept along the ground like a giant's fingers.

At first I'm so captivated by the beams of sunlight that break through the canopy of leaves and by the way the branches touch each other and create a net of leaves and twigs that I can't look beyond that. But as I follow the path deeper, so deep that there's nothing around me but trees and scrub and smudges of sky, I realize that this is the forest in my great aunt's painting. There's the big rock that looks like an old man lying down in front of the grove of milkwood trees, here are the four yellowwoods that twist together over the path.

How could I dream about a real place? It must be the heat. Maybe it's the fresh air, or there's something in the pollen that's drifting down in the sunbeams.

The sound of burbling water gets louder. I turn a corner and come across a pond surrounded by a low stone wall. It's surrounded by ferns, and deep orange clivias nestle in the shade of milkwood trees. Frogs croak between the waterlilies, and above the clear water, dragonflies dance.

It feels holy—like something gentle and nurturing lives here. Like I imagine my mother would have been, if only I remembered her.

I sit on the edge of the wall and wonder, did she like to sit here when she was pregnant with me? Is that why I dreamed of the forest? I lean over to splash water on my face. My necklace dangles in the water. A shaft of sunlight hits it, and sends a rainbow across the pond. It's so beautiful—the shining colors, flickering against the honey-colored stone.

Then silence—no wind, no frogs or birds, no rustling in the grass.

A swarm of bees flies out of a milkwood and forms a spiral over my head. They swirl around me, until their buzzing sounds like a thousand people humming. It feels as though they're welcoming me. Then they break out of the spiral, circle the pond, dipping across the center, and they're gone.

I've heard about bees—about how they could sting you to death. But these bees feel like protectors, watching over me. The wind picks up again, and a frog swims across the pond. A bird begins to crooo croooo. I tuck the necklace under my robe and it's warm. Warm, and shining like the rainbow.

When I get back to the house, there's a little boy

crouched next to the backdoor, dropping stones into Isi's water bowl. She licks his hand and then leans over to drink and he laughs as water splashes his leg.

"Hello," I say. "I'm Ebba. Are you Aunty Figgy's little boy?"

He buries his face in Isi's fur, his little arms around her neck, and doesn't say a word. I don't know how to talk to little kids, so I go into the kitchen to look for his mother.

I find her in the kitchen, chopping vegetables at the counter. The first thing I notice is that her left hand has a mark the same as mine. Her hair's like mine too, but it's pulled back into a bun and she's wearing a dark russet dress that brushes the floor.

"Aunty Figgy?" She looks up and smiles, but goes back to the carrots she's chopping.

"I'm Ebba. Did Mr. Frye tell you about me?"

Footsteps sound in the passage, and a woman comes in carrying a posy of pink pelargoniums. She's short and sturdy, with a lined face that is firm but kind. She's older than Ma Goodson—she's the oldest person I've ever seen. When she spots me, hovering in the doorway, she stops dead and her smile breaks her face into a thousand wrinkles.

"Ebba!"

I turn back to Aunty Figgy—but she's gone. The vegetables are still on the chopping board, but she's vanished.

The older woman gathers me into her arms. She's almost crying as she strokes my hair. "We thought you were gone forever. But you've come back to us, Theia be praised. Come, sit sit," she says, pulling out a chair. "I want to look at you. You're so like your mother."

"You knew my mother?" Who is this woman? I thought there were only two people on the farm—Leonid and Aunty Figgy.

"Of course. I was there when she was born. She was

tall like you, and she had your shaped eyes, but her hair was chestnut."

I sit where I can see through the open door into the yard. There's no sign of the woman or her child. "Where's Aunty Figgy gone?"

"I'm Aunty Figgy."

"But the woman in the long dress—and the little boy—they were here a moment ago. She was chopping vegetables. See? They're still there."

She frowns. Her eyes go to the half chopped carrots, the backdoor, then to the necklace around my neck. But when she sees my birthmark, she sinks into a chair and takes my hand in both of hers; I notice that her hands are shaking. "How long have you had this?"

Automatically I pull my hand away and hide it under my leg. "Since I was thirteen. The woman who was here— she had the same mark. And the same necklace."

She's still staring at me and without warning she jumps up from her chair and grabs the posy of flowers. I brace myself for another hug, but she is at the window sill, on her knees in front of a statue of a woman in a green robe.

"Thank you, thank you, thank you, Theia," she cries. "I knew you wouldn't leave us to die. Even though time is running out, I never doubted you would send her." She kisses the posy of flowers and arranges it in a glass at the statue's feet. "I knew you would be faithful to every word in the prophecy."

This poor woman is mentally ill. I've heard about old people getting confused in the head. I'm just going to have to be calm and gentle and hope Leonid comes in soon to rescue me.

But the old lady gets up as though nothing had happened, fills a kettle with water and puts it on the stove. Then she turns to me, and her whole demeanor has changed. She leans her stocky body against the counter, half closes her eyes as though she's thinking hard about something, and finally says in such a grave voice that I get quite a fright, "You're going to have to be courageous, Ebba. An important task is waiting for you." She lifts the necklace with one stubby finger and rubs the amulet lovingly between finger and thumb.

"It is home at last, praise Theia. You have brought the necklace back to Greenhaven. Ebba, your mother was wearing it when she died and it disappeared when you did. We thought the High Priest had stolen it, but it was with you in the Colony. In the one place we did not think to look."

At last she's talking about things that make sense. Now is my chance to answer the questions that have plagued me all my life. "What happened the day I disappeared? How did my mother die?"

"Your mother was a leader of the Resistance." She sees my blank face and explains, "The Resistance were a group of freedom fighters who fought the City Council over their unjust laws. She knew the Council would turn everybody out of the City when the Calamity came, so she turned the cellars under the house into a bunker, not only for everyone on the farm, but for other folk who had nowhere else to hide. But anyway, I'm getting off the point. To get back to that day—you were born very early in the morning. You were a beautiful baby, with those big green eyes, your hair already that vibrant red just like the Goddess's."

It's the second time she's mentioned a goddess. It must be part of her mental health problem—everybody knows the only god is Prospiroh. Or is that another lie told to us by the authorities?

"That same morning," she says, sitting next to me, "we heard on the news that the US, Russia, North Korea and China were about to deploy their nuclear weapons. Everyone flew into a blind panic. Caravans of refugees arrived at Greenhaven, begging to be given a place in the bunker. The Council passed an urgent resolution, banning anyone who wasn't a Citizen from the City. They sent the army to the gates of Greenhaven, to ensure we didn't take any refugees into the bunker. Your mother was outraged. There was still room for ten or fifteen more, but they were sending them away to die."

The kettle shrieks on the stove, and she stomps across the room and takes it off the heat. I try and imagine the chaos of that day—my mother holding me, feeding me for the first time, wanting to focus just on her new baby, while outside the farm gates, the army turned away desperate crowds, mothers and children, whole families, with nowhere to go as the world went into meltdown.

"Then what happened?"

She pauses, teapot in hand. "We heard shooting. Ali said she was going out to negotiate with the army. We begged her to stay, but she put you on her chest in a baby sling and left. 'They won't shoot a new mother,' she said. I can still see her, standing at the front door, insisting we keep going with the preparations. There was so much to take down to the bunker—food, water, everything we would need for a year. We even had to take some of the farm animals underground with us. So we let her go." She bites her lip. "I think about it every single day. I should have made her stay behind. When she didn't come back, Daisy went to look for her. The bastards had shot her. And you were gone."

"I just disappeared? Did the army take me? Maybe one of the refugees?"

"We had no idea. We searched everywhere. But then the lockdown happened, and we had to shut ourselves in the bunker or we'd all have been killed. All we could do was pray to the Goddess that someone, somewhere, was keeping you safe. And Theia protected you and now she has brought you back to us, in the nick of time."

I feel a little stunned. I've just met her and this is a lot—a lot—to take in.

"The Council is unpredictable," Aunty Figgy says. "I am not a Citizen, I was always here at your aunt's wishes. They could decide that I'm not allowed to stay here. It's vital that you know why you were saved. The Goddess…"

She stops mid-sentence, and peers into my eyes, her small black eyes so intense they seem to be alight. Does she read my confusion?

"If this were not an emergency, I'd give you more time before I told you this whole story. But we haven't got time—this may be the only chance I get to explain your heritage and your sacred task. I can see you've never heard of the Goddess. I bet they told you Prospiroh is the one true and only god. Well, I'll tell you this now, they were lying. There are many, many gods and goddesses. But Theia made the Earth, she alone is meant to be Goddess of the Earth. It was in perfect balance until Prospiroh colonized it and people became greedy, always wanted more land, more gold, more diamonds, more power. Just wait here. I need to show you something."

She leaves the room, her bare feet padding on the wooden floor. She's back a moment later with a leather bound book, the thick cream pages coming loose from the binding. She opens the heavy cover and begins to turn the pages, scanning through the handwriting broken up by drawings of plants and trees.

"Here," she says finally, pushing the book towards me. "See this section?" She points to a paragraph of writing. Below it is the outline of a familiar looking tree.

Where do I know that shape from?

"Read it aloud," she says, tapping the page.

"I…I don't know how."

"You can't read?"

The surprise in her voice withers me. It's not that she sounds scornful or unkind but...it feels like I've failed somehow. Why does she care so much?

"We didn't need to read in the Colony," I say. "And they told us that if it ever was safe for us to leave the bunker, there were no books or paper left."

"Hmmmmph. Of course they wanted to keep you uneducated. Just like the government during apartheid. Using propaganda to keep whites believing the lie that they were superior. Using inferior education to keep blacks and coloureds in line." She pulls the book back in front of her and finds the place with her stubby finger. "Listen." As she starts to read, her intensity is replaced by an unexpected calm and her voice takes on a soft lilt.

In the last year before the second Calamity,
a young woman will arise from deep in the Earth.
She will bear the mark of the Goddess upon
her left hand. To her will fall the task of reuniting
the sacred amulets. She will open the portal
to the gods, and balance will be restored.
The Goddess will return and heal the Earth.

While she reads, I compare my birthmark to the drawing in the book. They're identical down to the last twig. How can that be possible? That book must have been written long before I was born.

Aunty Figgy closes the book and leans back in her chair. Her eyes shut and for a moment she sits entirely still.

"Only four other women have had this mark on their hand," she says. "One of them was your ancestor Clementine, the woman you saw in the kitchen just now."

"She wasn't a real person? But she seemed so real. Was she a ghost?"

"Not a ghost. She is your ancestor—here to help you with your task. You need to understand something, Ebba.

You're not an ordinary human being. You're not a simple mortal like everyone else on the planet. You're the last living descendant of the Goddess. Her blood runs in your veins, and this birthmark is the proof."

Surely this is a fairy tale. How can I possibly be a mix of human and god? I examine her face.

She's dead serious.

She grips my hand and places it on the book. "You are the only person who can save the Earth from destruction in the coming Calamity."

I decide to humor her for now. Whatever she thinks or believes, I need to know—even if, like everything else I've been told until now, it turns out to be a lie. Information will arm me. Help me, at least, to understand how people expect me to behave. "How am I supposed to do that?"

"You need to find the three missing amulets. When you have them all, the Portal to Celestia will open, and the Goddess will be able to come back and restore the Earth."

She stops, lips pursed. "I can see you don't believe me. Look at the statue—she's wearing the necklace too. "

Going close to the statue, I crouch down to examine it more closely. She's beautiful, with bronzed skin and a shapely body. Her hair is as coppery and curly as mine, and around her neck is the exact necklace I am wearing, except it has four amulets hanging from it, not one.

I get up, my mind whirling. In the Bunker, they told us Prospiroh was the only god. They told us the world was dead and nobody could survive away from the Bunker. And none of that was true. Why should I believe a new story now?

She's watching me and she looks so anxious that I can't tell her what I'm thinking. If she's really ill, I should be kind to her. I sit down again and try and speak calmly so as not to upset her anymore.

"What will happen if I don't find them all? If the portal

doesn't open?"

"If Theia doesn't come back, Earth will be destroyed. You, me, Greenhaven, everyone, everything. We'll all return to dust. "

"Where do I find these amulets exactly?"

"They've gone missing over the past four hundred years. When your ancestors came to Greenhaven, the necklace was whole, but one by one they have been lost."

I think over the huge farm, the fields stretching to the foot of the mountains, the thick forest running down to the sea, the acres and acres of orchards and vineyards, the buildings piled high with farm equipment. "How can I possibly find them? "

"Your ancestors will help you. That is why Clementine was here."

I'm tired and confused and I can't imagine how a ghost will possibly help me search for something that has been lost for hundreds of years. And I must find three of them?

"Okay," I say, rubbing my eyes. "I'll think about it."

She sighs as she closes the book. "Don't think too long. There isn't much time."

Chapter Six

It's midmorning the next day when Mr. Frye's carriage rattles down the driveway, He comes sweeping in the front door, and greets me with a kiss on each cheek. "Right," he says. "I don't have a lot of time. Let's get this unpleasant business over with. Tell Aunty Figgy and Leonid to come to the sitting room."

I take a deep breath. "Mr. Frye..."

He raises one groomed eyebrow. "What is it, Ebba? I've got to get back to the office."

My confidence dissolves. What are the rules up here? In the Colony, we weren't allowed to talk to Mr. Dermond directly. We had to speak to our house mother, who told his secretary Ms. Cupido that we wanted an appointment, and she decided if he would have time, and usually he didn't. If we'd gone straight up to him, especially when he was busy, we'd have spent recreation running on the treadmill instead of watching Kinetika.

"Noth...nothing," I stutter, wishing I didn't care about the rules. But look what happened to Micah when he broke them. I have to do what Mr. Frye says.

"So run and fetch that pair of skabengas."

In the kitchen, Aunty Figgy is on her knees in front of the statue, her hands twisting her apron. Leonid rams the last piece of wood into the stove and slams the door, making sparks fly.

"Mr. Frye....Mr. Frye needs to see you."

Leonid looks like he wants to spit on me as he washes

his hands at the sink. Aunty Figgy gets up and she looks sick with worry.

I catch her arm. "I'm sorry," I mutter. "I don't know how to stop him."

"You haven't even tried," Leonid snarls as he dries his hands and throws the towel into the sink. "You're the long lost heiress. You could tell him you want us to stay."

"He's not going to listen to a sixteen-year-old girl," Aunty Figgy says. "Those Prosperites think that women are here to make food and babies, not decisions."

When they go, I slump down at the kitchen table and bury my head in my arms. If my sabenzis were here, we could go together—Jasmine could tell him what we want, and he'd listen to her. I look around as Isi whimpers. She's in front of the window, staring up at the statue. She looks back to me, and whines.

"What is it, girl?"

She jumps on her hindlegs and licks the statue, nearly knocking over Aunty Figgy's vase. Then she runs back to me and licks the back of my hand. I rub it on my robe, wondering what is going through her head. How intelligent are dogs? She seems to be wanting to tell me something, but surely that's impossible. But when she licks my birthmark again, I realize that she's telling me to talk to the Goddess.

I'm still not sure whether I really believe Aunty Figgy's stories, or whether I am the one who is going mad, thinking a dog can communicate, but at this point I'll give anything a try. "Help me, er...Goddess," I whisper. "Change Mr. Frye's mind." I nearly jump out of my skin when the kettle whistles. I jump up to take it off the hob but someone is already there.

It's Clementine, wearing the same long russet dress as yesterday, though now there's a white apron protecting it I watch her pour hot water into the teapot and put it on the tea tray. When she looks up at me I'm drawn to the sweet expression on her face, and the kindness in her large brown eyes. She gives me a little nod, then adds a cup and saucer, fetches a small jug from the pantry, and finally bends down to open the oven.

A heavenly smell fills the room. She takes out the pans, packed with steaming bread. A few seconds later, she's turned the loaves out onto a rack and is slicing one up. My mouth waters as she spreads butter and honey on the slices and cuts them in triangles. I'm hoping I'll be able to eat one, but she puts them on the tray and pushes it towards me.

She's disappeared, and Isi is standing at the door to the passage, whining. I get it. They're for Mr. Frye.

I hear his reedy voice shouting while I'm halfway down the dining room. Taking a deep breath, I push open the sitting room door and go in. He's pacing in front of the fireplace while Aunty Figgy and Leonid stand in front of him, as though they are naughty children. How dare he treat them like this? He's as bad as Mr Dermond or one of the guards.

"What is it, Ebba?" he snaps, but then he lifts his chin and sniffs the air.

Aunty Figgy catches my eye as I put the tray on the coffee table, and gives me a tiny nod of approval.

"Sorry to interrupt, Mr. Frye," I say, "but I thought you might like some of Aunty Figgy's bread. It's just out of the oven."

He's already taken a seat on the sofa and is helping himself to a slice. The butter has melted and mixed with the honey and they drip onto his fingers. He licks them clean and smiles at me. "Marvelous," he says. "Just marvelous."

Five minutes later, the plate is empty and he's leaning

back against the cushions, smiling.

"How many years have I been coming here and eating your bread, Aunty Figgy?" he asks with a little burp. "No one on the Island—in the whole Federation—can bake like you."

"It's a lost art," Aunty Figgy says.

"That it is. A lost art indeed."

"I'm hoping to teach Ebba," Aunty Figgy says. "But it takes time. It's not something you can pick up from a book. You have to learn from a master."

"Indeed," Mr. Frye says. "Indeed you do." His voice is dreamy.

"Leonid's a master beekeeper," Aunty Figgy continues. "Nobody can control the hives like him. You know how fussy they are. If Leonid goes, you'll have to shut down the hives. It would be sad—no more honey."

"That won't do," he mutters. "You'll have to stay. I'll give you..." He seems to be getting sleepy, as there's a long pause. "I'll give you six months. That's right. Six months. If you're still being...er...disrespectful, then it's back to Boat Bay for Leonid, and you, Aunty Figgy—remember the High Priest can expel you from the city any time—you're not a Citizen, no matter what Daisy den Eeden's will says."

Aunty Figgy is humming as she dishes up at dinner time. There's a fresh bunch of lavender in the vase in front of the statue. Even Leonid is in a good mood.

"Mutton bredie," he says, licking his lips. "My favorite."

I can't believe the flavors she's packed into the stew. Letti would be ecstatic. There's rosemary, garlic, and dried thyme, and along with potatoes and beans, a long green vegetable I can't identify.

"Veldkool," Aunty Figgy says as I prod it with my fork. "It grows wild. It's what the first people, the Khoisan, ate. My ancestors. Yours too, Leonid. You have Khoisan blood in your veins too, Ebba."

For a second I think she's going to tell me who my father is, but she continues: "Daisy's mother was a Griqua from the Northern Cape."

I've never had a clue about my heritage before all of this. Now I'm learning where I belong. How I belong.

"The Khoisan knew which plants were edible—and the ones that tasted best too," Aunty Figgy says.

In the Colony, food was fuel that we ate to keep going. Twice a day, the same thing—stew from protein pellets and dehydrated vegetables. There was no pleasure to it. But here food has magical powers. It turns enemies into friends, and soothes the angry. And it links you back to your ancestors and everything that happened to them.

As we tuck in, contentment fills me. This is almost like having a family.

The next morning, Hal arrives just after breakfast. He is like sunshine after Leonid's customary long face. I'm a bit shy as I greet him on the front stoep—but he seems so genuinely pleased to see me and interested in everything I say that I soon feel like I've known him for years.

"Mr. Frye says there's a river on your farm," he says. "That's why you grow such good crops here. It goes all the way down to the wall and into the sea. And he says there's a natural swimming pool. It's going to be stinking hot again today. I can't wait to swim. Have you been for a swim yet?"

I shake my head, wondering how he will react when he finds out I can't swim. Or read. He'll think I'm so backward.

"Shame, you must be finding this all so overwhelming. You're probably too scared to leave the house. I keep forgetting you've been underground all your life." He holds out his hand. "Come on, I'll look after you. You'll love it."

I hesitate, then take his hand. The people up here are

so huggy-kissy. In the bunker, we weren't supposed to touch anyone, ever. I'm going to have to try and loosen up a bit.

Isi watches us from the steps, her ears back, a slight ridge of fur standing up along her back. "Come on, girl," I call, wondering what is upsetting her. But she turns away into the house and we set off alone.

He leads me past the stable yard and the barn. "These old buildings are kind of creepy, don't you think? Like living in a museum. You must be looking forward to living in a normal house with other people. When you come and stay with Mr. Frye in his security village, you'll be close to us, and I tell you, you'll absolutely love it. I'll be starting work with my dad soon, but you girls have the best time. Nobody expects you to work for a living." He chuckles. "All you've got to do is learn how to be a good wife and catch a husband."

He's talking like it's been decided already. Both that I'll leave Greenhaven, and that I'll be getting married. In the Colony, we had to do exactly what we were told, but now that I'm a "Citizen," with my own property and land and even servants, I'd like to be able to make up my own mind about my own future.

"Come on," he calls, setting off through the field where fat-tailed sheep crop grass and a cow is grazing in one corner. "The river's this way. I'll race you."

I follow, loving the feel of the springy grass under my feet, and the sense of covering ground, moving forward instead of the relentless sameness of the treadmill we ran on every night to generate electricity. It feels almost as though I've been in a cocoon all my life, and now I'm a moth, stretching my wings for the first time.

We reach the forest, and he tears down the path. It's not the path I followed yesterday, and I really want to stop for a minute and feel how different it is in the Colony—

to listen to the wind, and relish the sensation of being shaded by the trees that stretch so far upward. But he's grabbed a stick and is bashing the bushes as he passes them, leaves and twigs breaking off with a sharp twang. Soon we're deep in the forest, and there at the bottom of the steep slope, glistening in the dappled sunlight, is the silvery river.

He's already standing barefoot in the water when I slide down the last bit of slope and land in a shower of small stones and sand.

"Isn't this just brilliant?" He grins.

Willows droop over the stream. Tiny fish swim in the rock pools, visible in the clear water. Birds are singing and the water gurgles over the stones. A few meters downstream, the river widens out into the natural pool, surrounded by rocks and boulders.

"Let's swim," Hal calls, stripping off his robe. He runs up the side of the highest boulder and stands there in just his undergarment, arms outstretched. I try not to look at his firm brown body.

"How amazing is this?" He jumps off, knees to his chest and lands with a splash. "Come in, the water is gorgeous."

He crosses the pond with strong rhythmic strokes. I'm too shy to let him see my underwear, and to tell him I can't swim, so I sit on the edge of a rock and dangle my legs in the water. It's enough to just soak my feet—even that is a novelty after a lifetime of sixty-second showers. And the feeling of the sun on my back is glorious; my muscles relax and stress drops away. This must be what heaven is like—in the fresh air, surrounded by trees, watching the water ripple through rock pools, listening to bird song...and a hot guy swimming, in just his underwear.

Jasmine would love it. She'd think he was gorgeous too, I know it. She and I always used to watch the guys at meal times and discuss who we hoped we'd be paired with, when the breeding program finally began. Letti never knew what was going on because she was too short sighted to see who we were discussing. Fez used to listen in, and although I never said anything, I think he was more attracted to the guys than to the thousand girls he saw every day. Though it was all academic really —they added something to our food so we didn't feel normal feelings. But those feelings are definitely flooding back for me now. I can't take my eyes off Hal's body as he twists and turns, dives underwater, and comes up on the other side of the pond, totally fearless. The water glistens off his short curly black hair like a thousand tiny diamonds, and it seems right somehow—he carries himself like someone born to wear a crown.

Then, out of the blue, the red haired woman— Clementine—emerges from between trees on the other side of the river. She puts down her basket and bends down to dig in the fallen leaves.

Hal splashes me, laughing. "Come on," he calls. "What are you staring at so intently?"

Can't he see her? Her rust-colored dress stands out clearly among the trees. "I thought I saw someone. Over there." I point to the spot. The little boy is digging in the leaves with a stick, and she's talking to him while she brushes the dirt off the back of his trousers. She looks up and sees Hal and she catches my eye and shakes her head.

"Come on." He laughs. "You're seeing things."

Am I? Is she in my imagination? How come Aunty Figgy couldn't see her? And why does she frown whenever Hal speaks?

"Hal, have you ever heard of a Goddess? A Goddess who made the world, and a sacred task and stuff?"

I try to make my voice light, but it's alarming how quickly he looks up and snaps, "Old wives' tales. All superstition, as far as I'm concerned, though my father would call it witchcraft. Who's been filling your mind with this rubbish? Is it the old housekeeper?"

"No...no..." I don't want Aunty Figgy in trouble again. "I...I found a book. I can't read very well though. I must have got it wrong."

"You can't read?" He jumps out of the pond and shakes himself like a dog. "I'll teach you if you like." He's so handsome, his big cheeky grin lighting up his face. He pulls his robe over his head and I get a moment to admire his perfect abs before his face appears again, and the folds of material fall around his body.

"I'd like that so much," I say, as he pulls me to my feet.

"Come on, then!" And he races off, up the path.

I follow him up the gully. Halfway, I turn back. Clementine is still standing near the river. She looks me in the eye and waves. She doesn't look like a witch. She looks kind.

Chapter Seven

The next day is Shrine Day and Hal told me he'd meet me at the Shrine. My stomach is already in knots when I wake up. The fact is, I won't know anyone there, besides Hal and Mr. Frye, and everyone will be looking at me, the new girl. They'll all know my story. How I was part of the Colony, lost for all these years. How I'm one of the wealthiest Citizens. How I'm Ebba den Eeden, one of the den Eedens. And I own Greenhaven. Maybe some of them will even be mad because my great aunt was the one who bought up all their properties when they were selling so they could move to their security villages, when they didn't think the world would survive, and now I have it all.

Besides. All those eyes on me staring at my red hair and my huge feet. Ugh.

I don't even know how they hold Shrine service up here in the City. What if I stand up when everyone else sits down? What if I don't know the songs?

Aunty Figgy narrows her eyes when I tell her where I'm going. She dumps a plate of eggs and toast in front of me with a hummmph.

Well, what exactly does she expect? She can't expect me to stay away on Shrine day, even if she doesn't approve. I'm a Citizen. I have to be there.

When Leonid brings in a basket of firewood, I ask him to get the coach ready, and he drops the basket next to the stove and puts his hands on his hips.

"I've got to take you to the Shrine?"

"Mr. Frye...um...Mr. Frye said I have to be there. He's going to introduce me to people—to the other Citizens, and I'm going to meet Hal's sister, and..."

His black eyes glint under those heavy eyebrows. "You've got to be kidding me." He starts to say something else, then clamps his lips, spins around and stalks off across the yard, Isi at his heels.

I try to read Aunty Figgy's expression, but she won't look at me. She fetches a piece of meat from the pantry, throws it onto a wooden board and starts chopping it so hard that each knife blow gets stuck in the board, and she has to wrench it out.

I gulp down my tea and slink off to get ready.

I stare in the wardrobes, trying to decide what to wear. I have no idea what the female Citizens wear. I can't wear my aunt's old pants and shirt. Aunty Figgy has washed my tunic and pants from the bunker, and I try not to look at myself in the mirror as I pull them on. Mr. Frye and Hal are both so polished and groomed, and I haven't a clue how to make myself look more like them. Maybe I shouldn't go. I could stay here and work in the kitchen garden.

But then the buggy comes along the driveway. The thought of Leonid's satisfaction when I tell him I'm not going decides me. I grab the white robe I wore during the Sacrifice and pull it over the tunic. I tie my hair back in a long plait, and, just before I leave, I take off my necklace and put it away in the dressing table drawer. I don't want anyone saying it's witchcraft. But my neck looks so bare, and both Mr. Frye and Hal wore gold chains around their necks, so I scratch in the old wooden box on the dressing table and find a pendant of a dove in a silver circle. I put it on, and I'm ready to go.

We drive along the road that runs against the base of the mountain. Everything is so dry and brown. Ruins of houses stand between khaki shrubs or on bare rocky ground. You can see where once there was a thriving city with shops and houses and busy streets but now nothing stands higher than the bushes. It's all ruined buildings, with collapsed roofs and gashes where the doors and windows once were. Lamp posts have fallen like twigs, and everywhere there are piles of rotting things—clothing, old washing machines and fridges, rusted cars, even the bones of dead animals. I think of the world we used to watch so enviously in the Kinetika, a world where people owned so much stuff, and were always buying more so they'd have bigger better things than the people next door. And here it lies, forgotten, when they're long gone.

We pass a group of circular brown houses with roofs rising into a tall point, clustered together in a ring like seeds in a sunflower. I'm longing to ask Leonid about them, but the people getting into buggies outside them are dressed like Mr. Frye and Hal, and after this morning he's not talking to me about anything, especially not Citizens.

This is the road Mr. Frye drove me along when he brought me to Greenhaven. How come Greenhaven survived? Why is my land green and fertile when the rest of the city looks like a desert?

It is supposed to be my home, but it doesn't feel like home yet. I can't feel any connection to my family. Home for me is where my sabenzis are, and they're deep inside the mountain that looms over the road, throwing it into shadow. I miss them so much—even Jasmine's outspokenness, which used to irritate me sometimes.

More buggies have joined the road. They're so smart, compared to ours. Leonid pulls the horses aside to let in a shiny navy blue buggy with a coat of arms, drawn by two shining white horses. We follow it as it turns up through a pair of gates, and up a steep hill, past fields where ostriches leave dust trails as they run across the scrubby grass. A pair of goats stands on a rocky outcrop while others tear away at a small shrub. The stumps of thousands of trees stick out of the ground like rotten teeth. This must have been a thick forest once. Did the trees blow over in one of the massive storms that led up to the Purification? Or was it the radiation from the nuclear missiles that got them? Maybe people just chopped them down for firewood.

At the top of the road, the Shrine glitters in the morning sun. It's enormous, plated in some kind of shining coppery metal, and suddenly I feel very small. When Leonid stops the buggy and opens the door, I pause.

"Scared, miss?" he scoffs.

"Not at all." I put my chin in the air and jump down onto the road. I watch the crowds of people thronging through the door and wonder if I can slip in and sit at the back, where no one will notice me. And then Hal comes through the crowd, beaming, with a girl about my age. Her hair is braided into an intricate pattern of stripes around her beautifully shaped head, showing off her long neck and high cheekbones. When she smiles, her teeth are a vibrant white against her mahogany skin. I've never seen anyone as exquisite in my life.

"Ebba, so glad you're here," he says, kissing me on both cheeks. "How are you? You must be feeling so nervous. Don't worry, we'll look after you."

"Move over, idiot," the girl says, pushing him aside and hugging me. "I'm Cassiopeia. Hal's sister. Everyone calls me Cassie. Now don't worry about the service today. You're going to love it. We'll show you what to do."

We climb the marble steps, Cassie chattering all the way. I'm too in awe of her to say anything, but that doesn't stop her. "I'm so glad you're here. It must have been terrible down in the Colony. We're going to be friends,

I just know it. Hal's told me all about you. He hasn't stopped talking about you since you arrived."

An usher opens the door and waves of incense and noise and colors flood out.

"Come on," Cassie says, taking my hand, and everyone in the crammed chamber turns to look at me. The aisle is endless, and it appears that our seats are in the front row. I'm cringing by the time we reach them, and I know my face is bright red. I glance sideways as we move into the row, and meet the piercing blue eyes of General de Groot at the end of the adjacent row. He nods briefly at me, but the pretty woman next to him smiles and waves.

Does she know her husband tried to have me killed? Does she have any idea that there are two thousand young people living inside Table Mountain, and that they're working twelve-hour days because they've been told the world is dead and it's what they have to do to survive?

Do any of these people here know anything about life in the Colony?

I know I'm not a member of the Colony anymore. But I still feel like one. I don't feel like a Citizen at all.

"Sit here," Cassie whispers, pulling me down into a cushioned chair. Down in the Colony, we sat on wooden benches in a grey rock meeting hall, no adornments on the walls or the stage or anywhere. But this Shrine has lush, velvet green seats. The walls are painted in rich reds and golds. Brocaded banners hang from the roof, and at the front is a marble stage set with a rich embroidered carpet in the middle.

A voice announces, "All rise."

A trumpet plays, the doors open, and in comes the worship leaders I recognize from the Colony. They're dancing ahead, as before, bells jingling on their feet and ankles, waving the gold incense burners so the smell fills the whole Shrine. Behind them comes a procession of four men dressed in white, with golden circles embroidered on their robes. They're carrying the High Priest on a golden throne.

Gone is the terrifying presence who came into the Colony and picked out the weaklings one by one. Now he beams like a proud father, and he has opened his arms as though he wants to embrace us all. They place his throne in the center of the carpet, bow, and step back. The music stops.

There is a pause. Nobody moves.

I want to storm onto the stage and demand to know why he lied to us, why he's having the Colonists killed when there's a whole world out here they could just be released into.

Cassie bumps me gently with her shoulder, as though we've been friends our whole lives.

"You okay?" she whispers. "Don't be nervous. I'll show you what to do when."

Next to her, Hal catches my eye and winks.

The High Priest is their dad, and they're so nice. I can't reconcile the two facts. Do they know what he does when he comes to the Colony?

The High Priest rises from the throne and steps forward to the edge of the stage. "Welcome. Welcome to you all, my dearest family." His smile is as warm and friendly as Cassie's. His eye catches mine, seated in the front row, and instead of the hatred I felt from him in the Colony, a flood of warmth sweeps over me, drawing me in.

"We are here to celebrate and to worship the One True God, Prospiroh," he says. "Let us start with a song of praise to Him who chose us to be His Elite, His Lantern in this dark, dark world."

The band strikes up and the congregation begins to sing. I know this song. We used to sing it in the Colony, but there it was a grey, lifeless dirge. Here it throbs with life and energy, sung by thousands of voices in celebration.

You, oh Prospiroh, are the source of all our joy.
Look with favor upon us,
As you did on the Day of Purification,
When the waters covered the Earth,
And you saved us.
You have given us land, shelter, food and water.
Your people prosper.
We praise and thank you, Prospiroh,
for your protection.

Then another Righteous steps forward. He is tall and thin and his eyes, deep set like the High Priest's, are a blue-purple. His skin paler than Hal and Cassie's. His pale hands twist together in front of his white robe. He looks torn, as though he hates being there, hates his white robe, hates the choir and even his father.

"That's Lucas," Hal whispers. "He's my half-brother. His mom is my dad's first wife." He gestures to a tall blond woman in the next row.

"Great God Prospiroh, you have given us so much," Lucas prays in a surprisingly melodious voice.

"Amen," roars the congregation.

"If you feel called to give back to the Lord Prospiroh, shout 'Amen, Prospiroh, Amen.'"

Again the congregation roars, "Amen, Prospiroh, Amen." Lucas looks up, and our eyes meet. There's a jolt of recognition, something electric between us. He is not smiling though, and I drop my eyes.

Then a weird thing happens. Someone in the choir begins to sing and we all join in. It starts off as the hymn I know from the Colony: "You, oh Prospiroh, are the source of all our joy." But as we reach verse seven, a voice begins to rise above the rest, and turn into a strange chant. One by one the other choir members join in, their voices soaring and swooping like birds at nightfall. The High Priest walks in front of them, waving his arms slowly in the air.

"Praise Prospiroh," he sings. "He is here, here with us. Raise your voices. Praise our Mighty God Prospiroh."

The congregation begin to join in the strange song, each person singing their own tune, but somehow it all melds into harmony. I don't have a clue what the words can mean. They're some language I've never heard. "Oh Tanamasante," the High Priest sings. "Release your songs from these people, oh Prospiroh." He is coming down the marble stairs, towards us.

All around me, people sway to the chant, their arms waving, ecstasy on their faces. Hal's eyes are shut and he's radiant, arms raised in worship. Cassie's singing too, as though she's not even part of this world anymore. The High Priest walks slowly down the stairs, chanting. When he is right in front of me, he looks straight into my eyes and places one hand firmly on my head. A jolt runs through me. I'm tippling over backwards. Someone catches me and lowers me to the floor. I can hear the singing going on around me, but I can't move. Can't think. Can't escape from this cocoon.

"Prospiroh! Prospiroh!" sings the congregation over and over..

The High Priest is standing over me, his hands lifted to heaven.

"Praise you for your daughter," he prays. "Praise you for this young woman upon whom you have poured your blessings." He leans over me and lays his hand on my neck.

I go cold inside. But he lifts the pendant around my neck for a second and then drops it back on my chest.

"Rise up, Ebba," he says, holding his hand out.

The paralysis leaves me. I take his hand and he helps me to my feet. I'm embarrassed, and I look around quickly to see how many people are laughing at me.

Most are still rapt in prayer, eyes closed, singing. Those who make eye contact with me are smiling, as though I've done something remarkable. As though I'm special.

A glow of pleasure moves through me.

Through the long sermon that follows, I ponder it. How could I just fall to the floor when he touched me? Why couldn't I move? Did he touch the necklace accidentally? It seemed like he was inspecting it, but why would he do that?

The service ends with a final hymn. While the band and choir are belting it out, the congregation are open-ing their bags and wallets. Stewards pass baskets along the rows and people throw in gold coins. I haven't got anything to put in, and I blush as I pass the basket along. I look up and the High Priest is watching with a smile. It's all right, he seems to say.

Then the service is over. Cassie turns to me with shin-ing eyes. "Wasn't that just fabulous? You were touched in a special way today."

Everybody feels that way, it seems. I've never seen so many hugs and kisses in my life. Hundreds of people want to embrace me. "Welcome home," they say. "Welcome to the City."

"But they don't know me," I whisper to Hal.

"It's because Prospiroh has blessed you so mightily," Hal explains, as one of the High Priest's five wives releases me from her huge arms. She's a large blond woman in an orange and purple robe, and like everyone else up here, she looks shiny with good living. "Indeed it is, Hal," she exclaims. "Ebba, you were lost and now you've been found. We are so glad to welcome you home."

They invite me to lunch. I feel bad for Leonid, sitting outside the Shrine with nothing to eat and nothing to do, but I don't know how to say no to the High Priest's wives. And anyway, I want to go. They're a huge family

—five wives and about twenty children—and I want to sit around a table and share a meal with friendly, happy, non-crazy people who like me just because I'm me. Not like Leonid who seems to dislike me precisely because I'm me.

Hal introduces me to his mother, Evelyn. She's the third wife, and the prettiest. Her hair is woven into braids, each ending with a gold bead. Her robe is as bright and richly patterned as the wall hangings in their Shrine, and she's soft and plump and smiley. I can't help liking her. When she links her arm in mine and takes me out of the side door of the Shrine, through a courtyard and into the compound where they all live, it feels like I've known her forever.

The only sour note is Lucas. He can barely look me in the eye when Cassie introduces us, pauses as though he's about to say something, then mutters, "Going for a walk."

He lopes off, all hunched shoulders and long legs, and I wonder what I did to upset him. Does he think I'm not good enough to eat with them?

"Don't mind him," Cassie says. "He's not normal. Can't handle people."

"He's an idiot," Hal says, with a sneer.

He grabs my hand and pulls me back onto the sofa. "Come on, sit down. We want you here. Don't we, Cassie?"

The servants bring in jugs of lemonade then. "Have some juice," Hal says. "You look so hot."

"That long hair of yours must be so heavy," Cassie says, lifting my plait. "When last did you have it trimmed?"

"Trimmed? As in cut? Never."

She gapes at me. "You've never been to the hairdresser? Mother," she calls, "Ebba's never had her hair done."

Evelyn is in the kitchen, but she peers around the door at me. "You poor thing. We must fix that at once. I'm going to call Pietro."

"Pietro's a genius," Cassie says. "Everyone says so."

Evelyn sends a servant down to the Shrine. Pietro is still there, and a few minutes later, he comes puffing in through the front door, beads of sweat on his upper lip. "Oh. My. God," he exclaims when he sees me. "Do you need a makeover or what? Don't you worry, I'm gonna find the Cinderella lurking there under all that hair and invite her to the ball."

"Come to the bathroom," Cassie says, pulling me up. She leads me through the courtyard to a large room lined with marble tiles. It's so grand, like something from olden days Hollywood.

I think of my bathroom at home, the wooden floor, the metal bathtub with the feet like claws. It seems so dowdy compared to this. Why didn't my great aunt smarten it up?

Cassie finds me a stool to sit on while Pietro opens his leather bag and whisks out a fabric cape, a comb, and a pair of scissors. He flips the cape open in the air and ties it around my neck. He undoes my plait, lifts my hair and lets it run through his fingers while he examines every strand. Then he swings me around so I can't see my reflection.

"Are you going to cut it?" I ask.

"Shh," he says, tapping my hand playfully. "You have to trust me. Now lean over the basin so I can wash your hair."

I watch Cassie's face as he gets to work. She's definitely approving.

When he's finished cutting, long red curls lie around the legs of the stool. I shake my head. The heaviness is gone. Cassie's right. This is going to be so much cooler in the heat.

"Wonderful," declares Evelyn, coming in for a look. She squeezes my arm. "You look gorgeous."

Hal tries to come in, but they shoo him away. "You can't see Ebba until the makeover's finished," Cassie says.

Next Pietro massages a mixture into my scalp. It burns, but he pouts when I tell him. "You have to suffer to be beautiful," he says.

While the lotion is drying he gets to work on my eyebrows. I squeal as he plucks the first hair, but he smacks my hand again. "What did I say about no pain no gain?" He purses his lips. "Now be brave, sister. The end result will be worth it."

He finishes attacking my eyebrows and turns to my nails. He tut tuts when he sees my birth mark. "Such a shame," he murmurs, stroking my fingers. "Such an ugly mark on such lovely hands. If you like I can find a tattoo artist to work on it? Turn it into a butterfly, or a unicorn perhaps."

I hide my hand under my thigh. "No thanks."

Cassie laughs. "Pietro wants everyone perfect. You won't believe the number of sit-ups he makes me do to get my tummy flat."

Evelyn puts her arm around his shoulders. "We can't do without him."

Pietro bats his eyelashes at her. "Thank you, darling."

When my nails are done, he washes the lotion out of my hair and takes me back to the courtyard. He makes me sit in the sun while three servants fan my hair to dry it. He outlines my eyes with kohl, and tells me to pout, while he paints my lips with a pot of red balm.

Cassie is getting so excited, hopping around us, getting in the way, clapping her hands when he finishes putting blusher on my cheeks. "That robe's not the right color for you," she says. "And what are you wearing under it?" She lifts it and inspects the tunic and pants I brought from the Colony. "Those are just ghastly. Look how thick the fabric is. Doesn't it scratch?"

"Take them off, take them off," Pietro shrieks. "Cassie, find her something decent to wear."

A moment later, Cassie is back with a beautiful sea green robe.

"Gorgeous." Pietro approves. "I've taught you well, Miss Cassie." He claps his hands and the servants drop the fans and leave. Then he and Cassie hold up the cape to form a barrier and I slip off my clothes and drop the silky fabric over my head. It feels so smooth and soft against my skin.

"Now what are we going to do about those sandals?" Pietro says, with his finger on his chin. "They are beyond hideous. Where did you get them?"

I blush. I was hoping he wasn't going to get as far as my feet. "From...from the Colony."

"Exactly! I knew it. Serviceable and durable. Ghastly. We'll have to find you something pretty and girly."

I try and hide my feet under my robe. But it's too late.

"What size are you?" Cassie asks. "I've got hundreds of shoes. Here, try these on."

She slips off her shoe and pushes it towards me. I knew this was going to happen. I'm bright red. "They... they won't fit me."

"Ebba!" she exclaims. "Your feet are ENORMOUS."

I hope Hal didn't hear her. It's embarrassing enough having them on show without having someone shriek about them.

Pietro pats my shoulder. "No worries, sister. I'll get the shoemaker to run you up some gorgeous sandals this week. And some robes. You deserve only the best. A beautiful girl like you."

Cassie claps her hands. "Ooooh, yes. This is such fun. You look fantastic. Can we do the reveal now, Pietro?"

He stands back and examines me from head to— well, not to toe, he can't bring himself to look at my sandals again. So he glances all the way down to the hem of my robe. He flicks up my hair around my shoulders, and pats his tummy, very pleased with himself. "I think we're just about ready. What a transformation. What a transformation!"

I can't wait to see what they've done to me. Cassie's eyes are shining as she leads me to the hall where there's a large mirror in a fancy gold frame.

"When I count to three, you can open them," Pietro says. "One, two...three."

I open my eyes and my mouth drops open. It's not me reflected there. This girl has a long neck, high cheekbones, and brown shoulder-length hair cut in a fringe. Her eyebrows frame her eyes, making them look bigger and greener. Cassie and Evelyn are delighted. They clap and laugh, asking me again and again if I love it.

I don't know how to answer them. I don't look like someone from the Colony anymore. I'm shiny and groomed like a Citizen. But what would Jasmine and Letti say if they could see me? What would Micah say? Would he even recognize me?

"You are gorgeous," Pietro exclaims happily. "You look like a million dollars, not a bedraggled witch."

When Hal sees me he stares and stares. I'm starting to get embarrassed. "Wow," he says finally, shaking his head. "It's a miracle."

"She looks like one of us," Cassie says happily.

Of course, Aunty Figgy doesn't like it. "What have you done!" she exclaims the moment I walk into this house. "Just look what they've done—you look ridiculous. You look like one of THEM!"

Who is she to tell me how I can and can't look? "I like the way I look. Everyone kept saying I was a witch because of my hair."

She shakes her head and squeezes her mouth shut

like she's trying to stop the words escaping. Her shoulders hunch as she picks up the broom and starts sweeping the kitchen floor, like she can sweep me out with the dirt.

"I was hot," I say. "My hair has never ever been trimmed. Pietro says I had the worst split ends he's ever seen."

She huffs. "There was nothing wrong with it, and the color was beautiful. And now they've gone and ruined it."

She leans the broom against the cupboard and stands up straight, hands on her hips. "You should be proud of your red hair. It's your heritage. It links you to the Goddess. If you forget your legacy, you forget who you are."

Not likely, I think. How can I possibly forget it when you're here reminding me day and night? But she's looking fierce, her little eyes watching me like an eagle with its prey, and I don't dare backchat her. Instead I break some news I'm sure will thrill her.

"I've got some friends coming over for lunch next Friday," I say. "There will be six of us. Can you please make a nice meal?"

Her face darkens. "What friends?" She almost spits the words. "That boy that's hanging around here—the High Priest's son?" She doesn't wait for me to answer. "The High Priest and his family are not your friends, Ebba. You're a den Eeden. And you're asking for trouble inviting people like that into Greenhaven."

"They're my friends." I try to sound more confident than I feel. "They're coming, whether you approve or not."

Later that day, I see her sitting in front of the statue of the Goddess in the window. She's got a look of utter concentration on her face and she doesn't hear me when I come into the kitchen. The sharp lemon-herb smell of buchu fills the room. I don't want to disturb her, so I creep away.

Aunty Figgy hardly speaks to me for the next two days.

She's muttering as she cooks and cleans—prayers to the Goddess for protection. It starts to get on my nerves. Why can't she just relax and be happy for me that I've made some friends? She just wants me to live here alone like an old lady, seeing nobody, doing nothing.

But the day before the visit, she comes into the sitting room where I'm practicing my reading. It's mid-morning and I'm expecting Hal. He's coming to give me another reading lesson, and I can't wait to see him. I've been practicing every spare minute.

"Ebba," she says. "Please listen to me."

I put down the book with a sigh. "What is it, Aunty Figgy?"

"I don't think you understand. Greenhaven land is sacred. You can't just invite any Tom, Dick, or Harry here. You've got to be very careful."

"Hal and Cassie aren't any Tom, Dick, or Harry," I snap. "They're my friends. And they're bringing some of their friends to meet me and to see the house. It's you who don't understand. You're so prejudiced against the High Priest that you won't listen to me. The people at the Shrine really made me feel welcome. And it's not like I'm going to let anyone damage my home. I care about it too, you know."

"Ebba." She speaks loudly and slowly, like I'm five years old. "Greenhaven is the only place on the whole planet where Theia is still allowed to reign. That's why I don't want you inviting Prospiroh's people here. They want to destroy us, Greenhaven."

I snort. "I hardly think Hal and Cassie want to destroy me, Aunty Figgy. I think you're forgetting that the High Priest saved me. I would be dead if he hadn't told Mr. Frye I was down there."

She shakes her head. "No good will come of it, no good at all."

"Well, I don't care. It's my house, and if I want to invite

my friends for lunch, I'm going to..."

She doesn't even let me finish. She turns on her heel and flounces out, leaving me seething.

At noon the next day, the grand table in the dining room is set for six. Aunty Figgy may be sulking but she's prepared a generous meal. There are loaves of homemade bread, dishes of roasted vegetables, goat's milk cheeses and pickles, butter and apricot jam, and a big fig, honey, and walnut cake. It's not sophisticated food like Hal's family eat, and I hope they don't think it's too simple, but my own mouth waters. It's much better food than anything I ever had in the Colony—and to be honest, I prefer Aunty Figgy's fresh food to the spread they laid out at the High Priest's house.

I run to the door as soon as I hear the High Priest's carriage coming down the driveway. Out jump Hal, Cassie, and their friends Pamza, Oliver, and Dax. They're laughing and joking as they come up the steps, and they greet me with huge hugs. Isi takes one look at the crowd, and runs into my bedroom.

Then someone else gets out of the carriage: Lucas.

"Sorry about him," Cassie says, gesturing with her thumb towards her half-brother. "Just as we were leaving, he came along and got into the coach. I told him he wasn't invited but he insisted on coming anyway."

Why is he here? Has he come to keep tabs on us? He doesn't like me. But astonishingly, Isi is greeting him like a long lost friend, running around his legs and barking. "You're very welcome, Lucas," I say, as he bends down and cuddles Isi. "Come inside. You must all be hungry. Would you like some lemon cordial?"

"I'm starving," says Hal. "I hope you've got some of that famous bread Uncle Fergis is always raving about."

Oliver sees the table and makes straight for it, cutting

a thick slice off the loaf and spreading it thickly with butter. "Can we tuck in?"

"You already have." Cassie laughs and smacks his hand.

They don't wait for me to invite them to sit down. They grab plates and start helping themselves. Everyone except Lucas.

"Wouldn't you like some bread and cheese?" I ask him.

He shakes his head. "I'm fasting," he says, as though he's rebuking me. He disappears down the passage towards the kitchen.

It's confusing. I thought Prospiroh was happy with abundance. Or maybe my food isn't good enough for him? And what is he doing in the kitchen? I can hear Aunty Figgy greeting him. Surely they don't know each other?

But Cassie and Hal and their friends have no problems with Aunty Figgy's cooking.

"Your kitchen girl is unbelievable," Pamza says. "I wish ours could make food like this. Where do you get the produce from?"

"She's not my kitchen girl," I say. "And it's all from Greenhaven. From our own farm."

They think that's incredible. They think everything about Greenhaven is astonishing. After lunch they want to explore and they swarm from room to room, opening wardrobes, unpacking trunks and drawers. Then the boys go outside to climb the big Ficus tree that towers over the meadow. Only Lucas is quiet. He's found a book in the study, and is sitting alone, away from the mess of dirty dishes at the dining room table, reading.

Cassie and Pamza find a hatbox in one of the bedrooms, and bring it into my room where we can watch the boys through the window.

"Here, Ebba, stop perving my brother and try on this hat," Cassie says, nudging me. She hands me a pink frilly hat and Pamza chooses a black pillbox hat with a veil.

"Incredible," Cassie exclaims as she fluffs up the ostrich feathers on the brim of her straw hat. "It's like something a superstar would wear in the Old World. It must have cost a fortune. I wish they still made movies. I'm sure I could have gone to Hollywood." She picks up the hand mirror to see what it looks like from behind.

Pamza's taken off her hat and is giggling as she tries on a brown wig she found in the bottom drawer of the dressing table.

It reminds me of Jasmine's curly brown hair. I feel a pang of longing. I wish she were here instead of these giggling girls who don't seem to have a worry in the world. What would she think of them? Would she like them? I know she wouldn't just scratch through my dressing table drawers without asking.

"He's so handsome," Pamza says. She stops preening for a moment to look out of the window.

"Who?" I ask, joining her at the window.

"Hal, of course. Just look at him. He's so athletic. He's climbing up that tree like a professional, and I'm sure he's never been in one before."

He sees us watching and waves from between the branches.

"I wish the High Priest would arrange his marriage," Pamza says wistfully, "and put us all out of our misery."

Cassie pulls a scarf over Pamza's head. "Here comes the bride," she sings. "I'd like to have you for my sister-in-law, Pamzy. Then I can be your bridesmaid."

"I bet if Hal could choose, he'd pick Ebba," Pamza says. "He talks about you all the time."

I don't know what to say, but she gives another giggle. "You're blushing, aren't you, Ebba?" And she tickles my cheeks with a lock of hair from the wig.

"Hal's too young. He doesn't want to get married yet," Cassie says, putting on one of the mini dresses she's found in the wardrobe.

Pamza laughs at the sight of her legs. "I can't believe they wore dresses like that in the old days," she says. "No wonder Prospiroh sent the Purification."

Cassie giggles. "Don't tell my mom and dad, hey?" She admires herself in the dressing table mirror. "It needs a necklace. Didn't your great aunt have any jewelry?" She opens the carved wooden box on the dressing table, and the next thing I know, Isi is halfway out from under the bed, growling, hackles raised.

"What's it, girl?" I ask, ruffling the fur at her neck.

She's staring at Cassie and her ears are back.

"Isi, stop it," I say. Then I see—the amulet is around Cassie's neck.

The room goes cold. There's an unfriendly force swirling up around me. The amulet shimmers on Cassie's elegant neck.

"I adore this. It's just amazing. Can I have it, Ebba?" she begs. "Please, pretty please?"

Isi edges towards Cassie, snarling.

"Hey, Ebba, can you put your dog outside," Pamza says. "It's scaring me."

But Isi is gone, running through the dining room towards the kitchen.

"It's just gorgeous," Cassie says. "Please, Ebba. I gave you that turquoise robe. Can't I have this?"

"Um...um, I can't give it away," I stutter. "I'm really sorry. I'd give it to you, I promise, but my mom gave it to me. It's the only thing I've got from her."

"Oh!" Cassie looks like I've slapped her. "I didn't know. You didn't tell me your mom gave it to you. It's just so pretty." She twirls it around her finger, wistful. "I've never seen another one like it. And it looks so awesome on me. Maybe we can swap for some more of my things?"

Isi is back, followed by Lucas. It's almost as though she

went to call him? Surely not. But Lucas comes into the room, unclasps the chain from Cassie's neck, and drops the necklace back in the box.

"It's a witchcraft trinket," he says, closing the lid firmly and shoving the box in a drawer. "Don't play with it." He marches out and goes back to his book. Does he really think it's something evil?

"Oh lighten UP," Cassie snorts after him. "You're not on Shrine duty now."

But the fun atmosphere is gone. Pamza throws her hat on the bed. "Let's go and see what the garden looks like," she says.

"No," says Cassie. "There will be bugs and scary stuff. It's wild out there. Let's stay here rather."

"Here's something cool," Oliver calls from the sitting room. He's tired of climbing trees and now he's found the gramophone, and is going through the records on the shelf.

"Hey," he shouts. "These are like over a hundred years old. I present to you The Ink Spots, with The Java Jive." He lowers the needle on the record and this funny old-fashioned music comes out, with four guys singing in harmony about coffee. "Drop a nickel in the pot, Joe. Waiter, waiter, percolator." Soon we're all singing it as we dance around the veranda. We collapse laughing at the end.

"This place is amazing," Pamza says. "You should develop it. Turn it into a holiday destination—experience life as it was in the olden days."

Lucas has been reading his book quietly, ignoring our laughter, but now he closes it with a bang. "There's a reason why Prospiroh brought down the Purification," he snaps. "This isn't the sort of place people should come to on holiday."

"Jeez," Hal exclaims. "You really do know how to ruin

everything, don't you? No wonder you don't have any friends."

"We'd better go," Cassie says, glaring at Lucas. "It's a long way home."

They pile into the carriage and I wave them goodbye, feeling a little deflated. They've left a horrible mess—cupboards unpacked, clothes thrown on the beds, the records piled on the sitting room floor. It takes me ages to tidy it all up. The last thing I put away is the book that Lucas was reading. He's left it open on the table. I pick it up curiously. The cover is buckled and stained as though it has been left outside in the rain. Inside are pages and pages of tiny writing scrawled across the lines like spider legs. I come to a page that is almost empty, except for three words in huge letters.

"Prospiroh versus Theia."

I can't read most of what's written after that, but it carries on for page after page. The water has caused the ink to run in some places, smudging the words, but I pick out the word "necklace" once or twice, and the name "den Eeden."

On the last page the big letters are back. It takes me a while to sound them out: First justice. Then peace.

"So they've gone, have they?" a voice says behind me.

It's Aunty Figgy, and she's looking particularly grumpy. "They made a fine mess, didn't they? And off they go, leaving you to clean up after them. Typical." She takes the book from my hands.

"Whose book is that?" I ask as she tucks it back into a shelf in the library.

She shrugs. "I have no idea. Daisy found it in the forest years ago."

The atmosphere in the house has changed. It was serene before. Now it feels like the house is rocking from too much noise and unpacking and twirling around to music. And what is Lucas playing at? I can't read him.

He's so stern and unfriendly. Is he on my side?

Thanks to him, my new friends all think my house is evil. I wish I hadn't invited them around. Maybe the whole thing was a bad idea, but I'm not giving Aunty Figgy the satisfaction of saying, "I told you so."

Chapter Eight

I forget where I am. When I wake the next morning, my old reflex kicks in, and I look for Jasmine's curly head. The pain that shoots through me when I remember we're apart is so sharp that for a second, I can't breathe.

Right now, my sabenzis are probably waking to the siren. Maybe Jasmine is looking across at my empty bunk and feeling as raw as I am. It's worse for them as they think I'm dead. The three of them must be trying to get on with their lives, trying to stay strong and pull their weight, so they don't get picked for the next Sacrifice.

As I lie on my pillows, watching the sunbeams creep through the shutters and throw stripes across the bed, I weed through the memories, trying to work out what was wrong with yesterday's visit. Was it just Lucas, watching me, judging me? Was it Aunty Figgy's disapproval that I could feel hovering over the house, even though she didn't come out of the kitchen?

Finally I realize what makes Hal and the gang so different from my friends in the Colony: my sabenzi had nothing, owned almost nothing. We all ate the same, dressed the same, did the same amount of work. We had to be interested in each other, to form bonds and make our friendships strong because we had nothing else of value. Hal, Oliver, Dax, Pamza, and Cassie weren't really interested in me except as an oddity—the girl who came from nothing and inherited so much. They only wanted to see all the stuff I owned, to giggle over the clothes and hats, to inspect even the smallest painting and piece of furniture, to play my records and rifle through my jewelry box.

Life is so complicated up here. I can't work out who to trust or who to believe when there are so many contrasting stories. Why does Mr. Frye go to the Shrine and worship Prospiroh if he's the den Eeden family lawyer, and the den Eedens are descended from the Goddess? Why does Hal's father allow him to visit me almost every day if he thinks my necklace is witchcraft? Maybe he doesn't know about it. What if Lucas tells him—and he bans Hal from visiting me? I don't think I could cope up here without Hal's kindness.

Maybe I should ask to go back into the Colony. Back to the safe world with the people I love. But I look at the trees outside my window, at the sky, the fluffy clouds, and stroke Isi's soft fur. How can I leave this behind now— now that I know the life in the Colony isn't necessary, that everyone should be let out?

There's a knock at my door. It's Aunty Figgy, with a cup of rooibos tea. "I remember your mother lying in this exact same bed," she says, with a soft smile. "You look so like her, now that your hair is brown."

"Isn't there a picture of her?" I ask. "Anywhere?"

"By the time of the Calamity, everything was digital," she says. "And when technology disappeared, so did all our photos. It's all gone." She picks up my robe from the floor and hangs it up in the cupboard. "I remember your mom in this dress." She smiles, taking out a red dress with a short flippy skirt. "She looked so pretty. Those were the days when we could wear what we liked—before they took over and made all these terrible laws..." She hangs the dress back and closes the door. "There might be some pictures of your mom in your great aunt's sketchbooks. She was always drawing her."

I sit up in bed. "Really? Can I see them?"

She laughs. "Of course. They're in the library. Shall I bring them to you?"

I've avoided the library. It makes me feel stupid, my bad reading. I'm practicing every day, but it's taking forever to learn.

Aunty Figgy comes back with a pile of soft covered notebooks, each tied with a ribbon. "I'll leave you to look at these," she says, putting them on the end of my bed.

"Aunty Figgy," I say, as she is leaving, "who was my father?"

Her back stiffens.

"Did you know him?" I add.

She pauses, then turns around. "No idea," she says, shrugging. "You mom never told us who he was." And off she goes to the kitchen.

I don't believe that she doesn't know. I don't believe her at all. But there's nothing I can do about it. She'll tell me what she wants to tell me when she wants to tell me—just like the High Priest, just like Mr. Frye. They seem determined to keep me in the dark as though I was a naive child still living in the Colony. But I'm not there anymore. I'm in the real world and I deserve to know. I need to know everything.

I open the first book. The sketches are beautiful—drawings of trees, flowers, people working in the fields. There are drawings of cars parked in front of the house and page after page of watercolor paintings of the Holy Well. There's someone sitting at a table, shelling peas. It looks like—it is—a young Aunty Figgy, before her face got so lined. There's a pregnant woman with a sweet face, looking out of one of the long windows in the sitting room. There's a series of sketches of the same woman and a little girl playing on the white sands of a beach. The mountain is in the background, and I realize with a shock that it was drawn before the waters rose—when Table Island was still joined to the Mainland.

I open another book. A-li...I sound out the name. This is what I've been looking for. There's my mother Ali as a toddler, running through trees, riding a tricycle, laughing at a dog—it looks like Isi, those three big black spots and ginger ears are distinctive, but Isi can't be that old, surely? She's asleep at my feet, but now she opens her amber eyes and thumps her tail. In a later book, I find drawings of my mom sitting on the stoep, asleep and heavily pregnant. And the last picture is of my mom feeding a new born baby. Of my mom holding, nurturing, loving me. Isi lies at her feet.

Looking at these pictures, I feel how much she loved me. But she's gone. The house, everything I own, feels like the dried out husk of a plant. The person that gave it life has gone before I got a chance to know her.

And then Hal comes back. Just as I'd decided he'd been banned from coming to Greenhaven, he arrives not on horseback but in the buggy. He jumps out smiling, and I run down the front stairs and, forgetting to be self-conscious, greet him with a hug.

"I've got a gift for you," he says. "My mother sent it."

"A gift? That's wonderful." I rip open the package. Inside is a pair of gorgeous turquoise sandals and three new robes. "That's so nice of her," I say, hugging him again. "Please tell her that I love them." I take off my ugly serviceable Colony shoes and slide my feet into the sandals. They're so soft and comfortable. Even my over-sized feet look elegant in them.

"Get in," he says. "We're going for a drive."

"Where are we going?"

"It's a surprise."

I shout goodbye to Aunty Figgy and get into the carriage.

He calls to the coachman and we set off. At the end of the farm road, we don't take the right turn towards the Shrine and the Colony. Instead we go left, along a road that climbs steeply up the forested hillside to a nek in the mountain range.

"This is all your land," he says. "Everything here is part of Greenhaven."

It's the first time I've seen the farm from this angle. I can see how enormous the forest is, how many millions of trees my great aunt planted. Where there is no forest, the ground looks fertile, but lies empty except for a herd of goats chomping the weeds. I could plant crops here, enough to send food down into the Colony so they didn't need to sacrifice anyone else, so they could get more to eat. Or they could come out of the bunker and live up here on my land. As we drive further up the slope, the ground becomes too rocky for crops, but we could build houses— maybe a cottage for each sabenzi group so nobody has to live underground anymore.

Every cottage could have its own piece of ground to grow the food the sabenzi groups will need to survive. I want to tell Hal about it, but he always brushes me aside when I talk about the Colony, as though what he can't see doesn't matter.

He's sitting next to me, and now he leans over and murmurs in my ear. "You're so far from everyone out here in the bundu. I worry about you."

His hand is just millimeters from my leg. His little finger brushes my robe.

My heart speeds up. Was that an accident? Is he making a move on me?

"I'm fine here," I say. "I've got Aunty Figgy and Leonid and Isi."

"I was hoping..." He moves his arm along the back of my seat. "I was hoping you would move to the compound.

My mother wants to look after you."

I wasn't expecting that. "Seriously? To move in with your family?"

"There's lots of room. You could share with Cassie or have your own bedroom. Then we can see each other every day."

"But...but the farm?"

"My father can find someone to manage it. It won't be a problem. It operated just fine all those years you were in the Colony, didn't it? Hmmmm?"

"My great aunt was alive then. She ran it. When she died a year ago, Mr. Frye let all the laborers go except Aunty Figgy and Leonid."

His hand slips over my leg. "Please say yes, Ebba," he murmurs.

I look at his hand, resting on my thigh, distracted by the unfamiliar feelings pulsing through me. I want so much to say yes. A part of me wants to say no. Which is stronger? Yes. Definitely yes. I think.

His hand is stroking my thigh. "Ebba," he murmurs, lifting my chin with his finger.

Is he going to kiss me?

My eyes linger on his face—his long eyelashes, the plumpness of his bottom lip, the dimples in each cheek. I can feel the energy pulsing out of him as his hand finds my shoulder and he moves his face towards mine. I break out in a sweat. Maybe no is stronger. Maybe.

I get up and open the window. "It's so hot in here. Where are we going?"

"To Constantia Nek." He reaches for my hand. "On the other side of the pass is Longkloof Harbor. It's where they hold the markets once a week. The view from the top is spectacular. You'll love it."

He's going to kiss me. But something is bothering me.

"Please come," he says quietly, looking into my eyes.

"I want to be with you every moment of every day."

I push aside whatever it is that's trying to shove its way into my mind. "I want to be with you too." He wants me to be with him forever. I'll be safe and loved. I'll belong.

He pulls me back onto the seat next to him, and presses his lips against mine. I wrap my arms around his neck and close my eyes as he kisses me as though I'm the only thing that matters in the whole world to him. His hands run down my back, pulling me against his warm, firm body. There is nobody to stop us, no guard to burst in and punish us. I should be enjoying it, but...

This doesn't feel right. Why aren't I happier? Cassie says every girl on the Island wants to kiss him, and he's selected me over all of them. He's from the most important family on Table Island. He's incredibly good looking. He's chosen me, and he's so certain about it that he's invited me to come and live with his family.

If I go, there will be no more Aunty Figgy talking crazy, no more Leonid sneering and despising me. It sounds perfect. I'm so grateful to his family—for caring so much about me, and yet....Why does it feel uncomfortable? Like I've got one of those spiky burrs Leonid calls duiweltjies poking at me.

"If I come and live at the compound, can I bring my dog?" I ask when at last we break apart.

"Dog?" He laughs as he pushes my hair back off my face. "Why do you want a dog?"

"I love her. She sleeps on my bed. She follows me everywhere."

"Twenty-six of us live at the compound, and that's just the family. There won't be room for a dog. And anyway, dogs are unclean. My father won't have one in the house. Maybe he'll let her come, but she'll have to be chained up in the yard."

Chained? My Isi? I swallow. "Oh."

"Come here," he says, pulling me towards him again. "Leave her at Greenhaven."

Leave Isi behind? It's...unthinkable. It's only been six weeks since I came out of the Colony, but she feels like family—like the last remaining member of my family. I can't leave her behind

"You'll forget about her soon enough..." He pulls me towards him and kisses me again.

The horses are starting to strain from the steep climb when finally we round a corner, and we're almost at the top. Greenhaven lies below us, a stripe of green in a sea of khaki vegetation. It's strange how it's the only fertile part of the landscape. It reaches right down to the grey wall that circles the whole Island, keeping back the sea. Keeping us safe from outsiders.

We reach the top and the other side of the mountain comes into view. The trees are all gone. The road drops sharply away, clinging to the bare mountainside, and below us is a long narrow inlet of sparkling sea.

"The people of Boat Bay are down there," Hal says. "It sucks that they live in the fjord. They just moved in one day. They didn't have permission to be there—no, of course not—they just invaded it on their plastic rafts with their houses that were literally made out of garbage, and when they got to the end of the inlet, they tied them all together to make that floating platform."

I peer over the edge trying to see what's making him so angry. The vivid blue of the inlet is broken at the end by a large Island. It's covered in soil, and there are patches of green at one end. It looks like they're growing vegetables on it. That seems incredibly resourceful to me, considering how hot and dry it is on this side of the mountain.

"But where do the people live? Surely they need a roof over their heads?"

"They used to live on that Island, apparently. But then they burrowed into the mountainside like rats, making houses out of any old junk that washed up on the beach. You'll see it more clearly when we go around the corner. My father wants to move them away. They're a security risk."

Aunty Figgy and Leonid come from Boat Bay. How are they a "security risk"? I look down at the rafts tied together, the rusty old boats and sagging shacks stuck into the mountainside just above the water's edge. Which house is Aunty Figgy's? Which is Leonid's? "If he moves them away, where will they go?"

"Who cares? They're poor. They must have displeased Prospiroh."

Does that mean I displeased Prospiroh? Because for the first seventeen years of my life, I was so poor, all I owned was a necklace and a baby blanket. I want to ask him, but I don't dare. I'm realizing he gets irritated when I question him about anything serious.

The coachman pulls off the road to let an army wagon past.

"I brought a picnic," Hal says, opening a hamper. "Have a sandwich."

But I'm distracted. The wagon is huge—ten oxen pull it, and it's laden with sacks. I recognize them—they're the ones we use in the Colony to hold the harvest that gets sent to the storage gallery. What are they doing out here, on a wagon?

"What's wrong?" Hal asks with his mouth full.

"Those sacks—they come from the bunker."

He's rooting around in the basket for another sandwich. "Mmmm," he says, "yum, these are so good."

"Hal," I say, shaking his arm. "Are they from the Colony?"

"Of course," he says. "What's the big deal?"

"Where are they going?

"They're going to the storage sheds at the Harbor."

"Why? There's a whole storage gallery in the Colony."

"Ebba," he exclaims, brushing crumbs off his robe, "why are you so hung up on a boring old wagon? We're supposed to be having a picnic. I wanted to show you the view of the City from up here, and you're spoiling everything. And look—now the weather is changing."

The wind is picking up and the top of the mountain is covered in grey clouds. At last the wagon has passed, and Hal knocks on the window. "It's going to rain. We should turn back."

"Yes sir," the coachman says.

The mood has changed along with the weather. Hal is tapping his fingers on the soft seat as he stares out of the window.

"I'm sorry," I murmur. "I didn't mean to annoy you."

"It's not you," he says. "It's the goddam weather. I wanted to go all the way to the Harbor to show you the sea." He leans back and puts his arm around me. "I could never be cross with you," he says. "Ever." And he kisses me again.

Again, that unfamiliar feeling.

Something is still nudging at my memory.

Something I had buried.

And then I remember what it is.

It's Micah.

Micah, the boy who was executed...

Lithe, slim Micah, with the shining black hair that fell in his eyes, who moved swiftly, and liked to know the answer to everything...the boy who was executed.

We were having a life skills lesson with the most boring teacher of all, Mr. Dermond. Jasmine and I sat near the back, and Micah sat a few rows ahead of us. He was the total opposite of me, always asking the questions that made the teachers angry. He waited until Mr. Dermond had stopped talking, and put his hand up.

"Is it true that the authorities add chemicals to our food so we don't get horny?" he asked.

Some of the girls giggled. Mr. Dermond stopped pacing across the front of the room and stared at him.

"What do you mean?" he snapped.

Micah folded his arms behind his head and stared coolly at Mr. Dermond from under his black fringe.

"It's just, sir, that we're teenagers. If you look at the movies, you can see that in the Old World, teenagers had sex all the time. Or they wanted to. But we all live together in cells, boys and girls together, and we're all celibate. We're not even playing with ourselves."

"Speak for yourself," one of his friends quipped, and all the other guys roared with laughter.

Jasmine hushed them. "Shh. I want to hear the answer."

Mr. Dermond looked around the room like the answer was hidden somewhere—under one of the benches maybe, or in one of the cracks in the walls. At last he said, "The authorities have determined that off-spring will only be born in selected years. The numbers of the Colony are carefully regulated."

"With respect, sir," Micah drawled, although he didn't sound particularly respectful, "I know that. But what are they doing to us to stop us wanting to have sex?"

"I know," said Fez. He sat forward on the bench, his skinny frame almost quivering. "They've put something in the protein pellets, haven't they? Or is it in the hydroponic water? What do you think, Ebba? Are the vegetables contaminated?"

"I can't see how," I said. "I'm sure you're wrong."

"Those people in the Old World were having sex because they were depraved," Mr. Dermond said. "That's why Prospiroh punished them."

"Oh puhleeze," Micah exclaimed.

"You," Mr. Dermond snapped, wagging his finger at Micah. "You're on dangerous ground. Very dangerous ground. If you know what's good for you, you'll stop asking about things you know nothing about and trust the authorities. You're just a fifteen year old boy. Who are you to question the High Priest and the General?"

"Yes sir," Micah said, saluting him.

Mr. Dermond's face darkened. He carried on with the lesson, but that night Micah didn't arrive for dinner. His sabenzis were frantic. I begged Mr. Dermond to tell me where he was, but he wouldn't say a word. Nobody would say anything.

We waited till lights out, when most of the guards had left.

"What do you think has happened to him?" I asked.

"He's so smart," Fez said. "I reckon they've taken him up to the top levels, to work with the General, or the High Priest."

Jasmine's voice wafted down from the bunk above me. "They won't want him up there. He'll cause trouble."

It was Letti who said what I was thinking. "They've culled him, for asking the wrong questions."

I cried myself to sleep that night, and every night for weeks. We never saw him again. And there hasn't been a day since then that I haven't thought about him.

"What are you thinking about, looking so sad there?" Hal asks.

I can't tell him about Micah. He won't understand. "My friends," I say. "My sabenzi group. I miss them so much. If I went and asked your father, do you think he'd elevate them? They could work on the farm. There's lots of space there, and they're all experienced at growing food."

"Ebba," he says smoothly, "my father thinks the sun

shines out of you, but that's one thing he definitely won't do."

"But he elevated *me*."

"You're different. You've been chosen by Prospiroh. We all have. That's why we live in the City and they live under the ground."

"But it's terrible down there. The sun never shines and they work all day, and they never see the sky and trees..."

"I love that about you," he says, taking my hand. "You're so thoughtful about other people."

His fingers are entwined in mine, and his thumb is stroking the back of my hand.

"But I miss them," I say, choking up.

"One day you'll understand the wisdom of Prospiroh's ways," he says, softly. "But for now, we must just be grateful for the blessings we have received."

Hal drops me home and I can't stop thinking about my sabenzis, working like slaves in the semi-darkness.

That evening, as we sit down to eat, I make a decision. "Leonid, I need the carriage tomorrow morning please."

He raises one eyebrow. "Where you going?"

"To the Shrine offices. I'm going to speak to the High Priest."

Aunty Figgy stops with the soup ladle in mid-air. "Keep away from him. He is not your friend."

"What do you want to talk to him about?" Leonid asks.

"I want to ask him to let my sabenzis out of the bunker. I want them here with me."

Aunty Figgy shakes her head. "Do you think he'll let them out, just like that? He'll manipulate and trick you. Believe me."

"You don't know him. He's not like that. He's actually really kind."

She snorts. "Kind? He tried to have you killed!"

"Well, he also saved me, and brought me back here to Greenhaven. And he's Hal's dad, and look how kind Hal is to me."

She and Leonid exchange glances but I ignore them. I'll do anything, anything to have Jasmine and the twins with me.

Next morning, dead on time, Leonid brings the buggy around. Aunty Figgy has ignored me all morning, but as I leave the house, she hurries through and catches me in the doorway. She touches the amulet necklace, closes her eyes, and begins to whisper.

"What was that?" I ask when she finally opens her eyes.

"I'm asking the Goddess to protect you." She smiles at me and there's love, real love, in her face. Although she's bossy and treats me like a child, she is on my side.

"Thank you," I say, squeezing her hand.

An hour later, we've passed the Shrine and the High Priest's home and drive a short way along a road that clings to the mountain like it's scared to let go. We go through a pair of metal gates and Leonid stops the carriage in front of a stone wall so high that nothing is visible on the other side.

What am I doing? I was expecting a building like their home but this feels like a fortress. I should listen to Aunty Figgy and just go back to Greenhaven. But my sabenzis are shut deep inside the mountain in a different kind of fortress, and I need to get them out.

A guard approaches the buggy and Leonid calls, "Miss Ebba den Eeden to see the High Priest."

The guard disappears into the guardhouse. He appears to be discussing the issue with someone. A moment later, a soldier comes over and salutes. "Follow me, Miss den Eeden."

It's Captain Atherton. Instantly I'm back teetering on the rim of the ventilation shaft, trying not to see the broken bodies splattered on the rocks. My stomach folds over, as sweat breaks out on my face.

He opens a door in the wall and gestures for me to go through it. But every instinct in my body says run. I glance back. Leonid is watching me from the carriage. Is he sneering at me? I won't give him the satisfaction of saying I told you so. I bite my lip, and go forward, through the door.

I'm in a courtyard. On the left, four flights of stairs rise up to a building fronted by columns. A pair of marble lions line each flight of stairs, and at the bottom, a statue of the High Priest riding a horse stands on a plinth. He's gazing towards the Mainland, shielding his eyes with one hand as though he's about to canter off to conquer the rest of the world.

"This way," Captain Atherton says, and once again I am climbing flight after flight of steps next to him, not knowing what awaits me at the end.

At last we reach the top, and pass through the rows of columns. He knocks on the arched door, and it swings open.

The offices have been dug out of the mountain side. It's the first thing I notice. It's like the Colony, which isn't surprising as it's carved from the far end of the same mountain. But where we had bare stone walls and a hard floor, everything here is luxurious. The walls are hung with tapestries and cloths. Rich carpets cover the floor. Instead of stale air and sweat, these rooms are filled with the sweet smell of incense. Light shines in through domed skylights.

I follow the guard past offices, where important looking men sit writing in registers or have their heads bent together in earnest conversation. At last we reach a door inlaid with gold discs in the shapes of sheaves of wheat. The guard knocks again.

"Come in," says a voice.

The door swings open and Lucas stands there.

"Ebba!" he says, wringing his hands.

I can't read his expression. Is he pleased to see me? I thought he disapproved of me.

"Please...er...come inside," he says. He leads me across the room to a sofa covered in a deep red rug. "Please...er, please wait here."

We may be in a cave but a huge window looks out over the mountainside. Waves crash against the granite wall, battering the rocks and throwing spray into the air.

I perch on the edge of the sofa, practicing what I'm going to say to get not only my sabenzis but everybody in the bunker released. How can I persuade him to give me what I want? I decide I should start with the smallest request and see how he takes it. I'll ask for Jasmine first, as she's just one person, and then the twins.

I'll leave today with all three of them. We'll be together again, finally able to grow into the people we dreamed of being. I've seen a box of old spectacles in a chest of drawers—there'll be a pair there that give Letti perfect eyesight. Fez won't ever get asthma when he's getting fresh air and sunshine. Jasmine won't have to be so watchful anymore—she'll be able to relax, maybe learn to ride the horses. She'd love that.

Lucas sits at his desk, hunched over as he scratches away in a book with his gold topped pen. His right foot jiggles. Why is he so nervous? Is it me or something else?

A door opens, and the High Priest comes sweeping in, in a voluminous white robe with gold sheaves embroidered around the neck. He glides across the room, holding out both arms. I stumble to my feet, heart thudding.

"My dear Ebba. How wonderful of you to come and visit me. Is this a social call?" He claps his hands. "Lucas, bring refreshments."

Lucas drops his pen instantly, bows, and hurries out of the room. The High Priest gestures towards two arm chairs set right in the window. "Have a seat, my dear. Now how are you getting on? It must be an enormous adjustment. It's such a lot for a girl your age to handle. So far you're doing splendidly."

He looks at me as though I'm the only person in the whole world who really matters. It feels weird, that just over six weeks ago he was inspecting me from top to toe with such loathing that he sentenced me to death. And now he seems to consider me so special that he's invited me to live with his family.

Is this what wealth does to you? In the bunker what mattered was what kind of person you were. Here it's all about the things you own and the power that gives you. Even though I told Leonid and Aunty Figgy that the High Priest has been kind to me, I really don't know how I feel about all of this. It's not right that some people own so much while others are hungry. I have so much, and I have to persuade him to let me share it.

"I'm doing well, Your Righteousness," I say. "Thank you for asking. You're right, it's been a huge change, but Hal is helping me so much. He visits nearly every day, and he's teaching me to read so I can keep proper records. We've planted the seeds for the winter crop and hopefully Leonid will transplant them next week..."

Everything seems of utmost importance to him. Nobody has ever listened to me like this before. His hands play with a set of dark red beads on a colorful string, running them through his strong fingers one by one. It's oddly soothing, and I think I'd like a set to play with.

As though he's reading my mind, he gets up and goes over to Lucas's desk. He opens a drawer and takes out a string of jet black beads on a tasselled cord. "For you," he says. "A gift from me and my family."

He's so kind. They're so kind, showering me with gifts. If he can give me a beautiful set of worry beads like this, he'll look kindly on my request, I'm sure. I run them through my fingers, feeling the cool smoothness, and begin to relax.

Lucas comes in then, with a tea tray. He has beautiful hands with long fingers. I can't help noticing that his hands are not manicured like the rest of the family's. They shake slightly as he pours the tea and his father frowns and sighs as the cup rattles in the saucer.

I'm as nervous as Lucas, but I have to take the plunge. "Your Righteousness..." My mouth dries up, so I take a sip of tea, and burn my tongue. "I have so much empty land. I need to develop it, but I don't have enough labor."

"Yes?" he says. "My dear, you don't need to come to me for something like that. Just ask Mr. Frye to organize you some new staff. He'll find some good people from the Mainland."

"I...I need someone who knows about horticulture. I was thinking about Jasmine Baartman. She was with me in the Colony. We worked together in the plant nursery and there's nothing she doesn't know about growing food. You see, if we can get skilled people to work with the plants, then I can focus on—"

"Jasmine Baartman?" He steeples his fingers together, cradling the beads as his hooded eyes search mine. "Hmmm. I wonder. Is this wise?"

"Oh yes, Your Righteousness." I cringe at the begging in my voice. I don't want to sound whiny, so I straighten my back and clear my throat. "You see, I have to have someone I know and trust. I need someone who will know what to do if I'm not there, especially if I accept your very kind offer to move to your compound." I know I'm about to be disloyal but I say it anyway. "Mr. Frye isn't very happy with the staff I have at the moment, and I'm not sure how much I can rely on them."

His eyes narrow. He's trying to read my face. I try to look serious and grown up, although my heart thuds against my rib cage.

He comes to a sudden decision, sits up, and writes something down in a small notebook. "As you know, Ebba, we have very strict immigration laws in the City. Any outsider who wants to live within the City Wall must fulfil certain requirements and apply for a permit. If we elevate—what is her name?"

"Jasmine Baartman, Your Righteousness."

"Yes, Baartman, she will not be given Citizen status. She may not dwell in your house, but must live in the laborers' accommodation, which must be separate from your house. You may not socialize with her. She may not leave your premises without her pass, which may be checked at any time."

He's not serious, surely. The Citizens can go anywhere they want, whenever they want, but Jasmine will be treated like black people were during apartheid, only good enough to be servants? I thought that kind of discrimination was outlawed sixty years ago. But what is the alternative? A life as a slave, working underground. Maybe if I agree to this, cruel though it is, he will let the twins out as well. I weigh up the options. If we're all together again we can make a plan about getting the rest out. "Yes, Your Righteousness, I understand."

"And you will have to pay a special tax for her. You will be required to pay to the Shrine forty percent of all your earnings from your land. This is payable quarterly. A bookkeeper will be assigned to you to oversee the financials. Do you still wish to go ahead?"

Forty percent! That's almost half, and I have no idea if I can afford it. All my earnings come from the land, but then, according to Mr. Frye, I'm very wealthy. I can probably manage on what is left, especially if I'm making more from the new land. And I'll have Jasmine with me. "Yes, Your Righteousness. I want to go ahead."

"Lucas," he calls across the room. "Make a note. See that...er...Baartman is equipped with the necessary papers and delivered to Greenhaven Farm. Now is there anything else, dear?" He closes his notebook and puts it down as if to say, "This interview is now over."

I take a breath, rubbing my sweating palms on my robe. "Please, Your Righteousness. I have another request. I grew up with my sabenzis—the four of us were together from babies. I...I...I miss them. It's lovely up here in the City, and everyone has been so kind to me, but there were four of us together down there and..."

"You'd like to pay a visit to the Colony? I'm sure that can be arranged. Lucas, check the diary."

I swallow hard and try to stop my voice cracking. "No, more than that. I want them to live with me, at Greenhaven."

"On your farm?" he laughs. "My dear, that's just not possible. We can't just elevate anyone at a whim."

"But I was elevated. And you've agreed to let Jasmine out..."

"Yes, my dear, I know that," he says. His voice hardens. "But you were chosen by Prospiroh. You are blessed in his eyes. And I'm allowing Baartman out only because of her skills."

Tears burn the back of my eyes, but I push them down. "But they're my family."

"My dear, don't whine. It's very ungrateful after all Prospiroh has given you. You must forget about them. We are your family now. And if Prospiroh so desires, you'll marry and start a family of your own. Don't you want that?"

Tears trickle down my face. I can't bear to think of Letti and Fez stuck down there in the bunker. What if there is another Sacrifice and they get chosen?

He leans forward and wipes my cheeks with his handkerchief. "Don't cry, my dear," he murmurs. "You're getting all upset about nothing. I'm sure we can make a plan."

"Really?" I sniff. "Can you make an exception, just this once?"

"My dear," he says, "it's not up to me. It is all in the hands of our Lord God Prospiroh. He has blessed you so richly already and now you ask for more? This won't please him."

"I'm sorry," I say, "but it means so much to me."

He stares out of the window, deep in thought. I'm mesmerized by his hands, the light catching the beads he threads through his fingers, the sense of power he exudes that makes me feel so insignificant.

"There might be a way," he says at last, turning back to me. "If you were prepared to make a small sacrifice—to thank Prospiroh for his generosity to you—he would look kindly upon your request, I am sure. "

"Anything," I say. "Anything."

His eyes are fixed on mine, and the rest of the room disappears as I focus on his pupils. He doesn't blink as he holds out his hands. Our eyes are locked, and although I don't want to, I let him take my hands in his. "Prospiroh commands me," he says, "to release your friends. They can be up here tomorrow, but you will have to pay a tithe…"

He pauses and I gulp. I'm already paying forty percent of my income for Jasmine. What more could Prospiroh want?

"Just a small thing," he says. "Prospiroh is a generous god. All he requires is the trinket you're wearing around your neck."

"This one?" I gulp, tucking it under my robe. "But it's not that special. I've got much more valuable jewels at home."

His stare grips me again, and I can't look away. "Then

you won't miss it. Take it off, and your friends will be with you by the end of the day."

From the corner of my eye, I catch sight of Lucas at his desk. His leg is jiggling faster and faster. Why is he so worked up? Is it because the amulet is witchcraft? But why does the High Priest want a witchcraft charm so badly?

"I can't give you my necklace." I clutch my hands over my robe, covering it. "It belonged to my mother. It's the only thing I have of hers."

"Oh nonsense," he scoffs. "Your house is full of things from your family. And you are choosing a commonplace little charm on a cheap chain, over your friends. What kind of girl are you, Ebba? I thought better of you."

What is it about the necklace? He was going to kill me in the bunker, until he caught sight of it. If it's just a commonplace little charm on a cheap chain, it makes no sense that he wants it so badly.

Does he want me to come and live with his family so he can get the necklace from me?

"I'll have to think about it," I say, getting up.

"It seems you are a foolish little girl after all. Foolish and selfish. Prospiroh sees your selfish, ungrateful attitude. You need to repent before it is too late."

He gets up. Dismisses me with barely a glance. The interview is over.

He's angry. Angry with me.

Lucas is holding the door open. As I reach it, I turn. The High Priest is standing against the window. Light is streaming in from behind him. He looks like a god himself in his white robe, with his hair glinting in the sun.

"Great favors demand great sacrifices," he says, opening his palms. "He who gives generously will be rewarded a hundred times more, overflowing, too great for measure." He glides across the carpet and disappears through a doorway.

I stare after him, wondering what I have to do to repent. All my life I've tried to keep to the rules, but the rules up here don't seem to be fair.

Lucas leads me back down the long passageway. He twists his hands together as we walk, barely able to look at me. I wonder what he's thinking.

At the top of the stairs, he shakes my hand. His fingers are cold, and he doesn't smile.

"You are going to need more staff," he says. "I'll arrange to have some laborers sent over to Greenhaven with the bookkeeper." He nods briefly and then he's gone, leaving me feeling as confused as I always do when he is around.

It's a relief to see Hal waiting at the colonnade. "They told me you were here," he says, taking my hand. "It's fantastic. When are you moving in?"

"Um...we haven't made a date yet."

"Then what were you talking about? I thought you were here to talk about coming to live with us."

"I can't move to the compound, Hal. I need to get the farm running properly. We were talking about staff. Don't be grumpy," I say, squeezing his arm. "I've got wonderful news. He's agreed to let my best friend Jasmine out of the Colony. She's going to be working with me on Greenhaven."

He stops dead. "You're kidding me. We agreed you'd move to the compound," he snaps.

I stare at him, trying to read his face. I've never seen this side of him before. "I never agreed to anything." His scowl deepens, so I lighten my voice. "Come on, Hal," I say, giving him a peck on the cheek. "Don't be an old grouch. Someone's got to grow the food you like to eat. If I'm not there—or someone I trust—there's no knowing what those two skabengas would get up to on the farm."

He looks slightly appeased. "OK," he says at last. "You

can stay there. Just until you get the farm settled. Then you're coming to live here, with us, where we can look after you."

We've reached the bottom of the stairs. I look back, along the row of windows carved into the mountainside. The High Priest is still standing in the window, watching us.

For once Aunty Figgy is pleased with me. "Well done, Ebba," she says when I tell her Jasmine is being elevated. "That's wonderful news. You need to be around your old friends, people you can be yourself with."

"I TOLD you the High Priest was a good man," I say, ignoring her jibe. "And look, he gave me these pretty beads."

She takes them but instead of admiring them, she opens the door of the stove, and chucks them into the flames. "That thing is not coming into this house! What did you think you were doing, taking gifts from him?"

I'm about to explode when Leonid asks, "Where is Jasmine going to stay? Is she going to be a full Citizen, like you?"

Is that a sneer as he says, "Citizen?"

I shift my feet. "She's not allowed to stay in the house with me. I was thinking she could stay in the laborers' cottages with you, Aunty Figgy?"

"She's going to be your servant? Lucky Jasmine."

"I tried! I asked him for the twins as well. I wanted to get them all out of the bunker."

"You obviously didn't try hard enough."

"It's better than nothing, Leonid," Aunty Figgy says, rubbing my shoulder. "Ebba is just one young girl. How do you expect her to stand up against the most powerful man in the world?"

I'd like to see you try, I think as he rolls his eyes. You have no idea what it's like in the Shrine offices.

As I lie in bed that night replaying the scene in the

High Priest's office, I wonder briefly if Leonid's right. Could I have tried harder?

I don't see when the High Priest had total control over the interview and when it ended. It's easy for Leonid to criticize me when he's not the one doing the asking.

A week later, an army wagon pulls up at the front door and Jasmine climbs down. She's looking around, bewildered, and I run down the stairs to greet her. Her face goes white.

"But you're dead! They sacrificed you."

I grab her in a hug and lift her right off her feet. "I'm alive," I shout. "I couldn't get a message to you, but I'm alive. And now you're out too, and you were right—the world out here wasn't dead. Look at it." I gesture to the grass, the meadow and forest, but she only has eyes for me.

She pulls away from my arms. "Are you sure this is you? You don't look like you anymore. "

"It's me." I laugh. "I'm so happy to see you."

Leonid and Aunty Figgy have come out to meet her. Aunty Figgy pulls Jasmine into a hug. "Welcome," she says. "I'm Aunty Figgy. Thank the Goddess that you've been released from that hell underground."

"They told us it was dangerous above," she keeps saying. "They told us we had to stay inside the mountain or we would die of radiation sickness, or malaria, or Influenza. I *knew* they were lying."

"Total bastards," Leonid says, shaking her hand. "Welcome to the real world or what's left of it."

"Come inside," Aunty Figgy says. "You must be tired and hungry. It's almost dinner time."

"What is this place?" Jasmine asks, pausing at the top of the steps. "Why are you here?"

I take a deep breath. How am I going to explain everything to her? As far as she's concerned, I'm nobody and nothing. Not that she thinks of me that way, but I'm the only one of the Colonists who had no background, no family, no memory box that a family lovingly put together for me. How do I explain who I really am?

"I inherited it," I say at last.

She gives me a blank look. "From who? You don't have any family."

"When the High Priest saw me in the Colony and he saw the necklace around my neck, he realized I was from the den Eeden family, and that I was the den Eeden baby that went missing. I wasn't meant to be in the Colony because I'm really a Citizen."

"What's a Citizen?"

"They're the people who live up here in Table Island. But anyway, the High Priest realized who I was and sent a message to stop the guards. I was literally hanging on the edge of the ventilation shaft."

She's too distracted by the sight of the hallway to listen to me. "This is all yours? Everything?"

"Yes. I inherited it all from my great aunt. She died about six months ago."

"And those people." She peers into the sitting room. "Aunty Figgy and that good looking guy?"

"They—they work for me." I straighten the edge of the carpet with my foot. I don't want to look her in the face.

"They're your servants?"

How do I tell her that she's my servant too? Luckily, she's distracted by my bedroom. "Who sleeps here?" she asks, running her hand up the carved posts on my bed.

"Me." I bite my lip. I don't want to have to tell her that her bed isn't anything like as grand as this one. I've made sure she has a comfortable bed in the cottage, with soft pillows and pretty blue linen, but it's not enough. Nothing can ever make up for the unfairness of the system.

"This bed is so soft," she says, sitting on the edge. "Will

I share with you or can I have a room all to myself?"

Why did it have to happen so soon? I wanted some time with her before she got the bad news. My face burns as I mutter, "I'm sorry, Jazzy. They're very strict up here. You're not allowed to sleep in the main house with me."

She sits up. "What do you mean, not allowed to? Who won't let me? Where are the guards? I haven't seen any guards."

"The only way I could get you out of the Colony was if you came to work for me. To work on the farm."

"I'm working for you? I'm a servant? I'm YOUR servant?" Her voice rises.

My face is hot with shame. "I'm so sorry. I don't make the rules. I...I have to do what the High Priest says."

She stares at me for a moment. Then her eyes trace the bedroom, big enough to house twenty of the bunks we used in the Colony. Her eyebrows rise as she sees my private bathroom, the fluffy towels, the heavy matching wardrobes.

"So where am I sleeping?" Her voice is cold when at last she speaks.

"I'm so, so sorry, Jaz. You're in the laborers' cottages, with Aunty Figgy."

The word "laborer" hangs in the air. She's about to explode, but at that moment Aunty Figgy sticks her head around the door. "It's dinner time," she says. "Come and eat."

Jasmine won't meet my eye. She sits down next to Leonid, and turns all her attention on him. He can't believe his luck, losing that sulky look instantly so he's hardly recognizable.

I can't bear to have her so angry with me especially over something I can't control. "I'm sorry, Jasmine," I blurt out. "I wish it were different. I don't make the rules."

She ignores me, intent on watching Aunty Figgy as

she takes the dinner out of the oven. "This smells amazing," she says. "What is it?"

"It's called Bobotie," Aunty Figgy says as she puts it down in front of us. "It's traditional Cape Malay food. The slaves brought the recipe from Indonesia in the 1600s."

I wait for her to respond, but she's too distracted by the smell. She closes her eyes and inhales, slowly. Leonid chuckles. I've never heard him laugh before.

"You're smelling the spices," Aunty Figgy says, reaching for the plates. "Cumin, nutmeg, cloves. All traditional Indonesian spices."

"And to think that all the time we were in the Colony eating protein pellets and vegetables, and thinking the world was nothing but ashes." Her curls bounce as she shakes her head.

It reminds me of Pamza trying on the brown wig that she found in a wardrobe. I thought then that everything would be all right again if only Jasmine was here with me.

"They lie about everything," Leonid says. "My dad taught me that when I was really small. He was one of the heroes of the Resistance."

"Ebba's mother Ali was a Resistance hero too," Aunty Figgy says as she passes the plates around. "Greenhaven was famous in the old days for standing up to the authorities."

"My great-grandfather was in jail on Robben Island," Jasmine says. "He was a freedom fighter, like Mandela. He fought the racist government who wouldn't give black people the vote."

"Serious?" Leonid pauses, fork in hand. "My mom's grandmother went to jail during the struggle too."

"Maybe they knew each other." Jasmine laughs. "Imagine they were friends. Do you think everyone had a huge party when they'd finally defeated the racist laws? I bet they danced together." Is she fluttering her eyelashes at him? Already?

Nothing I say has ever impressed him, but he is looking at her like she's the most fascinating person he's ever seen.

"And forty years later, it was all forgotten," Aunty Figgy says, untying her apron and sitting down at last. "Forty years is all it took for all those brave new laws promising equality and justice for everyone to be obliterated."

"Because of the Purification?" Jasmine asks. "You must remember it well. What was it like?"

"It was not a purification," Aunty Figgy says firmly. "It was a worldwide, appalling calamity that almost destroyed Earth. The Prosperites call it a purification because they don't want to face up to the fact that it was caused by people like them and their endless greed with no thought of caring for the planet. Billions of people died."

"How long before it happened did you know it was coming?"

"It was obvious that tension was rising between the world's superpowers. It wasn't just a war over land and refugees—it was a spiritual war between those who believed in equality and balance, and sharing what we had, and those who worshipped greed and wanted everything for themselves. Then the Prosperites hacked into the electoral system and gained control of the local government. Once they were in power, they stopped doing normal things like maintaining the roads and public buildings. They poured all our tax money into building security villages with underground bunkers for the very wealthy and digging a new set of Council offices out of the mountain. And of course they built that hideous Shrine to Prospiroh. We knew what was coming —they were going to prepare for the Calamity by making sure they stockpiled much more than they needed, even though it meant that all those people who weren't Prosperites would be left without food and water and medicine."

"Wow," Jasmine says. "So they were basically going back to apartheid, but this time they discriminated against people because they were poor, not because of race?"

"Exactly," Leonid bursts in. "And the wall. Tell her about the wall."

They're acting like I'm not even in the room.

"When they announced they were going to build the wall that would split the City in two, they said it was to hold back the sea if it rose suddenly," Aunty Figgy says.

"They lied!" Leonid punches the table so hard, his glass jumps. "They knew how much the sea would rise if the polar ice caps melted. They built the wall just above that height. It wasn't to hold back the sea. It was to keep out people trying to move to safer ground, so they could keep all the safe land for themselves."

"And the Colony?" Jasmine asks. "Why did they build that?"

"That was the most disgusting," Aunty Figgy says. "They spent billions of rands on digging out Table Mountain to build what they called a 'Haven.' They told ordinary people who couldn't afford bunkers that it was to keep the children safe for future generations. If that was true, they would have held a lottery, so any child could be accepted."

"It was a gene pool," Leonid interrupts. "Genetic farming. They only took the kids of high achievers. Your parents must have been experts."

"My mom was a scientist, and my dad was an engineer." Jasmine rests her chin on her hand and her voice is wistful as she says, "Imagine sending your tiny baby to live underground not knowing if you'll ever see them again."

"People were desperate," Aunty Figgy says. "The

Earthquakes had destroyed most of the City. There were too many refugees, and not enough food, and then the Influenza wiped out millions. And the sea was rising all the time. People would do anything to keep their children alive."

Jasmine sighs, and I know she's wishing she could go and search for them. "Where did the parents go?"

"Most people sold everything they had and trekked away from the Cape. It wasn't an Island then, of course, though the sea was already rising. But some people refused to leave. Miss den Eeden—Ebba's great aunt—was a very wealthy woman, and she decided right away that she wasn't moving into any security village either. She was going to stay put, in her house. She took her money and began to buy land. She bought more and more until she was the biggest landowner in the City. Everyone laughed at her. She was mocked in the newspapers. But she kept on buying land that people were selling for almost nothing."

"And my mother?" I ask. "Did she also refuse to go into a security village?"

"Absolutely. She was adamant. That's when she joined the Resistance—she was just a girl, even younger than you. She and Leonid's father Darius tried to persuade the authorities that everyone had an equal right to remain in the City. They said that if we all worked together, there would be enough to go around and everyone could be saved if the worst happened—not just the wealthy, or the intelligent. But the government wouldn't listen. The Prosperites went ahead with their plans. They said only the wealthiest had been called by Prospiroh to be saved. It was disgusting." She spits out the words.

"Why didn't ordinary people just flood the shrines and insist that they were also worshippers of Prospiroh?" Out of the corner of my eye, I catch Leonid and Jasmine rolling their eyes and my cheeks burn. That was not a stupid question. There is power in mass protest. That's exactly what Nelson Mandela and Jasmine's great-grandfather and Leonid's great-grandmother believed in. If everybody had put on a yellow star in Nazi Germany, how would the Nazis have known who were the real Jews? Would they have killed everybody? And if during apartheid here in South Africa, everyone had burnt their pass books, and whites had refused to require it or participate in the government's schemes, things would have been different...

"Because you can't be a Prosperite unless you are rich and entitled," Leonid says with a sigh.

"Ordinary people grew more and more angry," Aunty Figgy says, brushing his comment aside with her hand. "There were riots, and the authorities brought in the army. Hundreds of thousands of people died. Ali—Ebba's mother—and Darius worked day and night to organize protests against the authorities. Ali wanted to move some people here, onto Greenhaven. But the authorities surrounded the farm, with tanks and enough weapons to start another war. And then Ali was killed and Ebba disappeared, the Calamity we were all dreading finally happened, and we went into lock down."

By the time Aunty Figgy stops talking, dinner is over, and we all help clean up the kitchen. I scrape the leftovers into Isi's bowl and take it outside to feed her. It's quiet out here, and the animals are settling down for the night. I sit on the low wall around the duck pond and watch the reflection of the sky in the shallow water. The kitchen window is open and Jasmine's voice drifts out on the evening air.

"I can't believe I'm not allowed to stay in the house. It's like apartheid. All those years we dreamed about how we'd live if we ever got out of the Colony. We said we'd live together in one house, each with our own bedrooms, but connecting so we'd still be together, so we could talk to each other at night. And now it's come true, and I'm not good enough to live in her larney house."

Her voice bleeds hurt. I know how disappointed she is, I'm disappointed too. But there's nothing I can say that will make it better. She doesn't seem to believe me when I tell her I didn't have a choice. Have I made a terrible mistake bringing her out of the Colony? She's always been my best friend, but it seems I can't bridge this chasm opening between us.

The next morning things are still awkward between us. She doesn't look at me all through breakfast. If only Letti were here. She's always been good at handling Jasmine and her moods.

Aunty Figgy comes to find me when I'm collecting the eggs after breakfast. "Give her time," she says. "Leave her to work with Leonid for a while—she needs to make a big adjustment. She'll calm down in a few days."

It seems to work. A week later, she's thawed a little and I'm hopeful that things will come right between us. I ask her to come with me to look at the new lands that I want to develop. We set off through the orchard, Isi running ahead of us between the rows of apple trees.

We keep off the subject of the Colony and the Citizens. Instead we talk about the things we know about—plants, and what we can grow, and what will do best in which part of the farm. It's like old times again.

When we've decided what to plant where, we go back to the potting shed, and start preparing the trays for planting. It feels so good, being back working together at a bench planting seeds, though now we're up to our wrists in compost and real, sun-warmed soil. "Hey, Jazzy," I say, as I pat the mix into the trays. "There's this guy I'm seeing

—his name is Hal."

"Really? What's he like?" She looks up quickly, but she's interested, not judgmental—like old times. "Have you kissed him?"

"Jasmine!" I exclaim, swatting her away. "Of course not."

"You have!" She laughs. "I can always tell when you're lying. Is he good looking? Is he more gorgeous than Leonid?"

"Leonid!" I make a face. "Leonid's too grumpy. Hal's lovely—he's always cheerful and he's totally positive all the time. He's got the nicest family. They're the ones that gave me my makeover, and lots of new clothes. They have so much stuff because his dad is the High Priest."

"Wow." Her voice is suddenly flat and she rams the soil into the pot she's filling and bangs it against the table.

Why did I mention the High Priest? Why did I draw attention to my new clothes? She's still wearing the tunic and pants from the bunker—the same clothing she's worn her whole life, and I can't ask Hal to ask his mom to get me clothes for Jasmine. I've talked myself into a corner.

"I wish the twins were here," she says, after a while. "They're so vulnerable if the High Priest decides it's time for another Sacrifice. Can't you do something? I mean, you are dating his son."

I'm so relieved that she's not freezing me out again that I don't stop to think. "I tried to get them out. When I asked the High Priest to elevate you, I asked for Fez and Letti as well. He said only if I gave him my necklace."

She drops her trowel and stares at me, hands on hips. She points a muddy finger at the chain around my neck. "That necklace?"

My heart drops. Now I've totally blown it.

"He asked you for THAT necklace in return for the twins, and you didn't give it to him?"

"Aunty Figgy says it's sacred and..."

"That's ridiculous and you know it. You're making excuses." She jabs her finger in my chest. "You'd rather let Fez and Letti die than give up a piece of ugly jewelry."

"It wasn't like that," I mutter. My face is burning, and I can't find the words I need.

She sweeps her arm along the bench, sending the newly filled seedling trays clattering to the floor, potting soil and seeds flying everywhere in a cloud of dust. "I thought I knew you," she spits. "I really thought I knew you. But I don't recognize you any more, giving orders, making your sabenzis sleep in a cramped room while you swan around with a whole house to yourself. And worst of all, choosing your jewelry over the people who love you. No wonder you love mixing with the Citizens. You're just like them."

She storms out, slamming the door so it swings on its hinges. It feels as though it's our friendship she's destroyed along with the seed trays. If only she would try and see it from my side. But she's always been obstinate —things are black or white with no middle ground. If only I could find a way to cross this divide between us. When we had nothing we felt equal. Now I'm hugely rich and she still has nothing. I want to build a bridge to join us again, but I can't find anything that isn't against the law, or that she and Leonid won't tear down.

I'm about to follow her when a wagon rumbles up the driveway.

It's the staff Lucas promised to send. Talk about perfect timing—just when I'd said I couldn't get the twins out. One of them will be the bookkeeper the High Priest sent to make sure I pay my taxes. He'll be spying on everything we do.

Leonid will be furious about that. Just thinking about it gives me a headache. And as luck would have it, he's fixing the wire of the pigeon coop, right next to the vegetable garden, and Jasmine is already with him, no doubt telling him that I care more about my jewelry than two of the people I love more than anything in the world.

The wagon has rattled off down the drive, and Leonid's already taken them into the kitchen by the time I get there. I straighten my back, and go through the door, hoping I look like the confident, mature woman I certainly don't feel like.

"Good morning. I'm Ebba den Eeden. Welcome to..." I break out in goosebumps.

The guy with the straight black hair. It's Micah.

Jasmine is staring at him, her mouth open. "What are you doing here? They killed you."

"Do I look dead?" he says with a cheeky grin.

There it is. The chipped front tooth.

"You're thinking of someone else. I'm Mike Patel. I come from Bellville City, on the Mainland."

"But before that..." She shakes his arm. "I know it's you. How did you..."

I'm about to insist that it's him when I catch Aunty Figgy's eye. She gives a tiny shake of the head and her eyes flicker to the other two men standing in the kitchen, caps in hand. One of them is the spy.

"Must have been your doppelganger," I say quickly and shake his hand. "Don't take any notice of Jasmine. We once knew a guy called Micah who looked a bit like you. But actually, his nose was a different shape to yours. Anyway, welcome to Greenhaven."

"You can call me Micah, Michael, Mike," he chuckles. "I'm easy."

I move on quickly to the short little guy next to him. He's kind of round—his face, his belly, even his eyes are big and round like a baby's and his hair is blond and downy like a duckling's.

"Good morning, miss," he says in a squeaky voice.

"I'm very excited to be joining your staff. My name is Troy Julius, but everyone calls me Shorty, you can see why, ha ha. The High Priest sent me to do your books, ha ha."

"Thank you, Troy," I say, cutting him off mid-flow. He's the one to look out for.

The third guy seems nice—he's shy, and he keeps his eyes down as I shake his hand. "I'm Victor," he mumbles. "Thank you for giving me work."

He'll be no trouble. Even after their journey, he's as neat as if he'd just got dressed. And his hands are calloused. He's used to hard work.

"The first thing we have to do is find somewhere for you all to sleep," I say. "Leonid, the staff rooms at the back of the stables—do you think you three could clean them?"

He sighs and I clench my fists. The last thing I need is Leonid making me look stupid in front of my new staff. But he calls the new guys and they head off towards the stables. Maybe he's talking bad about me but he's doing what I asked, and that's better than nothing.

Chapter Nine

For the next few days, Shorty spends every moment—when he's not going through the farm books—hanging around, watching everything and getting in everyone's way. He chatters right through every meal, but it makes Jasmine's silence more bearable. I watch Micah as he goes about his work, his lithe body digging and chopping wood, his fearlessness as he brings the horses in for the night, his confidence as he milks the cow each evening. How did he escape? Why won't he tell me the truth? We were so close for so long, and now he's treating me like a stranger. Maybe he's got a girlfriend and he doesn't want to complicate things...and I've got Hal.

But if I had to choose...? I push the idea out of my mind. I am a Citizen, he is a farm laborer. We are not allowed to mix. End of story. Except, I know it's him. And I want to kiss that soft mouth again, and brush the hair from his eyes.

A few days later it's Shrine Day, and—no surprises—Shorty offers to drive me. I suppose he's going to report back to the High Priest what he's observed so far. As usual, he chatters right through breakfast.

"I come from the Mainland," he says. "I worked as a clerk in Stellenbosch Harbor, and I have to say I was very surprised when we arrived here."

"Why is that?" Leonid growls. He's taken an instant dislike to Shorty.

"Well, in the Mainland everything is dry. If it wasn't

for the goats and ostriches and the prickly pears, people would starve. And Table Island City is even worse, because it's all rocks and mountain. But then you get to Greenhaven, and there's trees and flowers and vegetables, and it's like being back in the day. How do you get it so green, Miss Ebba? How do you get things to grow so big? I mean, look at these tomatoes. I never saw such giants." He gestures with his knife to the slices of fried tomato on my plate.

"I have no idea," I say. "I only just got here myself, remember."

"Greenhaven land is sacred," Aunty Figgy says. "It belongs to the Earth Goddess."

Shorty's eyes flicker over to the statue in the window. "Her?"

"Yes. Theia. The one who made the world."

"That's witchcraft, isn't it? Or superstition. Ha ha ha. I didn't think anyone still believed those old tales."

Aunty Figgy glares at him. "Eat your eggs," she says.

How long until that piece of information gets back to the High Priest, I wonder, watching him gobble down his food.

Micah watches me from across the table. There's an electric current between us. Surely he feels it too. Why is he pretending not to know me? Does he also hate me because I'm a Citizen? Or does he hate me because I'm his boss?

Hal is waiting for me outside Shrine. "You look miserable," he says, searching my face. "What's wrong?" His voice is so kind and I melt.

"I had a fight with Jasmine, but please don't tell anyone." I have the urge to bury myself in his shoulder and sob, but Mr. Frye just waved to me from the top of the stairs, and I can't look weak in front of him. He'll insist

I leave the farm and move in with him and his wife. I don't
want anyone but Hal to know I'm struggling.

"You poor thing. You shouldn't let them upset you so
much. They're your servants."

"But Jasmine was my best friend. We've been best
friends for sixteen years. And overnight I've lost her."

"Ebba," he says, resting his hand on my back as we
walk up the first flight of stairs. "You're different from the
Colonists. It's tragic that you had to spend your childhood
in that hellhole, but you're out now, with your own people.
Of course the people who work for you will be jealous.
That's what always happens to Prospiroh's chosen people.
That's why we want you to come and live here with us
—to protect you."

Cassie runs over when she sees me, and gives me
the biggest hug and kiss. "I kept a chair for you. I've
been dying to see you again." She runs her fingers
through my hair. "The dye is fading. You must come visit
soon, so Pietro can hide the worst of the red. Maybe
tomorrow?"

"I can't come this week—I've got new staff to organize."

"Oh Ebba." She gives me a playful smack on the wrist.
"Leave all that boring stuff to Uncle Fergus. Let's have
some fun together."

It's so tempting. My stomach has been in a knot since
Jasmine arrived. She and Leonid have joined forces. Like
him, she's always been political. In the Colony, she was the
one who watched what was going on, who seethed with
anger when Major Zungu strutted around showing his
power by pulling out random people and punishing them.

I learned to keep my head down and blend in with the
crowd. But Jasmine would stare at him defiantly when
he shoved the boys against the wall, or hit them with the
butt of his rifle. More often than not, he would hone in on
her and force her to scrub the floors or go without food

for a day. Once he hit her, a sharp slap across her face. It didn't change her attitude. Instead it gave her a seemingly bottomless hatred for the authorities, and for the High Priest most of all.

As long as I'm friends with Hal and Cassie, she will stay cold towards me. Right now, looking at Cassie's sweet, laughing face, and the crowds of smiling people pouring into the Shine, the idea of leaving Greenhaven seems extra appealing. Surely I deserve to be as carefree and happy as Cassie and Hal and their friends are. Isn't it my birthright?

Too soon, the band plays the final verse of the last hymn. It's over for another week. Cassie and her mother beg me to come for lunch, but I don't want Shorty here any longer than necessary. Although I'm longing to have a happy relaxed meal with uncomplicated, welcoming friends, I get into the carriage and we set off for the farm.

"So, miss," Shorty calls as the horses set off down the hill. "What are your plans for the week?"

"We need to prepare the new lands. I hope Leonid can set up the old plough he found in the barn, and then we'll have to plant the seedlings. I want to get the three big fields under cabbages. Luckily, the storeroom has plenty of seeds."

"Table Island City produce is the best," Shorty says as we canter along the mountain road. "Across in the Mainland, people queue for hours on Market days to get their hands on it."

"But who is producing it?" I ask, trying to recall what Mr. Frye told me. "Aren't I the only farmer left?"

"The Colony of course, miss."

I go cold. "The Colony? You mean inside the bunker? The food they grow there?"

"Yes, miss. It's the City's chief produce. Almost all of the GDP of the City comes from sale of fresh produce grown in the bunker. Surely you knew that?"

Were we seriously working ourselves to death, twelve hours a day, so that the food we produced could be sold? To others? While we ate nasty pellets?

"And who gets the money?" I ask finally, when I manage to get my voice back. "Where does it go?"

"Goodness, miss, I thought everyone knew about it. It's how the Citizens make a living. They trade the produce of the Colony with the Mainland. It commands premium prices."

I stare at him, his words swirling in my head. They told us the food we grew was being stored for us to use, to keep us going if it ever ran out! How long have they been selling it?

"Are you all right, miss?" Shorty asks, turning around to check me out. "You're very pale. Would you like to turn back to the Shrine?"

"No, no." I can't face any of them, not knowing this. Not until I've thought it through and worked out a response. "Let's go home."

"Right you are, miss," he says, flicking the reins. "Greenhaven, here we come."

I watch the dry landscape as we jolt along the pot-holed road. We're driving through the narrow strip of land, crouched half dead between the grey mountain and the granite wall, spattered with ruined buildings and the stumps of trees. Once Cape Town was renowned for its beauty, but now it's become so hot and the rain is so scarce that it's more like a desert. But as we reach the top of the hill, I drink in the view of Greenhaven valley, stretched out green and lush in the foothills of the mountains and rising in thick forests to the pass that leads to Boat Bay. The pass where I saw the wagon loaded with bags of produce from the Colony.

So this is why they wanted us to believe that it was dangerous to come out. They need us below, working ten hours a day. Now I know why the storage gallery was out of bounds. So they could cream off what we grow and sell it.

It all makes sense. The bunker is running out of food because most of what we produce is being sold. Sold, so that Citizens can live a life of luxury.

I'm so angry I want to scream, but I can't let Shorty see that I'm upset. He'll report me to the High Priest. I pull at the neck of my robe, longing for a breeze. The heat is unbearable today, and Shorty drank all the water while I was in the Shrine. Why is he so damned annoying all the time. I wish I could fire him.

It's almost lunch time when we get home and I go through to the kitchen to get some water.

"Miss Ebba isn't well," Shorty says. "She went white as a sheet in the buggy. I thought she must have a bit of carriage sickness, but she's still pale so it must be a virus. Look at her..."

I wish he would just shut up.

"I—I just need some air. I'll be all right." I go outside to the water pump, and splash cold water on my face. I'm drying my face on my sleeve when I sense someone next to me.

"Micah!" I stand up quickly, pushing my wet hair behind my ears.

"Did something happen?" he asks. "You seem upset."

I look around. Shorty is still in the kitchen, chattering away. Victor has been cleaning the pigeon loft, and he's holding their water bowls, hovering like a little grey field mouse, waiting for us to finish at the pump.

I wish I could talk to Micah—tell him what I learned this morning. I need an ally here at Greenhaven. But he still hasn't admitted he is the person I know he is. I don't understand why he's holding out. And until he tells me the truth, I won't know if he really is on my side. I see him watching everything I do, drinking in the details of my life, but not in the gossipy way Shorty does, where you know he's just dying to tell the High Priest everything. No, this is like the old Micah—he watched, he analyzed, and when he was sure he could win, he stepped in, at precisely the right moment.

I'd better keep my mouth shut about the food until I've got proof. Shorty might be talking rubbish. If I'm wrong—if I spread rumors and the High Priest finds out, he'll be furious.

I've got so much to lose—Hal, my place in the Shrine, my new friends. So instead of confiding in him, which every corner of my heart wants to, I smile weakly and as we go back inside, I say, "It's just the heat. I'm battling to get used to it."

Aunty Figgy starts fussing around like a clucking bantam. "Go and lie down," she says. "I'll bring you your lunch on a tray."

Jasmine and Leonid exchange glances. They think I'm making a fuss over nothing.

"Don't you worry, Aunty Figgy," Micah says, fetching a tray from the pantry. "I'll take this through. I can see you're busy."

When he comes in a few minutes later, he lays the tray of food across my knees and looks at me with those deep brown eyes I remember so well. Why won't he admit we've known each other all our lives? He's about to say something when Aunty Figgy calls him away. He grins, that same chipped tooth grin, and he's gone.

Chapter Ten

Over the next few days, I ponder what Shorty told me. There's no disputing that I saw the wagon piled high with sacks from the Colony. But I don't know for certain what was inside those sacks. What if he doesn't have the whole truth? Ma Goodson always used to say, "There's two sides to every story." I don't want to be like Jasmine, jumping to conclusions about people, especially not the Citizens, when I am one of them. It could be dangerous for me.

I could just ask Hal to tell me what he knows, but he thinks I should leave business matters to Mr. Frye, as though my female brain is made of dandelion fluff. I'm going to have to see for myself what is going on. Even though the thought of spending a whole day alone with Leonid repulses me, I decide to go with him to the next Longkloof market where we sell our produce every week.

It's still dark when Leonid brings the wagon around to the front of the house the next market day. It's laden high with crates of vegetables, eggs, milk, and bunches of herbs. Wicker baskets with chickens and pigeons are tied on the sides of the wagon. He's full of attitude the moment I come out the door, looking me up and down and then pointedly at the empty seat next to him.

"Oh dear, miss," he says, "it's really not appropriate for someone of your status to sit with the hired help. Would you like me to fetch one of the armchairs? I could fit it on the back perhaps."

"Leonid!" Aunty Figgy snaps. "That's uncalled for."

I say nothing, though I'm seething inside. I climb up next to him. Before I'm settled, he flicks the reins and the horses set off. I almost fall off. I grab the bench and sit down, wanting to give him a sharp slap.

For the next hour, he ignores me. I go over every single exchange we've had in the months I've known him. Why does he hate me so much? Is he still furious that I let Mr. Frye blame him for spilling the milk? Surely he can't be that petty. Is it just because I'm a Citizen? Or is there another reason, something he's keeping from me, just another bit of information that I'm not allowed to know, like who my father is?

By sunrise, we're cresting the mountain. One of the High Priest's carriages is cantering along the road towards us. A guard blows a horn, and Leonid is forced to pull the wagon right to the edge of the cliff. I catch a glimpse of the sea far beneath us and grab the edge of the seat.

Leonid grins. "Scared?"

I'm not giving him the satisfaction. "No," I snap. He doesn't hear—the carriage has swept past, driving so close that it knocks the baskets that hang on the sides. The hens set up a furious clucking.

"Stupid peasants," the driver yells. "If you can't drive properly, get off the Island."

"Oxygen thieves," Leonid mutters under his breath. "Should shut them in the Colony and block up the air vents."

I don't say anything—there's a long day ahead, and I don't want to spend it fighting. The sun has risen and there's a stream of wagons and carriages on the road all heading for the market. The Citizens have sent their servants out early to do the week's shopping.

"How long till we get there?" I ask as we turn down the steep road that runs down to the end of the fjord. "Does it take a long time to set up the stall?"

He rolls his eyes. "I wouldn't expect you to do any of the work, miss."

"Actually, Leonid," I say coldly, "you people here above don't know what hard work is. You try living in the Colony, on your feet ten hours a day, growing food in hydroponic rotators and then spend two hours generating electricity on a treadmill. Then you can come and make remarks about me not knowing what heavy work is."

"No offense, miss." His voice is insolent.

I've had enough of him. I grab his wrist and yell, "What is it with you exactly? From the moment I arrived, you've been rude and hostile. I told you I was sorry about the milk jug. I don't expect you to like me, but I don't understand what I've done to make you hate me."

He flicks the reins so the horses break into a gallop.

I stare at his profile. He's squeezing his lips together like he's trying to hold the words in.

"WHAT IS IT?" I shout. "Let's just have this out once and for all. What have you got against me? Is it just because I'm a Citizen? Or is there something more?"

He rubs the back of his neck, glances at me, then away again.

"If you don't tell me this minute, I swear I am firing you, and you can get off right here."

He looks up again quickly and snarls, "It's...it's not you. It's old history."

"Old history? What do you mean?"

"It's your mother. Ali."

"My mother? You didn't know my mother."

"Your mother, and...and my father..."

"Yes, they fought together in the Resistance. So what?"

He stares at the slats of the wagon floor. I can barely hear his words. "It's more than that."

I stare at him. "Hell, Leonid, just spit it out! What's so bad you can't just say it? You were fine when I first arrived, but the moment Mr. Frye said my name, you decided you hated me. What is it? Is it because I inherited the farm? Did you think I wasn't good enough to be your boss because I came from the Colony?"

"It's not that....It's....I'm—you're—" His face is dark red. Is that anger or—no it can't be—it's embarrassment. "We're family. You're my half-sister."

"You're lying. We don't look anything alike." But then my eye catches sight of his bare feet, and he has the same long second toe as me, the same crooked pinkie toe. I run my eyes slowly up his body, trying to absorb what he's saying, looking for confirmation. Can it really be true? Have I found a real, living family member at last?

"I'm not lying." His voice is cold, eyes fixed on the road. "My mom found out my dad was having an affair and that his girlfriend was pregnant. They had a fight, and he packed his things and left. My mom cried and cried. She was already pregnant with my sister Alexia. He never came back." He spits out the last words.

"You don't know what happened to him? Did he die or—?"

"We know nothing. We had to go into the caves at Silvermine until the worst of the nuclear fallout was over. Millions of people died. My mother always presumed he was one of the unlucky ones."

We've turned off the main road into a square of land crowded with makeshift shelters. People mill around, unpacking their wagons and baskets, setting up tables in the shade of the wall that towers over everything. The wagon judders through the potholes. Each one shakes my stomach, but not as much as the news that Leonid is my half-brother. What will this mean for me? Are there more relatives? Will they all feel the same hatred for me that Leonid does?

There's no time to ask any more questions. He's

unhitching the horses and leading them to a quiet area away from the stalls.

Customers are already queueing up, and we barely sit down until the afternoon. The other stall holders stare at me curiously. I hear Leonid telling the sharp faced woman who sells soaps that I'm his boss, come to check up on him. No mention of our family connection.

We trade vegetables and honey and chicken for gold coins with the Citizens' staff, but there are so many hungry people with no money. They're trying to barter with things they've brought in from Boat Bay—carvings and furniture made from things that have washed up on the beaches, dried seaweed, dried snoek...nothing we really need, but I can't bear to see them hungry while we have so much. I try to give a hungry child a jar of honey and some nuts, but Leonid pulls me aside.

"What are you doing?" he snaps.

"Giving this child something to eat. She's starving. Look at her."

"You think your handout's going to help?"

"So what, you want to just let her starve to death?"

"You're all the same, you people," he says. "Feeling like a hero because you give a kid some honey. Only thing that will help her is destroying the vermin that run this city."

And that includes me, I think bitterly. Just say it, Leonid. You wish I'd never been elevated. You wish I'd been culled and thrown over the edge of the mountain.

At two o'clock, we're sold out. I've tried my best to look around and see if there are any stalls selling the grain from the Colony, but so far I haven't seen any of the Colony's bags. I'll have to go to the docks—maybe the sacks are being loaded onto a boat.

We join the queue of wagons and carts waiting to leave

the market square. "Please turn left," I tell Leonid, when he finally reaches the main road.

He sighs. "Why? I suppose you want to go to Boat Bay and cause trouble with my family."

"No, I don't," I say, coloring. "I want to see what produce is being exported."

His glare says he doesn't believe me.

I've had enough of him. "I'm not asking you," I say. "I'm telling you to take me to the Harbor."

I can feel his resentment smoldering as we set off along a narrow road that runs just inside the Wall. It's harsh and stony here and the Wall casts a long afternoon shadow, turning the air chilly. We turn a corner and the guard post lies ahead. Guards with guns stand at the gates, and there's a queue—wagons, buggies, people on donkeys, pedestrians, all of them waiting to go through.

Leonid scratches in his pocket and pulls out a small green book.

"What's that?" I ask.

"My passbook."

"I haven't got one. Will they let me through?"

"You don't need one."

Ahead of us, two guards are shouting at an old woman in tattered clothes. She's carrying a basket of linen on her head.

"What's going on?" I crane my neck to see. A guard grabs her by the shoulder.

"What's she done?" I ask, standing up to see better.

He pushes her against the wall. She knocks her head, hard.

"It's outrageous. I'm going to get the guard's name and report him to the High Priest."

"Lost her pass."

"They beat people up for not having a pass? I thought that died out with apartheid."

He doesn't answer—he doesn't need to. What he thinks of me, the army, the Citizens—it's all written clearly on his face. In his eyes, we're all one and the same. The apartheid state that died sixty years ago, and the new system run by the Prosperites.

His jaw is clenched as the guards punch her again and then shove her through the gate.

It's another fifteen minutes before we reach the front. The woman has disappeared. A guard approaches our wagon. "Passbooks," he snaps.

Leonid holds his out without a word. The guard checks it and tosses it back. Then he looks me up and down with one eyebrow raised.

"I'm Miss den Eeden of the farm Greenhaven."

"Go ahead, miss." He salutes, the cocky attitude disappearing instantly. "Enjoy your day further."

We're almost at the Harbor when we pass the old woman. She's sitting on the side of the road hunched over, holding her head. There's blood on her hands.

"What will happen to her?" I ask Leonid.

"She won't be able to go back into the City. She'll have to stay outside forever."

"What do you think she does for a living?"

"She looks like a laundry woman. She probably washes clothes for rich people." He doesn't actually say the words but his voice says, What do you care?

"So she'll starve?"

"Probably."

I grab the reins. "Go back. I want to help her."

He sneers at me. "You think your little handout is going to help?"

"Leonid," I say firmly, "go back."

"You're all the same, you Citizens. Throw her a few scraps to keep her quiet."

I jump down from the wagon and run back along the road. She's still sitting slumped on the basket, crying.

"Miss," I say, crouching down so we're eye to eye. "Can I help you? Can we give you a lift to your house? Have you got family we can take you to?"

Her eyes are sunken. She has a hacking cough and blood is trickling down her face. "There's no one," she mutters.

I can't leave her here, bleeding on the side of the road. And there's no one I can ask in Boat City to help. There's only one thing to do.

"Do you want to come with me?" I ask her gently. "Do you want a job in the City, on my farm?"

She doesn't answer. She just stares. Then slowly she nods.

I wave to Leonid. He turns the wagon and drives back up the road towards us.

"She's coming home with us," I say. "She's got no one here."

"They won't let her in," he says, gesturing towards the Wall. "Not without a passbook."

I look around for something. Anything. Then I see her basket of washing. I tip it up and search through it. At the bottom, I find a grand robe in saffron orange. It must have belonged to someone very wealthy. It's got a big stain across the middle, and it's pretty creased, but I tell her to stand up. I slip it over her head and it falls against her thin body. Her collarbones stick out like rods against the embroidered neckline.

I pour the last bit of water from our water bucket over a cloth and wipe the blood off her face. The wound is still oozing, but there's a red scarf in the basket. I wind it around her head in a turban, and pull it over, so it covers the wound above her ear. Then I take off my sandals and put them on her feet.

"Up you get," I say, heaving her onto the wagon. "You go in the middle."

She shifts up, next to Leonid. She's so thin that she takes hardly any space on the bench.

"Home please, Leonid," I say.

He rolls his eyes and sets the horses trotting.

"What's your name?" I ask as we near the border post.

"Sarie, miss."

"Well, Sarie, I want you to sit up straight and hold this book. Pretend you're reading it." I give her the book I brought in case I got a chance to practice my reading. She holds it upside down, so I turn it the right way up, and pat her knee. "You're not Sarie right now. You're Miss Sarah, my aunt, visiting from the Mainland. We fetched you at the Harbor. Understood?"

"Yes, miss." She manages half a smile before she doubles up coughing. She only has three teeth.

Leonid rolls his eyes again, but I ignore him. We reach the border post. A different guard comes over. The sight of the rifle strapped to his shoulder makes me sweat.

"Passes," he says curtly. "Hurry up."

Leonid holds his out and the guard checks it briefly. "You. Give me your pass," he snaps at Sarie.

I put on my snootiest expression and stand up regally. "I am Miss Ebba den Eeden of Greenhaven, and I do NOT carry a pass," I proclaim. "This is my aunt, Miss Sarah den Eeden, newly arrived from Stellenbosch. Kindly let us through."

The guard looks like he's not sure whether to believe me, but clearly he can't imagine why a Citizen would want to smuggle someone like Sarie into the City. He waves us on.

The moment we're around the bend in the road, Sarie is wracked with coughs. Her body is burning hot against mine. I've got to get her home and into bed.

Leonid doesn't say a word to me all the way back. I try and talk to Sarie, but she twists her hands together and answers in such a soft voice, I can't hear her. Halfway home, she falls asleep against my shoulder. What medicines will Aunty Figgy have to help her? In the Colony, I could have harvested some herbs and made an infusion, but this illness is worse than anything I've seen before. What if we can't help her? I push the thought out of my mind. We have to help her.

It's almost evening when we get home. Micah is washing himself at the pump. He waves to me as he sticks his head under the faucet. Aunty Figgy comes to the kitchen door to fetch the shopping we've brought from the market. She sees me helping Sarie down from the wagon, and shakes her head. "What have you done!" she exclaims.

"This is Sarie," I say. "She needs help. Please can you find me some medicine for her cough, and help me get her to bed."

"Ebba!" she scolds. "You can't bring her here. It's against the law." Her voice drops and she comes closer to me. "You can't go bringing just anyone onto Greenhaven. You don't know who this woman is."

"But she's got nowhere to go," I say. "She was beaten by the guards because she lost her pass."

"How are you going to explain this to the authorities? When they hear about her, they'll come here and arrest you."

"They're not like that, Aunty Figgy," I say. I'm getting irritated with her negativity. "I'll talk to the High Priest. I'll tell him that the guards were beating her."

"Just listen to yourself," Aunty Figgy says. "Do you think he'll care? He believes that people who are poor and sick are being punished by Prospiroh for their sins."

I stare at Sarie, biting my lip. She's standing next to

the pump, as thin as a corn husk, and her cough shakes her whole body.

"You don't know what diseases she has," Aunty Figgy whispers, shaking her head. "She's very sick. You can't have her in the house—she'll infect us all. She'll have to sleep in the barn. Or Leonid must take her back to the Harbor."

"If Shorty finds out you smuggled her in, he'll report you to the High Priest," Leonid says, as he comes back from the kitchen. "I told you so, but you didn't want to listen."

"You listen here," I say, grabbing him by the front of his tunic. "I have had enough of you. Just shut up. And you, Aunty Figgy," I say, turning to her with my hands on my hips. "I thought you were all 'Earth mother, the Goddess loves us and protects us, we need to care for all living things.' But I guess I was wrong."

"There's no need to take that tone with me, my girl," Aunty Figgy snaps. She grabs the crate of shopping and marches off into the kitchen.

Sarie twists her hands in the folds of the saffron robe. "I'm going now, miss," she mutters, looking at the ground. "I don't want to cause trouble."

"It's quite all right," I say firmly, taking her arm. "Aunty Figgy is just being bossy. Come with me."

I take her through the front of the house and put her to bed in the spare bedroom. I know it's against the law, but I'm certain the authorities will understand when I explain that she's ill. And hopefully Shorty won't see her until she's better, and I've had a chance to explain to the High Priest myself.

Sarie gets into bed and lies there, exhausted. Her forehead is wet with sweat and she's struggling to breathe.

"I don't want to be any nuisance, miss," she murmurs when I bring in a bowl of chicken soup.

"You're not a nuisance," I say, as I lift the spoon to her

lips. "Please drink some soup."

She turns her head away.

"I'm going to see what medicines we have for you," I say, putting the bowl down. "You rest quietly, and I'll come back just now with something to help you break your fever." I wipe her forehead with a damp cloth and go back to the kitchen. I have no idea what kind of medicine to give her. I'll have to ask Aunty Figgy to help me.

But it's dinner time. The guys have arrived, stamping their boots at the back door, their hair wet from washing off the day's dirt at the pump. Leonid and Jasmine are whispering together in the yard, and when she comes in, Jasmine is scowling. I can't leave the kitchen now without raising suspicion.

"How was your day, miss?" Shorty asks. "Did you enjoy the market? We were very busy here—Victor and Micah were ploughing the new lands, and I helped a bit, though I'm not much good with my hands, ha ha ha. Better with the books."

I bite my lip and remember that I have to act like there's nothing wrong. "Is that so, Shorty?" I say. "The market was busy too. It was interesting, but exhausting. And so noisy. I couldn't believe the number of people that were there."

"Why don't you tell us about yourself," Micah says to Shorty. "You were telling us a funny story this morning about when you were growing up..."

Shorty's baby face breaks into a grin. "Ja, that was hilarious. You're going to love this one, Miss Ebba. Once me and my brothers, we were making go-karts and we couldn't find any wheels, so we took the chassis off an old Volkswagen Beetle we found on the scrap heap and we built this double decker go-kart..."

I switch off, worrying about Sarie. How am I going to keep her hidden until I've had a chance to see the High

Priest? Maybe it would be better to drive through to Shrine first thing in the morning and confess what I've done. But what if he's angry that I've broken the law? What if he decides to punish me? Leonid's right. I should have thought this through before I acted on impulse.

At last Shorty's interminable story, and dinner, are over.

"I'll be off, if that's all right, miss," Shorty says, shovelling in the last mouthful. "I've got to go through the sales today from the market." He gets up and dumps his plate in the sink, leaving a mess of spilled gravy on the table cloth.

Victor puts his knife and fork neatly on his empty plate. "Excuse me, please. I have to feed the birds. Thank you for a delicious dinner."

"We need a plan of action," Micah says, when he's checked that Shorty and Victor are out of earshot. He closes the back door and leans against the counter, finger on his chin. "There will be consequences, Ebba. We need to be prepared for them."

"I'll go to the Shrine tomorrow morning," I tell him, trying to sound more confident than I am. "I'll ask to see the High Priest, and I'll explain everything. Hal will come with me, and I'm sure the High Priest will be fine with Sarie staying here until she's better."

"You're deluded, Ebba," Aunty Figgy says. "I vote we take her back to the Harbor, right now. If you want to help her, Ebba, we can find a family who will look after her in return for produce from the farm."

"Ja," Leonid grunts, "but how am I supposed to get her through the border post without a pass? I'm not getting arrested because Ebba decided to be Mother Teresa without thinking about how it affected everyone else."

Of course Jasmine has to say her two cents worth too. She's becoming as perpetually angry as Leonid. "I don't get it. You won't save Fez and Letti, when all it will cost to have them freed is an old necklace. Fez and Letti who have been our best friends, our sabenzis, our whole lives. Who are probably going to be chosen for the next Sacrifice." Her eyes fill with tears but she blinks them away. "And now you're risking all of us here by smuggling in a sick old woman. I don't recognize you anymore. The old Ebba would never have made such selfish choices."

"You don't understand, Jasmine," Aunty Figgy says gently, patting her hand. "That's not just an old necklace. It's priceless—it's absolutely irreplaceable."

"More valuable than two human beings? Honestly, I think Ebba's turned into one of Them already."

"It's not the time for personal attacks," Micah says firmly. "We have a problem and we need to focus on it until we find a solution."

Jasmine colors.

"Actually." Aunty Figgy holds up her hand to tell Jasmine to hold her tongue. "What she did showed a lot of compassion. Ebba, your mother would have been proud of you. But that doesn't alter the fact that what you did was impulsive and very possibly dangerous."

Then suddenly, there's a knock on the back door, so soft we almost miss it. Micah leans over and opens it. Victor stands there, looking at his feet.

"Excuse me, Miss Ebba. I—er—there's someone here. She's lying on the driveway..."

I have to think quickly. "It's my aunt! She must have come to visit me. I wasn't expecting her till later in the week. Micah, please help her inside."

Micah and Leonid hurry off, but Victor stands dithering on the doorstep, not making eye contact, but not moving away. What does he want?

"Thank you, Victor," I say. Then because I'm flustered, and he's still hanging around and I'm scared stiff that she's going to die. I say, "Please don't tell Shorty you found her."

"Of course not, miss. I'll get back to work if that's all right?"

"Perfectly all right. Thank you for bringing her."

He disappears back into the yard, and I rush through to get the spare bedroom ready as Leonid and Micah carry her through the front door and lie her on the bed. Her face is sunken and her breath rumbles in her throat.

"Do something," I beg, grabbing Aunty Figgy's sleeve as she puts a bowl of water and a cloth on the dressing table. "You must have some medicine or something."

Aunty Figgy crosses to the bed, and takes Sarie's wrist between finger and thumb. She holds up her hand to tell me to be quiet. "It's too late," she says at last. "Her pulse is weak. That gurgling noise is the death rattle."

I sit in the chair next to her bed, watching Sarie sleep. Her mouth falls open, and suddenly her rattling breaths stop. I lean forward. Is this it? I watch, trying to see if the sheet is moving even the tiniest amount. Then she gives a deep gasp and her breaths come fast and jagged before settling back into a regular pattern. Isi sighs, and goes back to sleep, her nose resting on my foot.

The night lengthens. Sarie's breathing follows the same pattern. A long pause, a gasp, but her breaths grow slower and shallower. The pauses last longer. And then just when the candles have nearly burned down and I think I need to go and fetch more, her breathing stops. No juddering breath following the silence. There's nothing. The room is quiet.

Aunty Figgy is sleeping in the armchair in the corner. She wakes, and puts two fingers on Sarie's scrawny neck. "She's gone."

"We must bury her, before Shorty and Victor wake up," I say. "Leonid and Micah will dig a grave."

We wash the thin body, brush her hair, clean and trim

her nails. I open my great aunt's wardrobe and take out a yellow dress with sunflowers on it. It's sunny and happy, and I think Sarie would have liked it. We dress her and wrap a scarf around her hair. Aunty Figgy rolls a small towel into a block and wedges it under her chin.

Sarie looks happy at last. The sunken face has relaxed and all the lines of suffering have smoothed out.

"It's late," I say, when we have finished laying her out and she is wrapped in a sheet. "Why don't you lie on the sofa until the grave is ready?"

"Just for a while." Aunty Figgy's eyes are sunken with tiredness. She goes to the sitting room and I sit on the window seat, watching over the still form lying on the bed. Isi jumps up next to me, and snuggles against my side.

The house is still. Death hangs over the house, like a hovering bird with open wings.

I imagine what will happen if Aunty Figgy's story is true. If I don't obey the prophecy. If I don't unite the amulets, and everything dies. I imagine how the world will disintegrate. And in my mind I see myself spinning through the silent universe, alone.

We bury her at first light, between two milkwoods, on the edge of the forest. The grey sky is streaked with pink as Micah and Leonid lower her into the grave.

Aunty Figgy prays.

Great Theia, welcome your daughter
back into the Earth,
the nurturing womb
from which we all are born.

And she scatters buchu and kooigoed over the white wrapped body until it's hidden under the fragrant foliage.

I stand a moment on the edge of the grave. "I'm sorry I failed you," I whisper, as I drop a small bunch of wild flowers onto her chest. "You shouldn't have died. Forgive me."

Leonid and Micah pick up the spades and start shovelling sand. My eyes fill. It's so wrong, just so wrong.

"Come, Ebba," Aunty Figgy says, pulling me away. "We need to get back to the house. Shorty and Victor will be in soon for breakfast."

I follow her up to the house. Jasmine walks beside me, but her face is grim and she turns it away from me.

Breakfast is awkward. We're exhausted, but we have to act like nothing's wrong. Fortunately, Micah keeps the conversation flowing. He talks about life on the Mainland, about his family in Bellville City, about his uncle who breeds goats and his cousins who are wheelwrights.

I wonder how he manages to make up so many details. I'm pretty certain he spent his childhood in the Colony with me but to hear him talk, you'd think he'd spent it playing with his cousins in the farm dam. His leg is resting against mine, under the table. Is it on purpose? I so want it to be deliberate. I want him to tell me the truth, to explain where he has been, to pick up where we left off, with that kiss that made my senses spin.

At last the meal is over. Shorty has shovelled the last mountain of scrambled eggs into his mouth.

"Very tasty, as always, Aunty Figgy," he beams. "Nobody cooks like you. Well, thank you very much. I'll be getting back to the books, if you don't mind. Such a lot to do. Such a lot."

"Fine," I say, getting up from the table. I'm so tired I couldn't care less what any of them do today. I just want to be with Micah, but I can't. He's got work to do with Leonid in the new lands.

It's still early, not eight o'clock yet. I don't want to think about Sarie anymore—that caved-in stomach, the exposed ribs, the knobbly old knees. I want to be in the forest where it's cool and calm. I want to hear the water rippling over the stones and the frogs croaking in the reeds. I call Isi and set off through the forest to the kloof where Hal and I went the day we met. I stumble down the steep slope, thinking about how different Hal is to Micah. What would Hal have done if we'd found Sarie when we were out driving? Would he have told me not to pick her up? Would he have reported me to his father? I'd like to think that he would have stopped and helped her too, but I know in my heart that he would have left her to die on the side of the road. Because that is Prospiroh's way. He selects a few and showers them with blessings. And the rest must starve.

I follow the river downstream, past the natural rock pool where Hal swam and I saw Clementine, and onwards down the path, winding through the thick bush.

The river makes another big turn, and there, looming up, is the Wall that encircles the Island. It's as tall as the highest tree in the forest. As it crosses the river, the base has been arched into a culvert, and steel bars reach down like teeth, anchored in the river bed.

I wade into the shallows, bend down and peer through. Outside there's a dirty beach, boulders, a ruined building... and the sea, beating against the rocks.

There's a bad smell. A seagull lies rotting on the sand. I turn back, feeling my way back along the wall to the river bank. My skin feels gritty after a night sleeping in my clothes. I need to wash. I wade through the shallows upstream until I reach the natural rock pool.

I hang my robe and underclothes over a rock and step into the water. It's cold, but I force myself to go deeper until I'm waist deep. I squat down until the water covers my shoulders then dip my head underwater and come up gasping for air. The shock of the cold water against my skin feels like a thousand pins stabbing me, but the pain is good. At least I'm alive.

Alive, like Micah.

The thought brings a cascade of memories.

One Friday night during recreation, everyone was watching a boring movie. Micah started a game of Hide and Go Seek. We were all too old of course, but it felt fun to play a kid's game again. Jasmine was It, and when she had closed her eyes and was counting to one hundred, we all ran to hide. We had the whole of the recreation level to hide in, but Micah and I found ourselves running down the same passage, and we reached a locked door. In the distance, Jasmine called, "Coming, ready or not," and I grabbed him. "What shall we do?" I whispered.

He opened a small square door in the wall, and said, "Get in."

I peered inside. It was the laundry chute, taking dirty washing from our sleeping cells in the level above us to the laundry level below.

"You're not serious," I whispered.

"Go on." He grinned.

Letti was shrieking nearby. Jasmine had found her already because she was useless at hiding. I refused to be caught next. So I climbed into the chute and next thing I was sliding down a tube, and ended up on a huge pile of dirty sheets and empty sacks from the storage chamber. I turned over just in time because Micah came shooting down and landed next to me.

We rolled around in the sheets, laughing. And then...he caught in a linen sack, leaned over, and kissed me. A long, lingering kiss that felt like a root growing in my heart. His skin smelled of sandalwood and soap. I wanted to lie in his arms forever.

But then the door opened and a guard stood there, scowling. He sent us back to the recreation room, and we both got shouted at by Mr. Dermond.

It was worth it for that kiss.

But the next day, he was gone. Nobody would say where. He was just gone.

I shake my hair, and stick my face underwater again, trying to wash away my tiredness and headache. It's then that the clasp somehow comes undone, and the necklace slips off. I try to grab it, but I miss and it sinks to the bottom of the pond. I can see it shining among the rocks, but I can't reach it. I wade in deeper, trying to reach it with my toes, but I'm frightened. It's fallen in a hollow and the water would be over my head if I went down after it.

What if it washes away? The culvert is just around the bend in the river. If the current washes it through the culvert, it will flow into the sea and be lost forever.

I don't strictly believe in the Goddess, but I'm desperate so I pray, "Goddess, help me."

And suddenly, like a miracle, Micah comes into view, whistling. He's carrying an axe—he must have come to chop wood for the stove. He doesn't wade in the shallows as I did. He jumps from rock to rock down the river bed.

"Ebba," he says, stopping abruptly as he sees me in the pond. "I'm sorry. I didn't know you were there."

My eyes flicker to my robe, neatly folded and out of reach. I'm waist deep in water. I cross my arms over my breasts, and try and hold onto my dignity. "Micah," I say, "I've dropped my necklace and I can't reach it. Can you swim?"

"Like a fish. All those years in the farm dam." He begins to pull his shirt over his head. "Close your eyes, you naughty girl," he says with a grin. "I don't want to corrupt your innocence."

I point to the place where my necklace lies. "It's between those rocks there."

He pulls off his pants and wades naked into the water.

I won't look at him. I won't I won't I won't. As much as I

want to, I won't look at that brown body that I remember so well.

He dives under the water. OK, yes, fine. I look. I can't help it.

And I catch a glimpse of a strong back crisscrossed by scars. Scars? What happened to him? He didn't get those in the Colony.

A moment later he surfaces, with the necklace in his hand. "Here you are," he says. "Shall I put it on for you?"

"Thank you. Thank you so much." My voice squeaks.

The moment he stands behind me and puts the chain around my neck, I start to shiver. It's not the cold. It's him. Even though he's not touching me, just his fingers sweeping my neck, I'm aware of every inch of skin, every atom of space between us. He fastens the chain, then he slowly turns me around. I smell his skin. Sandalwood and soap. No matter what he says, he is Micah. My Micah, from the Colony.

"You're cold," he murmurs. His fingers brush my shoulders. "It's time to get out."

His hands run up and down the side of my neck, his thumbs lingering over my collar bones.

"You go first," I say. I can't take my eyes away from his. I can't move.

"OK," he says, but he moves his hands down my back to the base of my spine, and presses me closer.

"I know you," I murmur. "You're Micah. *My* Micah."

"Shh," he whispers, pushing my body against his. I can't help it. My arms open and wrap themselves around his waist. I gaze into the deep brown eyes I have loved since I was a child.

My hands gently caress his scars. "You were injured. When? How?"

"Shhhhhhh," he murmurs. He takes my face in his hands and lifts my mouth to his. His kiss is long and slow, like the kiss we shared in the Colony, except this time my body isn't filled with a chemical to control my desire, and every part of me is alive with longing for him.

But suddenly, there's a voice in my head. *Ebba, get out of the pool.*

Clementine stands on the rock above us. Isi is there too, and the little boy is scratching her behind her ears. Something's different. Usually Clementine is placid and smiley. But today she's not calm. She's not smiling. *Come away, Ebba.*

"What is it?" Micah asks, turning around to see what I'm staring at.

She waves frantically. Picking up a handful of pebbles, the little boy throws them into the water next to us. They make ripples but Micah doesn't react. He can't see the child or his mother.

"It's nothing," I say, turning around so I won't have to look at her. She probably thinks that I'm being immoral, standing naked in a rock pool, kissing the most gorgeous guy in the world. And I don't care what she thinks. I've waited for this moment for five years. I'm not stopping now.

Micah kisses my eyelids, my lips, my neck. He cups his hands around my breasts and...

Stop it, Ebba... Her voice in my head is more urgent. *You need to go home.*

I wind my arms around his neck and kiss him again.

Suddenly Isi begins to bark. Micah lets go of me and ducks down behind the big boulder. "Get dressed," he hisses.

I look up to see Hal coming down the path towards me. Oh no!

What am I going to do? I should have listened to Clementine...

"Hal!" I exclaim, turning my back to him. "I'm just bathing

in the pool."

"So I see," he says with a strangled voice.

By the time I pull on my clothes and run up to the house, he's already back on his horse and cantering off. I shout after him but he doesn't look back.

Chapter Eleven

I pace under the pecan trees in the kitchen garden, trying to calm myself down. The Citizens insist that their women are modestly clothed in robes that cover their bodies at all times, so hopefully he was just shocked and didn't know what to say.

But...and I can hardly bear to think of it...what if Micah was too slow, and Hal saw us both naked in the pool? I know, I know. I should have got out when Clementine called me, I should have trusted her. But it felt so good to be back in Micah's arms. It's been so long, I thought he was dead, and he's come back to me. I hug myself, remembering the feel of him holding me, of his mouth against mine, of the way our bodies seemed to call out to each other and intertwine like two strands of a vine. I didn't lose him, even though I was convinced he was dead. He survived and found his way back to me.

If Hal saw us together, he'll be enraged. He considers me his property, I see that now. Right now, he could be reporting me to his father for kissing one of the laborers. I'm one hundred percent certain that it is forbidden for Citizens to have a relationship with non-Citizens. And if they ever do a full investigation and discover that Micah was thrown out of the Colony and somehow survived, they'll almost certainly finish off the job now. It's so dangerous for him here. Perhaps I should tell him to go back to the Mainland or Boat Bay, or wherever he's come from.

But how can I lose him for a second time?

Aunty Figgy comes out with a basket to pick vegetables. "You look exhausted. I'm going to brew you some tea," she says, breaking off sprigs of fennel and camomile. "Go and lie down and I'll bring it to you."

I wish I could tell her what's worrying me, but I dare not. She doesn't approve of me being involved in anything except running the farm and looking for the amulets, and I haven't even started searching for those yet. I'm not sure yet if I believe the story she's told. Me? Related to a Goddess? With a sacred task?

The clatter of hooves wake me from a deep sleep. I sit up, trying to work out why Leonid is taking the wagon out again?

Someone bashes on the front door and a man's voice shouts, "Open up. High Priest's orders."

I jump up, my heart thudding against my rib cage. They've come for Micah. I've got to warn him. I've got to send them away. I've got to think up something to say...

I run to the door, but Aunty Figgy has got there first.

"What do you want?" she demands, hands on her hips.

It's Captain Atherton. She only reaches his chest, but she glares up at him and he takes a step back.

"Ebba den Eeden. I'm here for Miss den Eeden."

I want to fall on my knees in gratitude. It's not Micah they want.

"Good afternoon, Captain." I try to keep my voice cool. "How can I help you?"

"You are ordered to attend the Council meeting."

He still makes my skin crawl. Every time I see him, I'm back in that long climb out of the Colony, convinced I'm about to die. But I must hide my fear from him. "In connection with what?" I say, putting my chin in the air.

"I am not at liberty to say."

"Hal's told them about Micah. My legs shake."

Aunty Figgy turns to me. "You can't go to the Shrine like that. It would be a disgrace. You need clean clothes."

Captain Atherton nods. "Five minutes only."

Aunty Figgy and I go into my bedroom and shut the door.

"I knew there'd be trouble, I just knew it," she mutters as she opens my wardrobe and chooses a clean robe. "Good Theia, protect her..."

I'm in so much trouble. And I can't tell her that Hal caught me kissing Micah. With shaking hands, I change into the clean robe and wash my face and hands in the bathroom.

Aunty Figgy keeps up a steady mutter of prayer as she unclasps the necklace from my neck. "You need this for protection," she says. "But they're going to try and get it away from you. We need to hide it."

"Where? How?"

She stands for a moment, pondering.

"Ah. I know," she says, opening a drawer and taking out a small tin filled with hair clips and bobby pins. "It's a good thing your hair is so thick and curly." She pulls my hair back into a bun, and secures it with a band. Then she takes the amulet, wraps the chain around it, and shoves it deep into the bun. She pins it into place. "Now be careful with your hairdo. Don't let it come loose."

Captain Atherton bangs on the front door. "Hurry up, please. The High Priest does not like to be kept waiting."

"I'm coming," I call. I clutch Aunty Figgy's arm. "I'm scared."

"I know you are. But the necklace will protect you. Wait," she says. "We need a decoy." She searches through my dressing table drawer. "This is all cheap costume jewelry," she says. "Nothing too valuable here. We want something that looks old. Now where is it? Ah, here." She takes out the pendant shaped like a dove that hangs on a heavy chain, and slips it around my neck. "Keep this under your robe. It might fool them." Then she pulls me into a hug, and pats my cheek. "I'm going to light a candle for you and pray. Now go."

The journey takes forever. I'm shut in the buggy with Captain Atherton watching my every move. The Council are going to interrogate me, and I have to think up something to say. The anxious thoughts of what might happen swarm in my head like wasps, each bringing their own sting. I can't focus. The only thing that comforts me is the memory of Micah's kiss. Those soft lips, brown eyes, his firm body.

The net of scars across his back.

What's going to happen to him? Is history repeating itself? He kisses me and then he gets punished and we're separated?

I can't lose him. I can't.

We arrive at the Shrine offices and my heart pounds as I climb the long flight of stairs. The stone lions look as though they want to pounce and eat me alive. Hal must be at home in the compound, just around the bend in the road. Is he plotting revenge against me and Micah?

Without a word, Captain Atherton takes me down a long passage, deep inside the mountain. The further in we go, the more my anxiety churns my stomach. Are they going to throw me back in the Colony? Are they going to take my farm away?

At last, we reach the Council chamber. It's a large, rectangular room, with a cold, sterile feel from the smooth white marble that lines the walls, the floor, the ceiling. Even the rough-hewn grey rock of the Colony was more welcoming than this. At the far end, the High Priest and General de Groot sit side by side at a large rectangular table. Next to them sit Mr. Frye and Major Zungu. Lucas sits there too, pen in hand. He doesn't lift his eyes from the pages of the thick writing book in front of him. Captain Atherton takes the last remaining chair, and I'm standing alone in the cavernous space. Five pairs of accusatory eyes glare at me.

"Ah, Miss den Eeden," the High Priest says, frowning under bushy eyebrows. "What is this we hear about you breaking the City law?" His voice echoes around the white room, seeming to come at me from all sides.

I break out into a sweat.

How do I answer him? I've broken so many laws in the last twenty-four hours. I've lied about Sarie having a passbook. I've brought her into the City illegally. I've let her sleep in my house, and although I'm not sure what the laws are, you're probably not allowed to just bury people in your garden.

And then there's Micah. Kissing a farm laborer is definitely an infringement.

But I don't want to confess to something he doesn't know about yet, so I stare at the hem of my robe, and I don't say anything.

"Has Prospiroh not been good to you, Ebba?" he asks, spreading his hands wide. "Hasn't Prospiroh blessed you, more than you could even have dreamed of?"

"He has, Your Righteousness," I mumble.

"And this is how you thank Him. You should be ashamed."

I bow my head, mind racing. I do feel shame, I do. But I'm not sure anymore that I should.

"Have we not been kind to you? Did I not rescue you from the jaws of death and elevate you? Did I not welcome you into my home, like a member of my own family, and feed you from my own table?"

"Yes, Your Righteousness."

They watch me. I'm a pile of dirt on their pristine floor.

"Is this the way you thank Prospiroh? By breaking the laws He has set up for your own protection? You're a child, Ebba. What do you know about governing a city like Table Island?"

"Nothing, Your Righteousness." I pick at my cuticles, wishing he would tell me what I've done. Has Hal told him? Am I going to lose Micah for a second time?

"And yet you break the law by bringing a diseased old woman into the City," General de Groot bellows, pushing his chair back so it screeches on the floor. "Do you realize she could have inflicted a plague on all of us? We could all have died."

I look up quickly. Oh thank the Goddess. He doesn't know about Micah. Hal didn't see him.

The High Priest scowls, his hooded eyes cutting into me. "Where would you be without us, Ebba?" he says. "Would you like us all to die? Is that what you want?"

"No, Your Righteousness."

"Perhaps you don't want to be here in the City," General de Groot says, banging the table with his fist. "Perhaps you want to go back into the Colony. Is that it?"

"No." I can barely whisper. The thought is too awful. To be back underground again, with no sky, no trees, no Isi. No Micah. No Aunty Figgy and her luxurious, amazing food.

"Perhaps you want to leave the City then. Is that it? You want to be exiled to the Mainland."

I'm choking up. "Please, Your Righteousness," I beg. "Please forgive me. I'm so sorry. I didn't think."

The High Priest narrows his eyes and stares at me for a long minute. The room is totally silent except for Lucas, scribbling notes in his book. They're calculating my punishment, I know. Sweat trickles down my forehead, but I'm too scared to brush it away. If they throw me out of the City, I'll have nowhere to go. I'll be totally alone.

He and General de Groot confer behind their hands.

I wish I could hear what they're saying.

Help me, Goddess, I pray. Please, Theia. Save me, save Micah...

Then Mr. Frye puts his hand up. "Your Righteousness," he says. "May I say something?"

The High Priest turns and looks down his nose at him. "What is it, Fergis?"

"I take some responsibility for Miss den Eeden's lapse. I should have spent more time teaching her our ways. She's very young, and she possibly needs more guidance than I realized."

The High Priest ponders this, steepling his hands. "Hmmm. You may have a point. What do you say, Miss den Eeden?"

"I'll try harder, Your Righteousness," I plead. "Please give me another chance."

"Mr. Frye," he says at last. "You are going to take a more active part in Miss den Eeden's education?"

"Yes, Your Righteousness," Mr. Frye says. "My sincere apologies for my lapse in this matter. I've been so busy, what with the..."

"Yes, yes, yes," the High Priest interrupts. "Spare me the details. You may go, Miss den Eeden, but next time you won't get off so leniently. If you break the law again, I will be forced to reconsider whether we want you here in our city at all."

"Thank you, Your Righteousness." Thank the Goddess it's over. I can go home. Home to Micah.

"One last thing..." The High Priest's hooded eyes search my clothing. "Before you leave, you are required to undergo ritual cleansing. Captain Atherton, take her to the Cleansing chamber."

A fierce middle-aged woman with beefy arms is waiting in a small ante room with a tiled floor. "Undress," she snaps. "Put your clothes here." She points to a slatted wooden bench against one wall.

"Undress? Everything?"

"The whole caboodle. Jewelry too."

She watches me while I take off my robe and undergarments. Last thing I take off is the dove pendant. I put it on top of my pile of clothes and stand in front of her, stark naked, feeling like a snail with its shell pulled off.

She opens a door and a cloud of steam pours out into the room.

She's going to torture me. "No, please..." I beg. "Don't hurt me."

"Shut up," she says, shoving me inside. "It's just a steam room."

She shuts the door and leaves me there with no light, just the glow from the fire, and the sizzle of the water on hot stones. I huddle on the bench wondering what she's going to do next. Soon my body is running with perspiration. Suddenly the door opens, and she throws a bucket of cold water over me. I scream.

She grabs a towel, and starts rubbing my back, under my arms, my legs, my chest. "Disgusting," she says, showing me the grimy towel. "You are filthy."

She scrubs me so hard my skin is red and raw, like I've been sandpapered.

"Take down your hair. I need to cleanse your scalp."

She's going to find the amulet.

"Um, um..." I mutter, my brain whirring. I can't argue with her. She'll never go against the High Priest's orders.

"Hurry up." She wipes the sweat off her hairy lip with her forearm. "Haven't got all day. Get moving."

"Um..." I've got to think of something.

"What is it?" She flicks the towel against my leg.

It comes to me in a flash. They're so scared that Sarie brought an illness into the City. "I...I caught lice from the old lady I helped. She was one of the Boat People. I let her sleep in my bed."

She jumps back as though she's been slapped. "That's disgusting," she shouts. She's already started scratching her head. "Get out of here. Go on. Scat!"

I get my clothes on again as fast as I can. By the time I'm dressed, she's already called Captain Atherton. "Lice!" she snaps.

The Captain looks disgusted. He marches me out of a back door and into the waiting carriage. "Don't rest your head on the seat," he snarls as he slams the door.

I'm traveling alone. He won't risk being in the carriage with me. As we drive away, I remember the dove pendant. It wasn't on my pile of clothes where I left it. Someone removed it while I was in the steam room.

Chapter Twelve

Isi is waiting for me at the gates of the farm, and when she barks joyfully and runs alongside the carriage towards the gabled home that my ancestors built, I feel for the first time as though I've truly come home.

When I find Aunty Figgy waiting on the stoep, a rush of gratitude fills me. She knows exactly what to do in a crisis. I would never have got through this without her.

"Oh praise be," she exclaims, throwing open the carriage door. "You're safe. I was so worried about you. I prayed the whole time you were gone."

I jump down and grab her in a tight hug. "Thank you. Thank you for everything."

"Ebba," she says as the carriage drives away. "You are trying to please everybody. It will never work. The only one you should be trying to please is Theia."

I sink down on the top step as she goes inside. Isi sits next to me and I put my arm around her, feeling her warm body leaning against mine.

Life up here is far more complicated and difficult than I could have imagined. The perfect life that Jasmine, Letti, Fez and I imagined can never come true. After the last twenty-four hours with Leonid's bombshell news, sitting up all night with Sarie, her burial, Micah kissing me at last, Hal seeing us, and the summons to the Council chamber, I'm exhausted. It's as though I've been thrown into a deep river. I've been able to keep my head above water for a while, but it's just a matter of time before I drown.

A few minutes later, Micah comes round the side of the house, whistling. I have to stop myself from running into his arms.

"Miss Ebba," he calls across the grass, "can you give me a hand, please? I have to bring the horses in for the night."

I'm terrified of the horses, but I'll do anything for a reason to be close to him in broad daylight.

"How did it go?" he asks calmly as he opens the gate and we cross the meadow to the far corner where the horses are grazing.

"He said he was disappointed in me, that I'm a disgrace, and that if I'm not careful, they'll either throw me out of the City or send me back into the Colony." I want to grab his arm, but I hold myself back. Who knows if Shorty is watching through the office window? "Micah, I can't go back there. I can't. You've got to help me. Tell me what to do."

He steps away from me, and says firmly, "Ebba, calm down."

"What do you mean, calm down? You weren't there. Afterwards they made me take a ritual bath. They..."

"Ebba, I know you're upset. But you need to control yourself. You can't just fall apart because the authorities shouted at you."

"You don't know what it's like."

He looks at me with one eyebrow raised, and I remember that he knows exactly what it's like to be in the worst possible trouble with the authorities. To be sentenced to death, to be thrown out of the ventilation shaft just as I nearly was.

"Sorry." I take a deep breath and unclench my hands.

"You've had a bad day, but you're home again, safe. They wanted to crush you, but you survived. You won this round. You're much stronger than you think."

"I don't feel strong."

"That's because you haven't been tested. In the Colony, they told you what to do, and you did it. Up here, it's different. You have power."

"What power? I'm only sixteen."

"You're underestimating yourself. You're extremely powerful. But you're afraid of it, so you pretend it doesn't exist."

"You mean—um—the power in the amulet?" I feel in my hair and pull the necklace out of its hiding place. "Aunty Figgy says it's very powerful, but I'm not..."

"I'm not talking about the amulet. Politically, you're very powerful. Socially, you're powerful. You're very wealthy. You own a lot of land, growing a commodity that everyone needs. And you can decide—do you accept the political status quo, or do you try and change the situation?"

I stop walking. He's mad. "Me? Change the status quo? What can I possibly do?"

"I saw you yesterday taking charge with Sarie. You were clever the way you smuggled her through the guard post. I wasn't sure when I first arrived if you would be able to break the rules. You've been so thoroughly brainwashed by Dermond and the other idiots who run the Colony. Don't ask questions, don't rock the boat...Jasmine found it easier to argue with them because—well—she doesn't shy away from conflict."

He turns and looks me straight in the eye. "Ebba, there's a long, hard conflict ahead. You can pretend you don't see it, and do nothing about the injustices around you, or you can join the battle for a fairer society."

He picks up a halter from a fence post and strides up to the horses grazing in the middle of the field. I hover at the fence. There's no way I'm going near those massive animals—they could kill me with one kick.

Is he right though? Am I afraid of conflict? Am I scared

of my own power?

He strolls up to the big chestnut mare as though she's no bigger than Isi and throws the halter over her head. "Come on, girl, time to get you to your stable. Ebba, you take her."

"No, I'm terrified of horses..."

"Come on," he says. "Being scared won't kill you." He leads the horse to where I'm standing and although I shy away, he stands firm and hands me the reins. The horse nuzzles my shoulder and I shriek and jump away.

"Just relax," Micah says. "Don't let her sense your fear. Act like you do this every day. Come on. I'll be behind you with Ponto."

I don't want him to think I'm pathetic, so I take the reins again. What if she runs away, or refuses to walk? But Isi trots by my side and the horse lets me lead her across the field, around the side of the house, past the kitchen gardens to the stables. I get her into her stall finally. Ponto's big hooves are clip clopping on the cement floor as Micah brings him in to his stall at the far end of the row.

I shut the half door and latch it firmly. I did it... I confronted my fear. And it feels so good. He's going to be so proud of me.

Shorty comes walking past the stables on his way to the kitchen.

"Gosh, Miss Ebba," he exclaims. "Did you bring that horse in by yourself? You want to be careful. My aunt nearly lost her foot once—she was at the market and a huge stallion kicked her. You're just a girl. You should leave the horses for Leonid or one of us guys."

"Shorty," I snap, "just put a sock in it."

"Sorry, miss." He looks quite crestfallen and for a second, I feel bad. Then I remember that he shopped me to the High Priest. He's lucky I didn't say anything worse.

Late that night, Isi wakes me with a sharp bark. Someone is tapping on my window.

It's Micah calling my name softly. My heart zings as I jump out of bed and open the shutter.

"Come outside and look at the stars," he whispers.

"Are you sure we're safe? If Shorty finds us, he'll report me. The High Priest said..."

"Relax. Aunty Figgy made them a nightcap. She adds something every night to ensure they sleep well." He chuckles. "They won't wake for hours."

I open the front door and we sit together on the edge of the stoep. I'm happy just to be back next to him, with no one around to spy on us.

"Isn't this fantastic?" he says, leaning back on his elbows. "I never get tired of the sky."

"Me either. I used to think about the sky all the time in the Colony. But I didn't think the stars would be so bright." I'm memorizing every line and angle of his profile, longing to run my fingers down that bump in his nose—he must have broken it when he fell—down the groove below it that ends in his velvety smooth lips. Why isn't he kissing me again? Have I read it all wrong? Maybe there isn't anything between us. Maybe I imagined it all. Or maybe he's just analyzing and weighing up options, as he always does, never diving into anything without thinking it through first.

"Why are you and Jasmine fighting?" he says suddenly. "Is it because you fancy Leonid?"

"Leonid!" I snort. "That's ridiculous. First, he hates my guts, and second, he's my half-brother."

"Your half-brother?" He sits up and turns to look straight at me. "You're Darius Maas' daughter?"

"Apparently. Although I don't look anything like Leonid."

"No," Micah says, "you don't look like Leonid, but you

do look a lot like your father."

"Do you know him?" I say eagerly. "Have you met him?"

He shakes his head. "Nobody knows where he is. He disappeared at the time of the Calamity. He got everyone safely into the caves on Silvermine Island, and then he was gone. I've seen a picture of him though. His hair was brown, and his skin was darker than yours, but you have the same mouth, and the same shit-stirrer chin."

"Why, thank you," I say, strangely pleased that he thinks I look like a trouble maker.

"You've got a pretty incredible lineage, you know," he says. "Your parents are both major Resistance heroes. They were incredibly courageous." He's looking at me in a new way—almost as though he admires me. What if he discovers I don't have a fraction of their courage?

"What's going on with you and Hal?" he says, abruptly. "Is he your boyfriend? Are you in love with him?"

I wish I could hide my blush. "He's just teaching me to read. He's been really kind to me—his whole family have been. But I'm not in love with him. Should I tell him not to come here anymore?"

Micah relaxes, and suddenly his arm is around my shoulder and I'm leaning my head on his chest.

"That will raise suspicion," he says. "You want the High Priest to think you're trying hard to be a good little Citizen. Be careful of the High Priest though. If he's being friendly, it's because he wants something from you. Same with his family."

His hand is stroking my shoulder, running up and down my neck, and we sit quietly for a while, watching the sky.

"Why were you so unfriendly to me when I came home today? I was miserable, and you gave me a lecture about politics."

"I'm sorry," he says. He lifts a curl of my hair and twirls

it around his finger. "I was just trying to protect you. If the High Priest finds out about us..."

There's an "us?" My heart gives a jump.

I imagine a life where we could be together, in the open. No hiding. "Can't we leave? We could make a new life in the Mainland—maybe get a small piece of land..."

He shakes his head. "My place is here, in Table Island City. We will be fine if we're extra careful."

"I'm trying to be extra careful," I say, "but the High Priest is watching everything I do."

"You've just got to be cunning. The High Priest thinks you're an immature young girl with no life experience. Let him believe that. Pretend to be the innocent girl— it's a brilliant disguise."

"So." I think about this for a bit. "If I were a gullible girl, I'd be—I'd be trying to say sorry to him and the Council for what happened today. I'd apologize to Hal for the shock I gave him."

"Exactly. You keep one step ahead all the time. You can do that." He pauses. "So that's it then? You're sure there's no one else around that you fancy?"

I reach up and pull his face down to mine. "Nobody else." And I kiss him.

Keeping one step ahead tests me to my limit. I have to play the naive girl, so that the High Priest and the Council don't suspect anything. I need to get back into Hal's good books by pretending I love him, even though it makes me cringe. And I must make sure Shorty doesn't realize that I am in love with Micah. That's going to be the hardest. After breakfast, I'm in the kitchen garden talking to Shorty about the number of eggs we are managing to sell per week when I see Micah walking towards us pushing a wheelbarrow. A huge grin attaches itself to my face and I can't wipe it off. Shorty looks at me strangely, then at Micah, who is whistling a song and pretending he hasn't seen me.

"What's so funny, miss?" he asks, with that half-grin people get when they're waiting to hear a joke. "Why are you laughing?"

"It's—it's just that Micah has a really strange walk," I say, trying to think of something, anything. "Haven't you noticed? He walks like a hobbit."

"A hobbit?"

"Funny creatures, hairy feet? A really old Kinetika movie?"

"Ah," he says sagely, rubbing his fluffy head. "Can't say I've seen any movies."

Micah gives me a dirty look from across the aubergines and I want to laugh. I turn my back on him. "Hal's got a beautiful walk, hasn't he?" I say to Shorty. "He's so tall and well built."

"If you say so, miss." And he goes back to his list of egg sales.

It takes all the strength I have to ignore Micah at the dinner table. He's sitting right opposite me, and I can feel my pulse speeding up as he passes me the sweet potatoes and his hand brushes mine. But Shorty is such a busy body, he doesn't miss a thing. Why can't he be more like Victor—so unobtrusive we hardly know he's there?

"I want to send a hamper of our best produce to the High Priest," I announce when there's a lull in the conversation. "After dinner, Victor, please pick a selection of the best vegetables. And Aunty Figgy, could you bake a couple of your loaves of bread, please?"

Jasmine glares at me, but I ignore her. I don't have the energy to fight with her tonight.

After supper, Aunty Figgy brings me fresh eggs, butter, and a bottle of honey and packs them into a basket with the vegetables. Then she gets to work on the bread. As the guys are leaving for the night, I call Shorty back.

"Shorty, please help me write a note to the High Priest."

He beams. "My pleasure, Miss Ebba."

I pass him the paper and pencil I found in the library and begin to dictate.

Dear Righteous Poladion,
I wish to apologize for my ungrateful and
inconsiderate behavior to you and your family
and to the Council. Yesterday you helped me
see how wrong I have been, and how selfish I was,
putting all of us in the City in danger.
I am truly sorry, and I hope you will forgive me.
Yours faithfully,
Ebba den Eeden.

When Aunty Figgy goes out to bring in the clean washing, I drop my voice. "Could you help me with another one? This one's a bit embarrassing." I look around to make sure that no one else can hear me. "Please, Shorty, tell me what I should say."

He leans forward eagerly. "Yes, Miss Ebba. I'll help any way I can."

"It's just—it's just that yesterday morning, I was skinny dipping in the pond, and Hal saw me." I put a sob in my voice. "Now Hal thinks I'm immoral, and I don't know how to put it right."

His eyes gleam. He clasps the pen in his podgy fingers. "Ah, let me think. Try this:

Dearest Hal,
I love you. Only you. I love you more than
all the gold in the world. Please come back.
I want to be with you, forever.
Your darling, Ebba.

I swallow. It's a bit much. How far should I go, playing the innocent girl? Shorty is peering at me, his blue eyes are big and round. "Don't you like that? I think it's lovely."

"It's just—it's just—won't he think I'm a bit forward? What if he doesn't love me back?"

"Hmmm. I'm sure he loves you, Miss Ebba." He pats my hand. "OK, how's this."

Dearest Hal...

"Is dearest OK?"

I nod.

"Dearest Hal,
I'm so sorry about yesterday. You mean so much
to me, and I miss you. I'll try to behave in a way
that makes you proud of me. Please forgive me."

"That's better."

"How would you like to end it? Yours lovingly? Yours faithfully? What about, 'Yours forever?'"

"Yours forever, Ebba," I say. If I'm going to lie, I may as well be bold about it.

He gives a satisfied grin and begins to write. He finishes the letter and passes it to me. I painstakingly write out my name in sprawling letters, and draw a heart after them.

Shorty is beaming. "That's lovely, Miss Ebba. It's a lovely gesture. I'm sure he'll forgive you."

I seal the letters in envelopes, Shorty addresses them, and I put them in the basket, ready for the morning.

That night, I'm about to drop off to sleep when there's a tap on the door. I open the door, eager, hoping it's Micah. But it's only Aunty Figgy, carrying an oil lamp. I thought she'd gone to bed hours ago. "Come to the kitchen," she says softly.

I follow her through the dark house, and find Jasmine,

Micah, and Leonid sitting at the kitchen table. Jasmine is winding a lock of her hair around her finger. I know that gesture—it's what she does when she's very upset. She won't look at me.

I know what this is about. They want to confront me about the hamper. I'm in trouble, again. But when Micah starts speaking, my heart nearly stops dead.

"We've received information," Micah says. "The High Priest has planned another cull for Friday."

I cry out, "Oh no! Letti and Fez! He'll go straight for them."

Jaz looks at me, strangely. I want to hit her. Does she think I don't care? I know it, he'll go straight for them. For the two people left underground that I love.

"The High Priest is doing this to teach me a lesson," I say. "Should I just give him the amulet? Then he'll let Fez and Letti be elevated too."

"Never," Aunty Figgy spits. "It's holy. If he gets his hands on it we'll never, ever defeat him."

Jasmine exchanges glances with Leonid. I know she's thinking what a bitch I am to count a piece of jewelry over my closest friends, and how crazy Aunty Figgy is. How can we make her see that it's more than that?

"Giving him the amulet is a short term solution," Micah says. "You might get your friends released, but what about the other people inside the bunker? He is going to cull them as soon as they outlive their usefulness. What will you offer him next time? We need a bigger solution."

"Like what?" Leonid asks.

"We infiltrate the Colony and rescue them," Micah says. "We start with Fez and Letti, as the first stage."

Jasmine looks up quickly. "Do you think it's possible?"

"There's a maintenance worker—Chad. He was part of Darius Maas's cell during the Resistance, and after the

Calamity, he got a job working for the City doing repairs. He noticed me in the Colony when I was a kid and he was brought down to fix the solar panels. He said that I asked questions and didn't accept the things they told us."

"I remember," Jasmine says. "Even then you were politically aware."

"He was sure they were going to try and kill me. When the guards came for me, he was ready. They whipped me, then dragged me along one of the ventilation shafts and threw me out. He found me half-dead on the mountainside and carried me to a cave. He'd set it up with food and water and blankets. He mended my injuries, and I stayed there for three months until my wounds had healed. Then he came for me one night and we trekked to the Harbor. He had a boat ready to take me to Silvermine Island."

I imagine Micah lying injured and alone in a cave for months on end. I could never survive that length of time on my own, especially if I was in pain. My admiration for him grows even more.

"Could we get in through the same ventilation shaft?" Jasmine says.

"Chad will get us in," Micah says. "We've been working on an emergency plan. He'll disguise us as maintenance workers. We find Fez and Letti, we get to the storage chamber, hide in the sacks and one of Chad's guys will load us onto the wagon that goes to the Harbor. From there we move them across to Silvermine, to stay with one of the families there."

Jasmine starts to look more hopeful. "You mean there are people out there who care about the kids in the Colony?"

"Of course. The Resistance didn't die with the Calamity. It's stronger than ever. Leonid is one of our most valued members."

Leonid? Grumpy, chip on his shoulder Leonid? He

rubs his hand through his curly hair, looking embarrassed at the praise.

"Can't you bring them here?" I ask. Before the words are finished, I know it's a stupid idea.

"First place they'll look," Leonid says. "Tear the place apart. When they find them, they'll kill them, and us. Well, you'll be safe, you're a Citizen."

"That didn't stop them shooting Ebba's mother," Aunty Figgy says. "Ebba's in even more danger because of her sacred mission."

Jasmine opens her mouth to say something but Micah taps the table. "Let's keep focused. So we're agreed then? We'll infiltrate the Colony?"

"Agreed." Jasmine and Leonid nod. I notice they're holding hands under the table.

"They'll never believe I'm a maintenance worker," I say. "I'll stand out a mile because of my hair."

"You can't come," Jasmine says. "You're one of them."

Her words sting. Jasmine and I have always been a team, on the same side in every dispute. She had my back, I had hers. Until now. And I can't do anything to change it. "I'd never do anything to hurt Letti or Fez, you know that, Jasmine."

"There's no place for that sort of nastiness, Jasmine," Aunty Figgy says firmly. "We have to work together. Of course you can trust Ebba."

"But she's sending baskets of food to the High Priest. I mean, how ironic is that. Sending food to the man we spent our life growing food for. "

"It's a decoy." Micah reaches across the table and takes my hand. "She sent the hamper so the High Priest believes she's a compliant little Citizen who is sorry for being so foolish. Can't you see that? If Ebba suddenly went against the Council in everything, we'd lose this place as our fortress. She has to pretend....And if you can't see that...?"

He looks at both Jasmine and Leonid, waiting. Waiting for what? Their response? Their acquiescence? I'm not sure either one of them can ever give me the benefit of the doubt. No matter what.

But Jasmine narrows her eyes as she takes in his words, his hand holding mine. Is her expression softening?

"You can't come though, Ebba," Micah says. "You'll stand out too much. Jasmine and I will go."

"I'm coming, too," Leonid says.

"No. They'll notice if three of us are gone from the farm. You stay here and act like everything's normal. Aunty Figgy, can you concoct some mixture that will put Shorty and Victor out of action for a few days?"

"Of course. It would be a pleasure."

Micah gets up. "So that's arranged then. Jasmine, luckily you're really small. You can pass as a boy if we cut your hair short. The maintenance depot is near the Shrine. We can travel through with Leonid tomorrow morning when he delivers the hamper. And with any luck, we'll be back on Saturday afternoon. Sunday morning at the latest."

Chapter Thirteen

We're up before dawn. The kitchen is filled with the fragrance of freshly baked bread. The hamper for the High Priest sits on the table, overflowing with fresh vegetables. I've picked fresh herbs and a bunch of yellow and orange nasturtiums and Aunty Figgy has added a pot of goat's cheese. Then she sits Jasmine down at the kitchen table and cuts her hair close to her head. She binds up her breasts with a bandage so she looks flat-chested. She finds her a servant's tunic and pants like Leonid's, and by the time she's finished, Jasmine looks like a twelve-year-old boy.

I sweep up the hair scattered on the floor. It feels like every chance of connecting with the old Jasmine has fallen away with her hair. She's a stranger, looking for reasons to distrust me. And I don't know how to win her back. If only she were more like Micah, weighing up facts and thinking them through before she jumped to conclusions. It's why I feel so safe with him—he's measured, and doesn't act on first impressions.

"Come and help me pick mushrooms," Aunty Figgy says to her. "Let's leave Micah and Ebba alone for a while. Ebba, make sure you don't eat any of the mushrooms at breakfast. I'm going to cook some poisonous ones."

"We don't want to kill them," I say, handing her a basket. "That will really get me in trouble."

Aunty Figgy laughs. "I'm tempted but don't worry. I'll just choose the ones that will put them out of action for a few days. We don't want them asking where Jasmine and Micah are."

Then Micah and I are alone in the kitchen.

"I wish you didn't have to go," I say softly. "It's so dangerous."

"It will be okay, babe," he says gently. "I've been training for this for the last two years." He winds his arms around me. "I'll see you soon," he murmurs.

My heart wants to tell him I love him. But I don't want to make the moment awkward, so I swallow my words. "I'm really scared the guards will catch you. You will be careful, won't you?"

"Come on," he says firmly, letting me go. "No point worrying about something that might not even happen. We're going to be fine. You've got a job to do too. Put a smile on your face and make like everything's fine. You've got to stop Shorty getting suspicious."

Leonid brings the buggy around then and it's time to go. Micah takes my face between his hands, and kisses my lips. "You're more powerful than you think. Don't believe anyone who says otherwise." He lifts the hamper inside and jumps in after it. Jasmine gives me a half wave and a quick, "Bye." Then she's up in front next to Leonid and they're off, hooves clip clopping down the driveway in a sound I've grown to dread because it so often brings trouble.

I swallow back my tears and wave them goodbye. "See you lunchtime tomorrow," I call trying to sound cheerful.

Aunty Figgy squeezes my shoulder. "Come inside. Let me make you some toast."

I don't feel like eating, but I don't want to be alone. I follow her into the kitchen and start laying the table for breakfast. Micah's mug still stands on the table. What if this is the last time he drinks from it? What if he never comes back?

"Here, light a candle and ask Theia to protect them," Aunty Figgy says, handing me a lighted twig from the wood stove.

I watch the wick catching alight, and the sweet smell of honey rises up from the beeswax candles. The flame burns straight and strong. "Keep them safe," I pray. "Bring them home unharmed, and find a place for my sabenzis to live in peace."

I can't bear to think about Fez and Letti moving in with strangers on Silvermine Island, and trying to make a life in this harsh world. I have so much, but I won't be able to share any of it with them.

Aunty Figgy is chortling as she chops the mushrooms. "A nice plate of these with sausages and eggs," she says. "They'll be vomiting for thirty-six hours. Shorty's so greedy, he'll be sick for forty-eight hours at least."

I sit at the table and watch the candle flickering. "Tell me more about the Goddess," I say. "How is my necklace linked to her?"

"Well, when the Goddess Theia was born," Aunty Figgy tips the mushrooms into a frying pan, "her father, the King of Celestia, gave her dominion over all living and growing things. Then he invited all the other deities to a party to welcome her. The four most important gods and goddesses brought her amulets, each imbued with special powers, to make up a necklace.

"She grew up to be beautiful, with deep red curls, and a gentle spirit. She watched over all the plants and creatures of Celestia, keeping them in balance so all could thrive. One day, when she was wandering in the mangroves, she met a tall, handsome man with a birthmark that covered the left side of his face. His name was Prospiroh and they fell in love.

"Theia became pregnant. Hot and uncomfortable, she wanted something to play with. She decided to create a world where all living things could live together peacefully. She called it Earth, and she spun a cocoon of spells around it so that none of the other gods could interfere with it. She watched over it, saw it evolving and developing, and made sure that everything stayed in balance.

"Her baby daughter was born and she and Prospiroh named her Bellzeta. She was as golden haired, passionate, and quick-tempered as her father.

"Now Theia's days were taken up with watching Earth, and caring for her baby. Prospiroh grew jealous. He decided to steal the baby and take her to his home in another world, where her mother would never find her.

"But Theia learned of his plan just in time. She had to find somewhere safe to hide the baby, so she bundled up some possessions, and using the powers of the amulet necklace, escaped to the one place she thought Prospiroh couldn't enter, Earth. She chose a village in a beautiful wooded area called the Forêt de Soignes."

Aunty Figgy breaks off to add, "It's all underwater now, of course. Anyway, Theia built herself a human life as a wise woman, a healer who knew which plants could cure which illnesses, and which herbs could heal a broken heart. She had a little cottage, and she loved her simple life among the people she had created. Her daughter Bellzeta was not so happy. Like her father, she always wanted more—more things, more love, more wealth, more attention. She was jealous of the attention her mother paid other people. She wanted her all for herself.

"Now, after a few years, Theia fell in love with a wood-cutter, a kind man who loved her deeply and took Bellzeta as his own child. They had a baby, a happy little girl with a sunny personality they called Laleuca. She loved to hear her mother's tales of the land of the gods, and would often beg to wear the amulet necklace, which fascinated her."

"I'm getting muddled with all these names," I say.

"Just remember the two children—Bellzeta, who was Prospiroh's child, and Laleuca, who was the daughter of the woodcutter."

"So Laleuca was half-god, half-human? But Bellzeta was full god?"

"Exactly."

The mushrooms are sizzling away, and Aunty Figgy pauses the story while she adds some sausages to the pan and a handful of parsley. "This will disguise the bitterness," she mutters. "Anyway, where was I? When Prospiroh discovered where Theia and Bellzeta were hiding, he was determined to find a way to break through the cocoon she had woven to protect the Earth. Finally he found a way in—through his daughter, Bellzeta. He could make contact with her mind and her heart, although he couldn't enter the Earth. He filled her heart with anger against the woodcutter and jealousy of her little sister.

"By the time Laleuca was seven, Bellzeta was a teenager and a beauty. She was passionate and rebellious and her mother had no control over her. Bellzeta became pregnant by the mayor of the village, a married man. Theia was angry when she found out, and they had a terrible fight. Bellzeta's anger against her family brewed.

"One day when Theia was busy in the village, Laleuca was playing with her mother's amulet necklace when Bellzeta called her. 'Come and pick herbs with me,' she said. Laleuca didn't want to be in trouble for playing with the necklace, so she hid it out of sight under her high collared dress. Bellzeta took her little sister deep into the woods and when they reached a deep ravine, she tricked the child into going right to the edge of the cliff. Then she pushed her over.

"Back home, she told her mother that a band of wild animals had attacked them and killed Laleuca.

"Her parents were grief-stricken. The woodcutter

suspected that Bellzeta had harmed her. Theia was torn. She did not want to believe that her eldest daughter could be so wicked so she believed her story.

"Theia sat in her cottage and wept. Not only was her daughter lost, but the precious necklace was gone too. Her depression grew until she was half mad.

"The woodcutter searched for his daughter day and night. He was sickened by the sight of Bellzeta and her growing belly. Finally the baby was born, but Bellzeta was not interested in it. She persuaded her mother to return to the land of the gods. 'There's nothing left for us here,' she said. 'We should go home.' So Theia asked her father, the King of the Gods of Celestia, to take her home. Without the necklace and its powers, Theia could never enter Earth again.

"When the woodcutter came home that day, Theia and Bellzeta were gone. He took the baby to the mayor's house and handed the baby to a servant. 'Your master's bastard,' he said."

"I don't understand," I say as she pushes the pan to the back burner and cracks eggs into a skillet. "You told me I'm a descendant of the Goddess. You mean Bellzeta's my ancestor?" I'm hoping it's not true.

"Never!" she exclaims. "Not a drop of Prospiroh's blood runs in your veins. No, the little girl Laleuca was discovered half dead in the ravine by an old woman searching for herbs. She took her to her cottage, and when Laleuca told her that Bellzeta had pushed her off the cliff, she decided to keep her hidden for the long months it took for her broken bones to heal. She was afraid that Bellzeta would try again to harm the child. One day she heard that Theia and Bellzeta had gone forever. Laleuca was well again, so she brought the little girl home to her father. He was overjoyed."

"Ah, that's good," I say. "She was back in her own home.

What happened next? Where do I come in?"

When Laleuca grew up, she married a farmer called Frederik den Eeden. She always wore the amulet necklace, and it stayed in the den Eeden family, but one by one, over the centuries, four of the amulets were lost. All except the one you're wearing now."

"Wait—so the den Eeden family are descended from the gods?"

Aunty Figgy nods. "That's right."

"And my necklace was created by the gods themselves?"

"That's right. That's why the High Priest wants it so much."

My mouth drops open, and I have a million questions to ask, but she brushes them aside.

"Shorty and Victor will be coming in any minute. Let me finish my story. Each time an amulet was lost, Prospiroh gained more power over Earth. Finally, when only one amulet remained, the Goddess' power was weakened enough for Prospiroh's followers to cause the Calamity that almost destroyed the world."

"Why did the High Priest elevate me? He could just have culled me and taken the necklace for himself."

"He doesn't want one amulet. He wants all four of them, united on the chain, and only you can locate them."

"But how am I supposed to find them if they've been lost for centuries?"

"Your ancestors will help you." She grips my hand. "You must be careful. The High Priest thinks they'll make him immortal. He'll do anything to get the amulets, but he's got to do it without spilling your blood, or their dark powers are released."

"Like what?" The thought of dark powers makes me shudder.

She pinches her lips together. "I don't know. And I hope

we never find out." She turns away, clashes the lid onto the skillet, and begins to slice the bread. "The thing is," she says, after a pause, "the High Priest can't find the amulets on his own. Only the girl with the birthmark has the power to enter the world of her ancestors and retrieve the amulets. That's you, Ebba. And when you have them all, united on their golden chain, the Gateway to the Goddess will open, and the holy balance will be restored."

This is like something out of a Kinetika. Goddess blood, sacred tasks, dark powers and now entering the world of the ancestors?

"What happens if I refuse the task?"

"There will be another Calamity. The world will collapse in on itself and implode into a ball of dust."

"No pressure then," I say ruefully. "And let me guess— the High Priest is a descendant of Bellzeta's baby? The one the woodcutter left at the mayor's house?"

"Exactly!"

Before I can ask another question, we hear footsteps in the yard, and Shorty and Victor come in for breakfast.

"Poor Jasmine isn't feeling well," Aunty Figgy says as she places a plate of mushrooms and sausages in front of them. "Leonid and Micah have gone to deliver the gift hamper to the High Priest."

Shorty's already got his mouth full. "Shame," he mumbles, spewing bits of sausage. "Hope she gets better. You not eating, Miss Ebba?"

"I don't feel well either." I take some toast and butter and chew slowly but I can barely eat it. I'm so worried about Micah and Jasmine hiding in the mountain, trying to outwit my mortal enemy. My immortal enemy. Will they come home alive?

Chapter Fourteen

It's been over a day since they left, and I'm so anxious, I can't sit still. I call Isi and together we walk right to the end of the new lands, but I hardly notice the newly furrowed rows or the seedlings that are coming up in neat rows where just two months ago there was empty fields. I can't stop thinking about Micah. Right now, if everything's gone according to plan, they are hiding in the grain sacks on a wagon, jolting along the road to the warehouse at the Harbor. Members of the Resistance are getting ready to break into the warehouse and get them onto boats. As long as Fez doesn't cough. If he coughs, everything will be lost.

When I return to the house, Hal's tying the reins of his horse to the meadow fence. I stop behind a tree and try and compose myself. He mustn't see me looking stressed. He can't see how much I hate him and his family. I have to play the part of the repentant foolish young girl, who can't behave properly unless I have a man to tell me what to do.

He watches me as I come down the driveway, his shoulders back, his chin in the air. I let my eyes fall to the ground. I don't want him to see the disdain I feel for him. He acts like he's Prospiroh himself, or Prospiroh's gift to humankind. I don't know what I ever saw in him—he's arrogant and...the word I've learned from Jasmine and Leonid...entitled. He's top of the heap and he's making sure he stays there by pushing everyone else down.

"I got your note and your gift," he says when I join him on the stoep.

I don't look up. "I hope you liked them," I say meekly. "I just wanted to tell you how sorry I am."

"Come inside," he says, starting up the stairs like it's his house. He leads me into the sitting room and points to the sofa. He perches on the arm of the chair opposite. I hope he'll just shout at me and go home. But he says nothing. His silence makes me nervous, but I've got to hold it together. I straighten my back and look up at him. "My workers are all sick," I say. "They've been vomiting for days."

"I thought I saw what's-his-name in the orchard."

Is he testing me? He's got to be. It's a trick so he can get me to incriminate myself.

"Shorty? Victor?"

He looks blank.

"You mean Micah? Can't be. He's got it the worst."

"Not Micah. The cheeky one—Leonid."

"Oh, he's over it. He got it first. Was vomiting for days."

"I'm going to come straight out and say this," he says, sitting forward. "I don't like that boy."

"Boy?"

"The new one. Micah. He doesn't know his place. You know what those people are like—they're animals. They're not like us. They can't control their urges. You can't risk swimming—er—naked when they're on the premises. One of them will attack you. And you know, they always kill the woman afterwards so they don't get reported to the Shrine command."

I force myself to stay calm. "I've got Isi to protect me," I say. "She won't let anyone come near me, I promise. The thing is, Micah's a good worker. You know how hard they are to find." He didn't see Micah in the pool. Thank the Goddess.

It seems to appease him. He crosses over and sits next to me on the sofa. His eyes are sad. "Do you care for me at all?" he asks, taking my hand. "You don't want to come and live in the compound, and it makes me doubt you. I thought when I saw you there that perhaps you were waiting for someone else to join you in the pool."

"Waiting for someone!" I do my best to look aghast. "What do you think of me, Hal? That I spend my days swimming naked with my workers in the river? I'm shocked." I take his hand. "You have to believe me when I say I care about you." I stroke his fingers. "But sometimes I wonder what you see in me. You could have your pick of any of the girls in the City. Pamza's crazy about you. She's so pretty. And I'm just a red-haired, ugly, awkward girl from the Colony."

"You're too hard on yourself," he says. "You look so much better since you got your hair cut and dyed."

I'm not sure how to take that. But I must convince him that I love him. "Sometimes this new life is so overwhelming. I know I behaved badly, and I disappointed your father and the Council, and I'm so sorry. Do you think he will forgive me?"

"I'm sure of it," he says. His voice is warmer. "He's a very forgiving man. He knows what young girls are like. He's got daughters of his own."

I lean my head on his shoulder. "It's hard, trying to get it right. I wasn't raised for this life, you know."

"I know, sweetheart. Mistakes are to be expected. What matters is that you're willing to learn. And I'll teach you everything I know, I promise. All I ask is that you keep away from the servants. You probably feel more comfortable with them, because of your background, but just remember, they're not our sort of people."

"Yes, Haldus," I say meekly.

Suddenly I hear horse's hooves on the driveway and my heart nearly stops. Is it the Shrine guard? Oh Goddess. Have they been caught?

"You're so jumpy," Hal says, peering out of the window. "It's only Mr. Frye."

What does he want? Has he heard something? Why is he moving so briskly?

"Good morning, Ebba," Mr. Frye calls, walking straight in without knocking. "I've come to see how you're getting along. I haven't been keeping a close enough eye on you. Let's start in the kitchen. Can you call all the staff together, please?"

I follow him through the hall, Hal on my heels. I've got to create a distraction. If he finds they're missing, it will be the end. He's on the Shrine Council—he'll be obliged to report me to the High Priest.

"I...I sent a hamper of produce to the High Priest to say sorry," I say trying to distract him. "Did he get it? Did he like it?"

"Yes, yes. Now come along. It's time your staff got pulled into shape. You're too soft, my girl. Too soft." And he sweeps through the dining room, down the passage and into the kitchen. "Call everybody together, Aunty Figgy," he snaps. "Full staff meeting."

She puts down the pile of washing she was sorting and hurries outside. I watch her cross the yard, wondering what he will do when she comes back with nobody but Shorty.

The only person who appears is Victor. He staggers up to the back door, white as the sheet Aunty Figgy was folding.

"Good morning, sir," he says. He sways and grabs the back of the chair. "Don't come any closer," he mutters. "Vomiting and diarrhea. Haven't felt so ill in a long time."

Mr. Frye pulls out his handkerchief and covers his mouth. "Hal, we'd better get you out of here," he says, stepping away from Victor. "Your father will not appreciate you bringing home an illness like this."

"But Mr. Frye," I say, pulling out a chair, "can't you stay a while and help me with my planting schedule? I'm struggling so much with the routine, and Leonid says we need to repair the barn, and I need to sort these things out now."

"Another time, Ebba," he says through the handkerchief. "Come along Hal, and don't touch the doorknobs."

I'm weak-kneed with relief as they ride away. The last thing I need right now is to be arrested, or worse, have Hal insisting I move into his father's house.

Chapter Fifteen

Micah and Jasmine don't come back.

We wait all that day, and through the endless hours of the next. By the evening, I'm frantic.

Leonid is in a filthy mood, lashing out, even scolding Isi so she runs off and hides under my bed. I know he thinks I should just have given the High Priest the amulet. Then the twins would be safely at Greenhaven, and Jasmine would be home in his arms. He's got it easy, I think bitterly as we eat our evening meal in silence. There's nothing standing in the way of their love. They can be together forever—they can even get married if they want to. But Micah and I will always have to hide our love. It will always be illegal and as long as we love each other, he's in danger.

I'm just grateful that Shorty and Victor are still feeling too ill to eat with us. The last thing I need is perfect Victor nibbling away at his food, while Shorty talks nonstop about nothing with his mouth full.

"It's Shrine Day tomorrow," Aunty Figgy says as we finish eating and wash our plates at the sink. "You'll have to go."

"Shrine! I'm whining, I know, but I can't."

"You have to. You have to go there and act like you're a faithful Citizen filled with respect for the High Priest and his Council."

I drop the wash cloth and turn to face her. "How on Earth can I carry that off? One look at me and they'll _know_ I hate them."

"Ebba," she says, gripping my shoulders and looking me in the eye, "you can't let them see you're upset. You have to pretend everything is going perfectly. Jasmine, Micah, the twins—their lives may depend on it. And your life too."

I know she's right, but...

"And make sure everyone sees that you're in love with Hal," Leonid says as he goes out the door.

"But I'm not," I wail. "How can I pretend to love him when Micah is in a dungeon somewhere or dead even." I burst into tears.

Aunty Figgy holds me for a while, rocking me. Then she gently pushes me away from her chest, and wipes my eyes with her apron. "You have to be strong. You are the chosen one, Ebba, the one written about in the Book of the Goddess. You wouldn't have been chosen if you weren't equal to the task. Now I'm going to make you some chamomile tea and you're going to sleep soundly until the morning, and then you're going to go to Shrine and find your friends. Micah and Jasmine are perfectly smart enough to find a way to escape, and so are the twins, from what you've told me. The goddess will make sure you are in the right place at the right time, so trust her."

Isi seems to know how upset I am. When I go to bed, she jumps up next to me and rests her head on my chest. Her amber eyes look at me adoringly, and her tail thumps on the bed as I stroke her soft ears.

What would I do without her?

Just before ten the next morning, Leonid turns the buggy up the steep hill to the Shrine. I'm expecting him to still be irritable and snappy, but he's more resigned this morning, and kinder. "See what you can find out," he says. "Best scenario is they reached the Harbor. The twins are probably safe on Silvermine Island. Maybe Jasmine and

Micah are struggling to get back into the City."

I look up at the Shrine shining in the sun, the crowds of Citizens pouring in through the tall metal doors. My courage fails. "Let's just go home rather."

"You have to go in, Ebba." He stops the buggy near the steps. "Come on, think of Jasmine and Micah. You can do it. You're your father's daughter."

The mention of Micah nearly makes me start crying. I don't. Instead, I pull down my robe and make sure my turban is tight. Aunty Figgy has hidden the amulet inside my bun, secured with six hair pins, and she's wound a turban around my hair to make it doubly safe. She's found another necklace in my great aunt's jewelry box. This one is an old silver coin with an eagle on the front. From a distance it could pass as the amulet, especially if I keep it under my robe. "Good luck," he says softly as he closes the buggy door behind me.

I plaster a smile on my face and walk as regally as I can to the entrance of the Shrine.

Hal is waiting for me at the door, dressed in a golden robe. He beams from ear to ear.

"You look so handsome," I tell him, kissing his cheek. The feel of his skin makes my flesh crawl.

He takes my hands in his. "And you are beautiful, my darling. I'm so happy." Why is he so happy?

The bells are ringing, and we have to hurry to our seats. Pamza and Cassie are sitting next to us, dressed in vibrant robes of reds and purples with garlands of silk flowers around their necks. "What's the occasion?" I whisper.

"Shhhhhhh," Cassie hisses. She winks at Pamza.

The band starts to play and the High Priest is brought in on his golden throne. On the podium, the worship leaders beam over the congregation. Everyone is singing and dancing and clapping hands and I join in, pretending to be swept up in the unusually festive mood. The huge brass incense burners puff out clouds of fragrant smoke, and the drums beat faster. It's obvious, now that I can stand back and observe what's happening, that the worship leaders are using the drums to work the congregation up into an emotional frenzy. The incense, the music—they're devices to hypnotize the Citizens, to keep them compliant.

Finally the High Priest is at his place in the center of the stage. He rises, walks forward with arms outstretched, and booms, "My dearest children in Prospiroh, welcome, welcome to this joyous occasion." Then he turns to the front row where I'm standing next to Hal. "I'm going to ask two fine young people to come onto the stage. Haldus and Ebba, please come and join me."

Me? And Hal? Why?

Everyone is beaming, except Pamza, who looks like she might cry, and Lucas, who is his usual worried, leg-jiggling self, seated behind the High Priest on the podium.

"Go on," Cassie whispers, giving me a shove.

Hal holds my hand tight. "Come on, my love," he murmurs, and we walk up the stairs and onto the stage. The High Priest greets us with kisses on each cheek and then takes our hands. We stand in a row, the three of us, and I look out over the congregation of happy Citizens, and wonder what is going on. All this for a gift basket? They must really believe I'm repentant.

"There is no occasion as joyous as the joining of two healthy young people," the High Priest booms. "I'm happy to announce the marriage of Miss Ebba den Eeden of the farm Greenhaven with my son, Haldus Poladion."

What? Is he serious? Black spots shoot across my eyes. My knees give way, but Lucas jumps forward and catches me from behind.

"Be brave," he whispers in my ear.

Lucas. He can't have said that. I'm hallucinating from the incense.

Hal turns to me with a delighted grin. "Isn't this a wonderful surprise? Are you OK? You're so pale?"

"i—i'm shocked..." Sweat breaks out on my forehead. I remember I have to be the good obedient girl. "I'm delighted, but—it's so unexpected." I force myself to smile, as wide as I can, and I move into his arms, although every part of me is screaming "run, run."

We kiss. The congregation breaks into applause.

"Come, my dear." Hal's mother, Evelyn has come onto the stage. "Time to get you ready."

"I don't understand. What am I getting ready for?"

"The wedding, of course. Your clothes are waiting in the Sanctuary. Pamza and Cassie are your bridesmaids."

"We're getting married NOW?"

"Of course! Come along, we have lots to do. Pietro is ready to do your makeup and hair, and wait till you see your robe. It's wonderful."

Hal is so excited that he's almost hopping from foot to foot. "Hurry, Ebba, I can't WAIT!"

I look around the crowded Shrine for an exit. What am I going to do? There's not a single person I can turn to. Pietro's going to take my hair down and find the amulet. He'll take it to the High Priest and then it will be gone. When we're married, I'll have to do exactly what Hal says. I'll have to live here at the compound. He may never let me go home again. The room is getting hotter and hotter. The drums won't stop thudding—they sound like they're right inside my head. I've got to get away. Should I run? But Micah and Jasmine—I can't endanger them...

My mind will be clearer if I'm away from the incense and drums, so I let Evelyn take my arm and lead me through the interleading door into the sanctuary where the worship leaders get dressed.

Pietro is waiting in front of a mirror, with his scissors and makeup bag at hand. "Congratulations," he beams.

"What a beautiful couple you're going to make. Hal tells me you're the love of his life, Ebba. I'm so happy for you, so happy."

Evelyn comes forward with a white silk robe, so soft it's like a cloud. Golden embroidery of wheat sheaves decorates the hem and neckline. "Isn't this lovely?" she says, holding it across her open arms. "I embroidered it myself, just for the day when my beloved boy would be married. It's my gift to you."

"It's—it's beautiful." I'm not lying, even if I wish I wasn't saying the words.

"Here, darling, put it on."

Pietro lifts my old robe over my head and Evelyn slips the silk garment in its place. It's soft as butter, falling around me in soft folds. I swallow, trying to control my rising anger. How much longer must I play the compliant girl? Will I have to marry Hal, just to protect everybody?

"Hal hasn't even asked me to marry him," I say, licking my dry lips. "I thought he would propose, and we'd be engaged for a while."

"Oh silly girl," Evelyn smiles, taking a pair of shoes from a box. "In the City, his Holiness arranges weddings. Here, put these on."

I'm tempted to kick Pietro in the teeth as he bends down and puts the silver sandals on my feet.

"You won't believe what we've done to the wedding chamber," he says, looking up at me with a smirk. "Silk flowers everywhere—a person would almost believe they are real they're so gorgeous. Just...so...gorgeous. And satin sheets on the bed. I bet you can't wait, huh?"

"You're so blessed," Evelyn says. "Every girl in the City wanted to marry Hal. Now sit down, darling, and let Pietro do something about your hair."

He leads me into a chair and flicks the cape around my shoulders. "So let's see what this turban is hiding." He starts to unwrap it.

"Leave my hair," I snap.

"Don't be silly," he says, smacking my shoulder. "You have to look wonderful for your new husband. Stop making a fuss. There isn't time."

"Calm down, dear," Hal's mother says. "Just do everything we say and it will all be perfect."

Yes, do everything you say—for now and for evermore, I think. I'll never be my own person, ever again.

I look for an exit—maybe I can run for it, reach the buggy, and tell Leonid to drive like the wind—but General de Groot will send his guards after me. I don't stand a chance.

Pietro pulls off my turban. "Dear, dear," he says. "Just look at your hair. You haven't been using the olive oil conditioner, have you? I heard you'd caught lice..." He's checking my hair line and behind my ears. "I don't see any sign of them. Nope, all clear. Now let's take down this ugly bun..." He takes out the first pin and Hal's mother reaches over and undoes the clasp of the eagle necklace Aunty Figgy tied around my neck.

"I've brought you some of my own jewels," she says. "My gift to you, on your wedding day. First let me take away this old necklace. It's very girly, but you're a woman now, a married woman." And she beams at me.

She thinks I can't see her, but she's reflected in the mirror. I see her cross the room, open the door, and pass the necklace to one of the soldiers in the Shrine. Any moment now the High Priest will discover that it's a decoy. He'll come through and demand the real amulet.

Pietro pulls out the second hair pin. I've got to act now.

I leap out of the chair and tear off the plastic cape. "I'm not marrying Hal. I'm not getting married!" I shout. "I'm too young. You can't make me."

Evelyn stares at me. "Stop making a fuss," she snaps.

"You should be lucky that Hal has agreed to marry you. It's not like you have suitors lining up at your gate."

"I don't want to get married to anyone. You can't force me without my consent." My voice has risen to a scream.

"You're just a stupid little girl," Evelyn snarls, slapping the side of my head. "Do as you're told."

That does it. I grab the scissors from the table and jump up facing them. "I'm not getting married. I'm too young." I hold the scissors up like a weapon.

"Sit down," Evelyn shouts. "You ugly brat. Sit down and shut up."

Pietro grabs me by the shoulders. I'm pushing him away when Evelyn tries to pull my hair. I lash out, and the scissors slice across her arm. I drop them, horrified. "I'm sorry," I gasp. "I didn't mean to stab you."

Evelyn screeches as blood gushes onto the floor. She runs to the door, screaming for the guards. Pietro takes one look at the blood and passes out on the floor. I'm about to run when the door opens and three guards rush in, followed by the High Priest, Hal, and the worship leaders.

"She stabbed me," Evelyn bellows. "She attacked me with the scissors."

It seems everyone is shouting and pushing except the High Priest. He points one finger in my face and snarls, "Get her out of here."

They drag me out of the sanctuary, and down a flight of stairs.

I look back. Hal is watching from the doorway. He looks heartbroken and for a second I'm heartsore for him. It wasn't his fault. He might not be the person I want—Micah—and he might seem entitled—all right, he is entitled—but he has always been kind to me. His father forced both of us into this wedding, and neither of us were ready for it.

Chapter Sixteen

They take me down endless twisting passages and throw me in a cell. It's carved out of the same grey rock of the Colony, with thick metal bars across the front. The door clangs shut and I'm alone. There's a sleeping platform, a bucket toilet, and nothing else. Just hard rock.

I huddle on the platform, and pull my legs up to my chest. I stabbed the High Priest's third wife. I shamed his son in front of everyone. I thwarted his wishes. What's going to happen to me now?

I feel like a snail, waiting to be crushed under the High Priest's shoes. I wonder how long it will be until the execution. Will they give me a trial first? Or will he send Major Zungu to shoot me? Or perhaps it will be a public execution, with all the Citizens watching and cheering? They might even burn me at the stake, like a witch.

It must be late afternoon when a guard brings me a meal.

"What's going to happen to me?"

The guard pushes his face close to mine. I flinch from his sour breath. "I hope you're going to be executed, you filthy scum. They should never have let you out of the Colony. You're like cockroaches, the lot of you. You should hear the language from that other lot. That boy's got a mouth on him—wouldn't believe the filth coming out of it. Disgusting at his age."

"What boy?"

"The one who thought he could just walk in here and let the cockroaches out. They caught four of them in the storage chamber, hiding in sacks, trying to escape on the wagon. They're being executed tomorrow morning. Good riddance. The world doesn't need ungrateful little shits like you lot."

I can't let him see the relief that pours through me. The foul-mouthed boy can only be Jasmine. They were caught but they're still alive—and while they're alive, there's still hope.

The cell door clangs, and he's gone. I search the cell for a way out, anything, but there's nothing. The gate is triple locked. The bars are so thick there's no way I can bend them. Maybe we're not going to escape. Maybe I must just resign myself to being executed in the morning, alongside Micah, Jasmine, Letti and Fez. At least I'll die with my sabenzis, with Micah, who I have loved all my life.

Maybe I'll be united with my mother at last, and all my ancestors?

I fall asleep, curled on the rock platform. When I wake up, my body is stiff and sore. The guard is snoring in his chair at the end of the corridor.

I don't know what's going to happen or how this is possible but...I can't die. I have a sacred task to perform.

"Where are you, Clementine," I whisper. "Why are you so far away?" I take the amulet out of my hair and rub it between my fingers. "Help me, I beg you."

There's nothing else to do, so I keep focused on the amulet, on Clementine, on the Goddess. Help me, help me, I repeat, again and again in my head.

Distant footsteps echo down the corridor. I hang the necklace around my neck as the guard wakes with a snort. His key turns in the lock and then the central door into the corridor clangs open.

"Good evening, Righteous," he says. "This one is a right little bitch. Pardon my language."

It's the High Priest. What does he want with me? I imagine a torture chamber, and his enjoyment as he watches me suffering. "Please, Goddess," I breathe. "Be with me now." I pull my knees up tighter and hug them. "Don't let him hurt me. Make it quick."

But it's Lucas talking. "How are you, Stan?" he says in his surprisingly melodious voice. "I've brought you a bottle of something to warm you up. I know what a depressing job it can be, keeping guard over traitors like this."

"Thank you, Righteous," Stan says. "You going to have one with me?" I hear liquid pouring in a cup.

"Not for me, thanks," Lucas says. "I'm here on official business."

"Ah," Stan says. "Final prayers and such."

"Exactly. You enjoy it. You've earned it. Share it with your friends—who's on duty tonight? Is it Kobus?"

"That's right, Righteous. Kobus and Jaco. Jaco's looking after the other four. Kobus has gone to relieve him—bathroom break. He'll be back soon."

Their footsteps approach. Stan unlocks the cell door. "Get up," he snarls. "The Righteous is here to hear your confession."

I've got nothing to lose anymore. No need to be nice. I stay seated and sneer at Lucas. "Here to gloat, are you? I'll tell you straight, you self-righteous shit bag, I'd rather die than marry anyone in your family."

The guard slaps my head. "Watch what you say."

Lucas holds up his hand. "That will do, Stan. I'll take it from here."

"Right, right," Stan says, backing out. He triple locks the cell door. "Call me when you're ready to leave, Righteous."

He goes back to the desk, and I'm alone with Lucas.

"So what do you want?" I ask, glaring at him.

He shrugs. "Nothing."

Nothing? What does he mean nothing?

I stare at him suspiciously. "Well, get out then."

"I thought I'd just sit with you for a while."

I point to the floor. "Fine. Sit then, if that's what you want."

He sits down, jack knifing his long legs under him. He puts his hands in his lap and sits. And sits. He just sits. He doesn't say anything. He doesn't even jiggle his leg or twist his hands together. He's completely calm.

I watch him for a bit. This must be a trick. But then his stillness begins to fill the room, and I begin to quieten down inside. I lean back against the wall and let my thoughts wander. I wonder how the four of them are bearing up. I can imagine Jasmine is enraged, storming around the cell, cursing and banging on the bars. Fez is probably trying to work out an escape plan. And Letti—warm, loving Letti, she's probably trying to make sure Fez is all right, and that everyone is as comfortable as possible. What about Micah? Is he thinking of me? Is he dreaming of what might have been, in an ideal world? If there were no Prosperites, no need for the Resistance? Where we could live together on Greenhaven, and run the farm and have our friends around us, filling the long table on festive occasions. I wanted a chance to really get to know him as an adult, and we've had so little real time alone together.

And in my heart I have to admit—although I resisted what Aunty Figgy was telling me—I wish I'd been able to find the three missing amulets. Imagine if I'd found them, and that the Goddess had come back to restore the Earth to what it once was. Flourishing, balanced, full of life and growth, not this dry, broken shell of a world that people destroyed through their greed.

I wish I'd explored every inch of the forest, stayed long

enough to see the arum lilies bloom by the river, climbed more trees, learned to swim in the pond. Made love to Micah. Felt our bodies mold into one. I wish I could live long enough to reach old age, to see Greenhaven flourishing again and have sons and daughters to extend the den Eeden legacy.

Without realizing it, I'm rubbing the amulet on the back of my left hand. It runs across my birthmark.

A shadow falls across the floor. Clementine is standing inside the cell by the door, holding a lamp. Her little boy runs over to Lucas.

"Hello, little fella," Lucas says.

I blink. Did Lucas just talk to the little boy? But nobody can see him except me. Not even Aunty Figgy.

The child climbs into Lucas's lap and curls up. He falls asleep almost instantly. Lucas sits for a while, quietly, looking at the little boy. His face has softened. He catches my eye and smiles.

"I'll be going now," he says. "You've got company."

Clementine picks up her child and Lucas stretches his long legs. I'm expecting him to call the guard, but he takes a set of keys out of his pocket and unlocks the door. Then he's gone, down the passage, and I hear him unlock the second door. The guard still snores. He's left the cell door open. But what use is that? I'll never find my way out of the maze of tunnels they've dug into the mountain.

Clementine sighs and sits next to me on the platform. Her little boy is fast asleep, breathing with his mouth open. His dark curls are tousled. She slowly uncurls his chubby fingers and pulls a piece of paper out of his hand.

It's a map.

Lucas has drawn me a map.

"Thank you," I whisper as Clementine hands me the lamp. I follow her through the unlocked gate and down the passage, trying to move as silently as she does. The guards are asleep, one with his head hanging on his chest, and Stan slumped over the table. Lucas must have drugged the wine—the bottle in front of them is empty.

Lucas.

I would never have thought it. He was on my side all along. Like me, he has also been playing a part in front of his family—like when Cassie wanted my necklace and he told her it was witchcraft. Did he know that Micah was part of the Resistance when he sent him to work on the farm? Ma Goodson used to say, "Still waters run deep," and it's true. I totally underestimated him.

The keys lie on the table, centimeters from Stan's head. Can I get them without waking him? Millimeter by millimeter, I stretch my hand out and pick them up, trying not to let them clink together. Stan stirs and I freeze, covering the lamp.

"What's 'at?" he mutters. "Wha's going on?" Then his shoulders drop and he begins to snore again. My heart thuds as I try the second gate. It's unlocked. I slip through. I lock it behind me, but which is the right key? They all look the same, but Clementine taps one. I put it in the lock and it turns, locking the guards inside the corridor. No one will find them until the next shift begins—hopefully hours from now—though I have no idea what time it is.

I tiptoe down the passage, stopping at every turn to check the map. Am I in the right place? I could get lost down here among the twisted passages that all look exactly the same.

Then just as I'm beginning to think I've gone hopelessly wrong, I hear Fez cough. I creep along the wall and peep around the corner. There they are—Micah, Jasmine, Fez, and Letti, locked in a cell halfway down a corridor. The guard's desk is right in front of it, and he's wide awake, playing with a pack of cards.

I reverse back up the passage and study the map. There's an exit route marked—if I go back a few meters and take the right hand fork, I'll eventually reach a door that seems to lead straight into the yard at the back of the Shrine offices. That part will be easy, but first I've got to find a way to get them out, right under the guard's nose.

"I wonder what Ebba's doing tonight." Letti's voice echoes down the passage.

Dear Letti, I think. She's so loyal.

"I bet she's trying to rescue us," Fez says. He sounds tired, and he coughs again.

"I wish we'd got out," Letti says wistfully. "I wanted to see the world, just once before I die. It sucks that we didn't even make it as far as the wagons."

"I wanted to see the sea," Fez says with a sigh.

"Ebba's house is by the sea," Jasmine tells them. "There's a huge wall, but just on the other side is the ocean. You can hear it at night. You should see her house. It's enormous. She's stinking rich." She pauses, and then she says it: "She's not one of us anymore."

I peep around the corner. Micah is lying on the sleeping platform, staring at the ceiling. Why isn't he defending me?

"I think they've brainwashed her," Jasmine continues. "We were always a team, the four of us. But once she got Greenhaven and started hanging around with the Citizens, we didn't matter anymore..."

Micah interrupts her. "Ebba is one of the bravest people I know," he says. "She's walking a tightrope between doing what's right and not pissing off the Council. So give her a break."

"It's not her fault she inherited a fortune," Letti says. "You always see things in black and white—but there has to be more to her decisions, things you can't see. I bet she's trying to rescue us right this minute."

Jasmine shuts up. I can't see her, but I don't think she's quiet because she agrees with Letti or Micah. Once she gets an idea in her head, nothing will budge it.

The guard finishes his game, stacks the card and then gets up. He's heavy set, with bulging muscles—he could break my neck just by twisting it. He lumbers to the end of the passage and back again. To and fro, to and fro. I try to measure how long he takes with each lap. Not enough time to dart in behind him and let them out.

I'm stuck. There's nothing I can do. They're so close, but I can't get to them. "Help me," I whisper. "Clementine, help me."

The child wakes up, rubbing his eyes. Clementine puts him on the floor and whispers in his ear. He runs off down the passage towards the guard's table. Reaching it, he looks back at his mother and laughs, then he sweeps the cards onto the floor. Clementine blows, and the cards flutter down the corridor.

"Damned wind," the guard grumbles. He bends down to pick them up. She blows again, they scatter further afield, and he lumbers after them, counting aloud as he picks them up.

Once his back is turned, I sprint down the passage and toss the keys through the bars. Jasmine catches them as they're about to clang on the ground.

I run back to the desk and grab the guard's chair. I'm back behind the corner by the time he gets the pack of cards together. He can't believe his eyes when he sees his chair gone. "Kobus," he grumbles. "Don't play stupid buggers. Bring it back."

He shuffles down the passage towards me, cursing. I count the steps, listening as he gets closer and closer. As he reaches the corner, I bring the chair down hard on his head. He yells and the second he lifts his head, I smash the back of the chair into his nose. Blood streams down his face but it doesn't hold him back. He grabs the chair and hurls it at me. I duck out of the way. As I bend to pick it up, he seizes me around the neck with his arm. I'm gasping for breath, kicking, trying to get him in the groin. He's squeezing tighter. My eyes are bulging and black spots shoot across them. "Kobus," he yells. "Kom gou."

Just as I'm about to pass out, Jasmine leaps onto this back and gouges his eyes. He drops me and I fold double, coughing my lungs out. Micah punches him under the chin so his jaws connect with a crack and he collapses, unconscious.

"Quick," Micah whispers, grabbing the guard's ankles. We drag him into the cell and Fez locks the door.

"You fantastic girl," Micah says. "I knew I could count on you."

But there's no time to linger. I greet Fez and Letti with a quick hug and then start checking the map again. What is the quickest way out?

"Look what he left on the table," Jasmine whispers, grabbing the gun. "Should we shoot him?"

"We have to go," I hiss. "Fez, bring the keys."

Please, Theia, please let there be no more guards in the prison tonight. Give us enough time to get away.

We sidle along the passages, pausing at every turn to check. At last, we reach the exit. Fez finds the right key, we unlock the door, and we're out.

It's the middle of the night. There's a lamp in the guard house, but the rest of the Shrine yard is in darkness. We keep to the shadows, creeping along the walls until we can see through the window of the guard house. There are two guards inside, both sound asleep. Good old Lucas, I think as I see the empty wine bottle on the floor next to them. He thought of everything.

We slip through the gate and it's over.

We're free.

I want to hug and kiss Letti and Fez again. I want to confront Jasmine about not believing in me. But Clementine is outside the gate frantically waving as she runs across the road and up the mountainside.

"This way," I whisper, grabbing Letti's hand.

"Where are you going?" Jasmine hisses. "We should be going to the Harbor."

"The road is the first place they'll look," I whisper.

Micah nods. "You're right. Let's go."

As silently as we can, we climb the mountain. The moon is full, throwing enough light to see the path. Enough light to be seen by.

Fez stops again and again to cough. The higher we get, the more he wheezes from the effort, and Letti keeps stumbling on rocks she can't see. She's going to injure herself. And with all the stopping so Fez can get his breath back, we're taking too long.

"Get on my back, Fez," I whisper, bending over. "Don't argue." He jumps up. Micah piggybacks Letti, and we keep climbing. All night we climb, stopping to rest when we're too tired to go any further.

As dawn breaks, the sky over the Mainland turns pink. It won't be long before the darkness fades

"We need to find somewhere to hide," Jasmine says. "They'll see us from the road."

But where? It's just rocks now, grey, impenetrable rock with sparse scraps of dry scrub, too small to hide behind.

It grows lighter. I glance at Micah, concentrating on where to place each foot, his face red with the effort of carrying Letti. It's getting steeper. Soon we may not be able to climb without ropes.

As I'm about to resign myself to certain discovery, Fez gives a yelp and drums me with his heels. "There's a cave."

We scramble the last fifty meters on hands and knees.

As the sun rises in a great golden ball over the Mainland, we reach the dark opening and crawl inside—just in time. In daylight, my white robe will stick out like a bull's eye against the grey mountain.

Micah checks the interior of the cave. "It's a good hideout," he says. "We're high enough to see if anyone's coming."

Every muscle in my body aches. I want to throw myself down and sleep for a week. The twins sink down against the wall and fall asleep almost instantly.

"You two sleep as well," Micah says to me and Jasmine. "I'll keep watch."

He settles down just inside the entrance where he can see out without being seen from below. Exhausted as I am, I need to connect with him again. I sit down next to him, and he puts his arm around me.

"Hey, babe," he says. "I knew you'd rescue us."

"I didn't do it alone. Lucas helped me—helped us," I say.

He doesn't look surprised. "Apparently Lucas used to hang around at Greenhaven sometimes when he was younger," he says. "That's what Aunty Figgy told me. I think we can trust him. He's not like the rest of his family."

I lean against him, too tired to talk, just happy to be next to him, watching the sky brighten over the purple-blue mountains of the Mainland. This world is so beautiful. Despite everything Prospiroh's followers have done with their greed for more wealth, more things, they haven't been able to destroy it completely. There is still hope. If only I can find the missing amulets, it could be restored completely. Up till now I haven't searched for them at all—I've been so tied up in the farm, and Micah and Hal, and then Jasmine arrived...but if we survive this, if we get back to Greenhaven, I'll start searching in earnest. This world is too beautiful to be destroyed.

Micah takes my hand in both of his. "No matter what happens," he says, "I want you to remember that I love you. I've loved you since we were little kids."

I look deep into his brown eyes, reading the love shining from them. "I love you too." And my heart rolls over with joy.

We might be caught today and executed. But this moment—watching the sunrise with Micah—this moment is perfect. Our friends are out of the bunker, we've escaped the dungeons, and he loves me. He really, really loves me.

I fall asleep next to him. A couple of hours later, Fez and Letti's excited voices wake me.

"So much color!" Letti exclaims. "The sky is so huge. "

Fez is pointing at the ocean. "You mean this was all once land?" he asks. "All the way to the Mainland? People lived there, in houses?"

"I was lucky," I say. "Greenhaven was just high enough to escape the rising water."

I'm dying of thirst. Talking about water isn't helping.

Jasmine is scrambling around at the back of the cave. "There's a little stream of water running down the rock face," she calls.

One by one, we put our faces up against the rock and let the water trickle into our mouths. No water has ever tasted sweeter.

Jasmine waits until I've finished drinking. "Ebba," she says, avoiding my eyes. "I'm sorry about the things I said. I know you risked everything to come and rescue us."

I'd like to just say, "It was my pleasure" and "Of course I forgive you," but I can't. It's not that simple.

I try to explain. "You think I'm selfish not to give the High Priest my necklace, but he wants more than that. There's a spiritual battle going on and…"

She looks at me sideways, to check if I'm serious.

"The land I inherited—my wealth—it's not mine. It belongs to my family. To the den Eedens. I can't just throw it all away. I've got to look after it. I've got a holy task—there's a prophecy about me, in Aunty Figgy's Book of the Goddess."

"You don't believe all of that Goddess stuff, do you?" she asks curiously. "Surely it's old wives' tales and superstition. It's like the High Priest. He doesn't actually believe in Prospiroh. None of them do. It's a scam to get inside our heads and manipulate us into doing what they want."

How can I explain about Clementine? About the Goddess? The amulet?

"I do believe it," I say, and even as I assert it, I realize that I'm speaking the truth. "There's a battle between Theia and Prospiroh for control of the Earth." I watch her carefully. She's never going to believe me. "I'm a descendant of Theia, and it's my duty to fight for her—to try and regain some of her power. My ancestors are helping me."

"Surely you don't believe..." She stops and looks at my face. "My word, you do actually believe it, don't you?"

Fez and Letti are listening with awe. "You're a descendant of a Goddess, Ebba?" Letti asks. "Are you serious?"

"How awesome is that?" Fez says. "That's why you look different. Is the mark on your hand part of it?"

"Yes. And my amulet necklace. It was made by all the most important gods. They gave it to Theia when she was born."

It sounds ludicrous. Even I have to admit that. And it's not like I've got proof, apart from Clementine and her child who nobody can see except me and—it seems—Lucas. How do I persuade them of something they can't see?

Then Micah is standing behind me, with his arm around my waist. "Your turn to be on watch, Jasmine," he says. "And Ebba's right. We are in a battle. Whether the High Priest believes in Prospiroh or not, or where Ebba's necklace comes from, is incidental. The High Priest is a corrupt dictator and we need to overthrow him and the General and let everyone back into the City."

It's one thing we all agree on.

It's afternoon and we're hungry and anxious, and wagons of guards are still leaving the Shrine searching for us. "We should get going," I say to Micah. "When they don't find us near the roads, they'll start searching up the mountain."

"We have to wait till dark," he says. "They'll see us as soon as we start moving."

So we sit and watch them scuttling down below. Will the sun never go down? Does the army never knock off work?

Late afternoon, they start moving up the mountain. There must be a couple hundred guards, with guns. They're spread out in a line, sweeping upwards, checking every rock and bush for signs of us. They're heading straight for the cave.

"Shit," Jasmine says. "We'd better run for it while we've got a head start. If we just keep moving upwards, maybe they won't catch us."

"They'll know where we're going," Micah says. "They'll be waiting at the Harbor. They'll surround Greenhaven too."

Fez's having a coughing fit. We'll never be fast enough if we're piggybacking Letti and Fez. They're holding us back. I think it, but I can't say it.

Letti sees my worried glance. "Leave us here," she says.

"Never," I exclaim. "We stick together."

"Then we'd better run." Jasmine is adamant. "Come on, let's get started."

Micah holds up his hand. "Wait. There's one more option. I can be a decoy—if I go out now, I can lead them away from the cave. They'll follow me. I'll get to the Harbor and send word to Chad—the maintenance guy who let us in. He can come and fetch you."

"But you'll get killed," I exclaim. "They'll shoot you."

"I've got a gun too, remember. And I know the mountain better than they do. And I've escaped before." He counts his advantages off on his fingers.

Jasmine slowly nods. "It's our best chance. I think you should do it."

"Maybe we should take a vote," Fez says. "Everyone in favor put up your hand."

Four hands go up. I'm the only one who thinks it's a terrible idea.

"That's decided then," Jasmine says.

Micah pulls me to the back of the cave. He takes my hand. Looks into my eyes. "I'll be back for you, I promise," he says.

I squeeze his hands, trying to think of something, anything, to say that will express the surge of feelings rising to my throat. "I'll wait for you," I say at last. "I'll never ever fall in love with anyone else."

And then he kisses me. Our love for each other, our whole future together—I feel it all in his kiss and the way his arms enfold me. It's bitter sweet and I can't let him go. I can't lose him.

But he pries my hands away from his waist and pulls away. "See you all on the other side," he says, tucking the gun into his waistband.

We watch him crawl across the mountainside until he's a good fifty meters from the cave. Then he stands up and begins to run up the mountainside, zigzagging away from us towards the nek. The guards shout and give chase.

My heart is in my throat as I watch him run. He's like

a buck being chased by a pride of lions.

Will I ever see him again?

When he disappears around a rocky outcrop, there's nothing left to do but wait.

"Who would have thought?" I say. "In all our conversations about the world above, we never imagined we'd be hiding out on the mountain, being hunted by hundreds of guards."

"At least we're together," Letti says. "It was awful in the Colony after you left. We thought you were dead, Ebba. And when they came for Jasmine, we thought she was being taken away to cull. I cried and cried."

"I'm really hungry," Fez says. "How long till someone rescues us do you think?"

Jasmine is closest to the cave mouth. She peers out. "There's someone coming."

"Is it Chad?" Fez asks, jumping up. "Thank goodness. Hope he brought food."

She pulls back into the cave. "It's a guard."

I sidle to the opening. "Can we get away?"

"No. He's too close. Oh shit. There's another one. And two more. They're heading straight for us."

My heart drops like a stone in a well. There's no other way out.

"You two run for it," Letti says. "At least let some of us get away."

"Never," Jasmine says. "We're sabenzis. We belong together."

"We need to get as far back as possible," I whisper, grabbing Letti's arm. "Come on, hide."

But there's nowhere to hide. We shrink against the back wall, waiting for the inevitable.

"We're such easy targets," Fez mutters. "I hope they just do it quickly."

I'm holding Letti's hand. She's shaking. Jasmine can't sit still. She's running her hands over the wall, kicking the stones.

"Be quiet, Jazzy," I hiss. "There's no point in drawing attention to ourselves."

"I refuse to give up," she snaps. "There has to be a way out of here. How did you get out of the cell?"

"My ancestor—and Lucas."

"Well, Lucas isn't here. Can your ancestor help now?"

"I thought you didn't believe in her."

"Well, we're really desperate. I'll believe in the tooth fairy if it finds us a way out."

I lift my hand to my neck, and rub my amulet against my birthmark.

"I know," Jasmine exclaims suddenly. "The water. It's getting in here somehow. It must be going somewhere."

"Listen," Letti whispers. "The guards."

They're right outside the cave. We can hear them talking. We huddle at the back while Jasmine keeps searching the rock face behind the stream.

"Someone's been here lately," we hear a man say. He's at the entrance, silhouetted against the light.

"Help me," Jasmine hisses. "See if we can break away some of the rock."

We've got nothing to lose. We bash on the wall, pushing, shoving. Nothing gives.

"Goddess help us," I beg.

"There they are!" the man shouts. "Got them!"

"Damn it!" Jasmine screams. She's so frustrated she stamps her foot. The rock under our feet wobbles.

"Come out," the guard commands. "Don't make me come and get you."

"Jump!" Jasmine yells. We leap into the air and thunder down on the floor. The rock moves, but it's not giving way.

The cave darkens. Guards block the entrance.

"Help us," I plead.

Then suddenly Clementine is with us. She leans her back against the rock and shoves.

"Jump," Jasmine shouts again.

We've got one last chance. Seconds. The guards are inside the cave. We gather our energy and thunder on the rock with all our weight.

"Got you," a guard yells, grabbing the back of Fez's tunic.

Something gives. The rock totters and falls, opening a sink hole.

"Go," yells Jasmine, grabbing Fez's arm and they jump.

"Go on, Letti," I shout.

She half jumps, half falls down the hole.

The guard grabs my shoulder. I wrench myself free, shove him backwards, and jump.

I'm falling as Letti screams below me. I land with a smack in a pool of freezing water. Jasmine grabs me as I surface. "Get away from the opening," she gasps. "Hurry."

My feet find the bottom of the pool. Thank the Goddess, the water is only up to my ribcage. We're in an underground river. We just have to follow it and...

A gun fires. Bullets bounce off the wall next to my head. The sound echoes round and round the rock chamber till it sounds like a thousand guns are firing at us.

"Come ON!" Jasmine hisses, pulling me into the dark tunnel.

"I'm scared," Letti whimpers when we've taken a few steps. She grips my hand. "I can't swim."

"It's the dry season," I whisper. "We'll be able to walk."

"To where?" Fez's voice is tight. "Where will it take us?"

"I've read about underground rivers," Fez says, with chattering teeth. "They don't stay underground for long —they come up to the surface."

"Do you think they'll come after us?" Letti whispers as

another volley of shots peppers the water.

"Not without ropes," Jasmine says. A bullet whizzes past her head and she grabs Letti's hand. "Come on. Keep moving."

None of us want to go into the darkness. But there's no other way. We couldn't climb back up to the cave, even if there weren't guards there with guns. Staying where we are in freezing water will mean certain death. The only way is forward. We may still die. But at least we tried.

"I'll go first," Jasmine says. "I'm the shortest."

No one argues. Letti goes behind her, one hand on her shoulder, followed by Fez. I grip his right shoulder and we begin to trudge down the tunnel in single file. It's slow going. And once the dim light from the shaft has faded, each step seems to take a lifetime.

"How long do you think the tunnel is?" Letti's voice sounds above the rushing water. "How many steps?"

"I bet you it will be five hundred," Jasmine says. "What do you think, Ebba?"

I think it will be thousands of steps, but Letti's voice is wavering, so I grab the first number that comes into my head. "Three hundred seventy-four."

"Six hundred eighty," says Fez.

"Okay," Jasmine says, "we'll have a competition. The person who comes closest to the number gets one of Aunty Figgy's malva puddings all for themselves. Agreed?"

"Agreed. Wait till you taste her pudding," I call to Letti. "It's sweet and sticky—with dates and honey in it, and pecan nuts, and you eat it with a big dollop of fresh cream. It's like something the gods would eat."

"You're on," Fez says, with a cough. "A whole pudding just for me."

"Fine," says Letti. "I bet 1,488."

Damn it. She's probably right. We start to count as we walk. We've got up to the two hundreds when the current gets stronger, tugging us forward.

"The water's higher," Jasmine says. "It's up to my shoulders."

"Keep going," Letti says behind her. "Just keep going. Keep counting."

"Have you noticed something?" Fez asks as we reach three hundred ten steps. "The water is louder."

I listen. The rushing sound is much louder. And the current is swirling around us.

I clutch the amulet with my left hand and talk silently to the Goddess. "Goddess. Theia. You made everything in the world. You made this watercourse, the water, the rocks. You can save us. Don't let Prospiroh win. Find us a way out, before we drown. And keep Micah safe."

A few steps on and Jasmine stops. "It's up to my chin."

"It sounds as though two streams are converging just ahead," Fez calls over the rush.

"That's it," Jasmine says. "We're screwed. We tried out best, but we've failed."

"We could try going back?" I suggest. But as I say it I know it's impossible.

"We'd need pulleys and ropes," Fez says.

My teeth are chattering and I jog in place to warm myself up. I'm so cold my brain is going foggy.

"There is a way," Letti says. "We can't go back. We can't stay here. We have to go forward. We should just lie on our backs and float."

I gulp. Seriously? When none of us can swim?

"There's at least a chance we'll survive that way," Jasmine says. "It's the only chance we have."

"Let's just lie back and pretend we're in our bunks, dreaming of how the world used to be, before the Calamity," Letti says.

"At least we all got out of the Colony," Jasmine's voice sounds thin against the roar of the current. "One day in the world above is worth a whole life time below."

I think of her and Leonid laughing together as they washed the dishes in the kitchen of Greenhaven. Of Micah. My love.

"One day," I say, "we'll have a whole beautiful new world. Everything will be green and fresh. The birds will sing. We'll live together on Greenhaven. We'll marry whoever we want and our children will play together, climbing the trees and swimming in the pond."

"We'll pull down the wall and let everyone onto the Island who wants to be here," Jasmine says. "Who knows, you might even find the amulets, and the Goddess might come back and heal the Earth."

"I'm going," Jasmine calls. Her voice grows fainter as she floats away. My heart is in my throat. For all our fighting recently, for all the ugly things we've said and done to each other, she's still entwined around my heart like a vine. The four of us belong together.

"See you on the other side," Letti says with a small laugh, then she's gone.

It's only Fez and me left. He turns and gives me a quick hug. "We've got a 50% chance of making it, I reckon. Bon Voyage."

There's no one left. Just me, alone in the dark. "Take me home," I whisper. "Take me home." The current pulls me away.

Chapter Seventeen

It's so dark. So cold.

How much longer?

Goddess, how much longer?

Downstream, Jasmine is still counting, as though we were still taking steps. "Six hundred and forty six, six hundred and forty seven, six hundred and…"

When will we reach the surface? What if we come out in the sea? Or in the Shrine?

How will the twins survive on Silvermine Island? It will be night when we reach the surface, if we ever reach it. Fez won't survive a night in wet clothes. No one in the City will help us. They'll take us straight back to the Shrine.

Think calm thoughts. Keep calm. It will all be all right.

The rush is getting louder. There's less air. I put my hand up—my fingers brush the roof.

"Hey?" Letti squeals. "Hey…" Her voice disappears.

"Letti?" I call. "Letti?"

I take a deep breath as my forehead scrapes the roof. Goddess. Help us.

It's the end. After all this. The end. The water pushes forward, faster and faster. My lungs are bursting.

Then suddenly the pressure releases. I open my eyes. I'm moving up, propelled by the force of the water. I shoot out into the open, and gulp for air. For a moment all I can do is breathe. Then Fez coughs. I stagger to my feet. Letti is hugging Jasmine.

We've all survived. I am weak with relief as I stagger through the waist high water to hug Fez.

The first stars are twinkling in the evening sky. We're in a clearing, surrounded by trees. A frog croaks in the reeds. There's a familiar sense of tranquillity, of mystery. Isi comes running through the trees, and jumps up, her front feet on the parapet, barking with joy.

My heart almost explodes with relief.

We're in the Holy Well.

We're home.

Aunty Figgy bursts into tears when we creep through the front door. We've had to wait in the forest for Shorty and Victor to go to bed and we're freezing. She grabs towels and builds up the fire in the kitchen stove. She finds us clean clothes and oohs and aahs over Letti and Fez. Her face lights up when Fez tells her he's hungry. "You need feeding up," she says, rubbing his scrawny arms.

I ask her if there's news of Micah, but she has heard nothing. "The army were here this morning searching for you. They've put guards at the gates to stop anyone leaving or entering."

"I'm sure he's fine," Jasmine says, patting my shoulder. "If anyone knows how to survive, it's Micah."

But no matter what they say, or how much they try to reassure me, I've got a bad feeling. What chance does one person have against a group of soldiers with rifles. And how long before the army decides to do another search of the house?

Aunty Figgy feeds us scrambled eggs on toast, and rooibos tea with honey. I smile as the twins taste it tentatively and then wolf it down, remembering how I felt when I first saw normal food. "So where's the famous malva pudding?" Fez asks when he's cleared his plate.

"Tomorrow, tomorrow." Aunty Figgy laughs.

We're warm and fed, and the twins are nodding off. I take them to the spare room and they collapse onto the bed and are asleep almost at once.

Jasmine sneaks down to call Leonid. "I knew you'd make it," he says, almost smiling at me. "When I heard you'd stabbed Hal's mother and knocked out the hair-dresser, I knew you'd be okay." He pats my shoulder roughly and I know that for the first time, I've earned his respect. Jasmine's too maybe.

"Seriously? You knocked a guy out?" she asks.

I'm tempted to say, "Yes, of course," and show her my muscles, but I say, "I didn't touch him. He fainted when he saw the blood."

"Still," she says, "you fought the High Priest's wife. I underestimated you." She gives me a quick hug. "Sorry. I should have believed in you more."

Jasmine always says what she means, and she hates backing down, so I know her apology is genuine.

We'll never see eye to eye on some issues—she sees things as either right or wrong, either black or white, while I get caught up in the shades of grey. But that doesn't mean we can't be friends, and that we can't get over our disagreements. "That's OK," I murmur as I hug her back.

"We've got to make a plan," Leonid says, leaning against the table. "We have to ensure everyone is safe."

"Where will you go?" Aunty Figgy asks. "You all are fugitives."

"We can't stay here?" I'd been so relieved to be safe at home, leaving again hadn't crossed my mind.

"Not even you, Ebba. You attacked the High Priest's wife."

"I didn't mean to stab her. It was an accident."

"They need your produce," Leonid says. "As long as you stay on the farm and deliver your taxes, there's a good chance he'll leave you alone."

Aunty Figgy nods. "You're right. He needs Ebba to find the missing amulets."

"Whatever. So Ebba should stay. But the rest of you..." His eyes fall on Jasmine and his face softens. "It's not safe for you here. We'll have to get you to Silvermine Island somehow."

It's only been a month since she arrived, but it was love at first sight for them. If she went to Silvermine, wouldn't he want to go with her? How could I run the farm without him? He's indispensable.

But thank the Goddess, she says, "I'm staying. I'll put on my ordinary clothes. They won't recognize me."

"But your hair?" Leonid says. "You cut it all off."

"Wait," I say. I run to the cupboard with the hats and find the wig Pamza was playing with when they came for lunch. "Here," I say, putting it on her head and tucking the curls behind her ears. "If they come searching the farm they'll never realize you were the 'boy' who escaped from the cells. Just don't let Shorty see you without the wig."

"That leaves the twins," Aunty Figgy says. "We won't be able to get them out yet. The guards will be searching every buggy entering the Harbor and every boat leaving too. They'll be on high alert. We've got to find somewhere to hide them."

"Somewhere Shorty won't find them," Jasmine says, bitterly.

"I know. Come with me," Aunty Figgy says, getting up from the table. She takes us into the study and points to the ceiling-high mahogany bookcase. "Push this to the right," she orders.

We put our shoulders to the cupboard and shove as hard as we can. Just as it feels like my head is going to burst, the cupboard shifts an inch, and then it slides away from the wall, revealing a trap door in the floor.

Jasmine is already in the gap, and she grips the iron

ring recessed into the door and tugs. It lifts up, revealing a musty, pitch black hole.

"What's down there?" I ask. It looks far worse, more frightening, than the watercourse. Who knows what spiders and snakes might be lurking there.

"It's the bunker," Aunty Figgy says. "It's where we went during the Calamity."

Aunty Figgy hands us two oil lamps, and Jasmine climbs down the ladder into the darkness. Leonid and I follow.

The bunker must have been part of the cellar once. It smells like soil, and the air is cold. Aunty Figgy passes down brooms and dustpan brushes.

"Sweep up the worst of the dust," she calls.

The floor is made of Earth, so I can't see what point sweeping it is, but I attack the spider webs that hang from the ceiling beams. There's a living area, with a small kitchen to one side. The second room is a bedroom, with eight beds in a row. We focus on this room, brushing the dust off the mattresses. Jasmine goes back up the ladder, and fetches bed linen. We get to work making up two beds.

There are packets of candles in the storeroom, and I place a candle into each of the sconces that are set into the walls.

We go through the third door into a bathroom. Here huge rain barrels loom in the semi-darkness. There's a pair of basins, and behind a door, I see a toilet.

"It's weird down here," Jasmine says as we clean the bathroom. "It's like being back in the Colony."

"I can't believe we spent sixteen years living like this, never breathing fresh air." I wring out my grimy cloth in the soapy water Leonid has brought down from the kitchen. "I couldn't bear to go back, even for an hour."

"Here, come and fetch these," Aunty Figgy calls from

the trapdoor. "They may have to stay down there for a while."

I take the warm clothing and basket of food she passes down the ladder. There's hot tea in a flask, and a tin of rusks, sandwiches, and the last of the peaches from the orchard. They won't go hungry, that's for sure.

Finally we're done, Aunty Figgy wakes Fez and Letti and they climb down into the bunker. Although they don't say anything, I can see how disappointed they are to be back underground.

"It won't be for long," I promise them. "You've just got to stay here until the High Priest stops searching. He'll never find you here, not ever."

I feel awful about leaving them there, but we have to. We close the trap door and push the bookcase back into place.

I'm exhausted.

Nothing—nothing—has ever felt as good as my soft bed.

Chapter Eighteen

The next morning, Shorty greets me with a huge smile. "Praise Prospiroh you're home, Miss Ebba," he says. "We were so worried about you, weren't we, Victor? We've been so unwell, but I was just saying to Aunty Figgy last night that if you weren't home today, I was going to go to Mr. Frye and beg him to speak to the High Priest. We heard all about the wedding, and I must say, I don't approve. I mean, you're just a young girl. What are you, fourteen, fifteen? You can't be expected to make grown up decisions, and surely you're too young to get married. Not that Mr. Haldus isn't a charming young man, but you're just too young, isn't she, Aunty Figgy? I mean, what's the rush? You can wait a year or two surely?"

I want to hit him.

"Where's Micah this morning?" he continues, buttering his toast. "Is he all right? I thought I was going to die, I got so nauseous. I hope he's feeling better."

"Micah's still unwell," Aunty Figgy says calmly. "I'm going to take some mint tea and dry toast to him." She points to the tray ready laid on the counter. I realize she's been pretending to feed and nurse him for days to put Shorty off the scent.

Victor as usual says nothing, just smiles and eats so quietly, we hardly know he's there.

I need a break from Shorty's incessant chattering so I tell him to go with Victor and Leonid to clear weeds in the new field. He looks surprised. "But I've got to do the books, miss," he says.

"Shorty, just do as I say," I snap, and his big eyes open wide with surprise.

"Yes, yes, at once, miss." He jumps up, toast in hand, and hurries out the door.

I'm worried sick about Micah. Did he escape? Or is he lying dead on the mountainside? Perhaps they shot him and left him there, and he's too badly injured to reach help.

Jasmine sees me picking at my cuticles. "You're making yourself sick with worry," she says. "You need really hard work to make you sweat and get your mind off him. Come and work in the kitchen garden. You can turn over the compost heap."

I get a pitchfork and jab it into the compost heap, imagining that it's the High Priest I'm stabbing. Jasmine works on the seedlings in the greenhouse. She comes out to check on me every now and then and I'm grateful. This is the old Jazzy who has my back.

At around eleven o'clock, we hear horses on the driveway. Jasmine runs to check who it is. But I already know. It's got to be Captain Atherton.

I keep digging, though my stomach is knotting. Then Aunty Figgy opens the kitchen door and calls, "Ebba, Ebba."

But it's not Captain Atherton. Major Zungu is storming down the pathway, followed by Mr. Frye, all red faced and flustered as he tries to keep up.

"How can I help you, Major?" I say coldly, ramming the pitchfork into the ground and resting my elbow on it.

"You're under arrest," he snaps, grabbing my arm.

I try and pull away but his grip is like a handcuff.

"Please, Ebba," Mr. Frye says, flapping his arms like a frantic chicken. "Just do as he says. It will be better in the long run."

They propel me to the carriage and force me inside. Mr. Frye sits between me and the door. Major Zungu takes the seat opposite where he can watch every move I make.

The driver whips up the horses and we set off at a smart gallop. Isi runs after the carriage, barking wildly. The coachman flicks her with his whip. "Don't you dare touch my dog again," I yell, banging on the window.

We reach the gates of Greenhaven. As we turn into the road, Major Zungu reaches forward and grips my amulet. "What's so special about this?" he says, leering at me.

"Nothing," I say, grabbing the chain. "It's just an old necklace from my mom."

He pulls harder. "The High Priest might decide to forget about your indiscretion if you presented this to him," he says.

"Leave it. It's mine."

He tugs again. The clasp breaks and the amulet comes loose. He shoves it into his pocket. "Where are your friends?" he snarls, jabbing his finger into my chest.

"My friends?" The empty chain feels hot under my fingers.

"The prisoners. Where are they?"

"I haven't seen anyone," I snap. "I don't know what you're talking about. Give me back my amulet."

"If you tell us what we need to know."

A flood of rage washes through me. I leap on him, scratching his eyes. "The Goddess is with me," I yell. "Give me my amulet."

He punches me in my stomach, but I'm exploding with anger. I smash the heel of my hand into his nose.

"The Goddess is with me," I scream again. I grab his robe, reaching for the pocket. "Give it back!"

He throws me against the window. The glass breaks and a shard slices my scalp. The horses whinny, tossing their heads.

"Control the bloody horses," Mr. Frye yells to the coachman.

I attack again. I want to rip out his windpipe, but he blocks me, so I sink my teeth into his bicep.

"You little bitch," he yells. He grabs my arm and twists it behind my back. "Where are they?" he yells. "Where are your friends?"

"Don't harm her," Mr. Frye screeches. "Don't harm her."

The horses break into a full gallop. The carriage rocks as they career down the road. The Major jerks my arm upwards, pulling it out of the socket. I'm forced forward into a bend. Blood drips onto the floor from my head wound.

I stamp my foot on his sandal. "Give me my amulet."

"Bitch!" he yells, slapping me across the head.

We hit a pothole with a jolt that knocks me backwards, almost breaking my arm. The carriage rocks and he loosens his grip. I'm propelled against the door. It bursts open, sending me flying.

I hit the road, grazing the skin off my arms and legs. The impact rolls me onto my sore shoulder, then over again, into a ditch.

"Stop! Stop!" Mr. Frye screams. "Don't hurt her."

"Stop the coach," Zungu shouts.

The amulet. I have to get it.

The coachman stands up, yelling as he tries to control the horses. They hit another pothole and the carriage jolts to the left, runs on two wheels, and then rights itself before rocking towards the other side. The coachman loses his footing and goes flying. The horses snort with fear, their necks arched, their tails flying behind them. They misjudge the bend in the road. The carriage is on two wheels again. It's going over. It lands upside down in the ditch, the horses struggling on top of it.

A horse is screaming. Major Zungu is crawling out of

the window. He sees me and gets to his feet. I turn and run for the wall.

I've got to get back onto Greenhaven land. Can I get over? My injured shoulder can't take my weight. I jump as high as I can and grip the top, hanging on, gasping from pain. The Major is right behind me. "Get away," I snarl, kicking out at him. I hear his jaw crack and he yells. I take the gap, dragging myself up. I teeter for an instant and topple over.

I land with a thud on the Greenhaven side. Staggering up, I start to run, every step jolting my shoulder. Blood trickles into my eyes. I wipe it away and keep going, through the furrowed new lands, through the gate, into the orchard. My breath is jagged but I'm bolting like the horses.

When Leonid reaches me, I'm ready to collapse. He throws me over his shoulder and carries me home.

Chapter Nineteen

Aunty Figgy is beside herself when she sees I've been injured. I try not to scream as she and Leonid push my shoulder into position and tie it in a sling. Then she sends Leonid and Jasmine to see if they can find the amulet in the wreckage of the carriage.

"Her blood has been spilled," she mutters as she pours warm water into a bowl and helps me to lift my torn robe over my head. "The amulets are all lost," she mutters. "Goddess, protect this child." I try not to flinch as she cleans each cut and scrape, and applies a stinging red lotion to each wound.

When she's finished, she fetches a clean robe and helps me into it. Then she carefully arranges four candles in a circle in front of the statue of the Goddess and lights them, crooning a prayer over each one, her hands clasped in front of her. She unties a bundle of silver kooigoed from the herbs drying on the roof beam, lights one end in the stove, and waves the fragrant smoke around me, praying under her breath as it twists and turns, surrounding me in a swirling fog. I have never seen her so distressed or praying so hard. "Protect her, protect her," she repeats again and again, until the sprigs of herb have turned to ash, and the room is thick with the smell of African sage.

She pours five drops of liquid into a glass of water, turning it a blackish green. "Drink this," she says. "It will help with the pain and send you to sleep. Let me help you to bed."

It feels so good to be resting against the pillows. She is burning more herbs, cleansing every corner of my bedroom when there's a knock on the door.

Isi growls.

Victor puts his head around the door. "Miss Ebba, I heard you were in an accident," he says. "I hope everything is all right?"

I'm about to answer him when there's a noise from beneath the floor. It's Fez coughing.

"What was that?" Victor says, stepping right into the room, and looking around. "Did you hear that?"

"It's just Leonid," Aunty Figgy says coldly. "He's weeding outside the window. He's caught a cold. You should not be in Miss Ebba's bedroom."

"Sorry, sorry," he mutters. But as he's leaving, Fez coughs again. "Miss, there's someone under the house," he says. "Do you want me to check? It could be someone coming to attack you."

My head is throbbing so badly I can't think. "I didn't hear anything," I mutter.

"It's no trouble, miss," he says. "Let me go into the cellars and see if there's someone hiding there."

"If Ebba was in danger, Isi would be barking," Aunty Figgy snaps. "Now go and do your work, and don't poke around outside her window. She needs to rest."

"Yes, miss, sorry, miss." He's almost groveling as he backs out the door. Isi watches him on high alert. Why has she taken this sudden dislike to him?

Aunty Figgy follows him down the passage. She's back a short while later. "He's gone at last, nosy parker. He's busy in the pigeon coop."

"The pigeon coop?" I ask. "He's supposed to be working up by the dam."

The truth hits me like a punch in the stomach.

"He's the spy," I gasp. "He's been sending messages to

the High Priest with the homing pigeons. " We've been such idiots, focusing on Shorty, thinking Victor was too colorless and insignificant to matter.

Aunty Figgy's jaw clenches. "I'll sort him out," she says, narrowing her eyes. "Stinking little runt." She marches off, footsteps pounding the floor.

I'm lying there, imagining Major Zungu coming back with a battalion of soldiers, breaking open the floor and dragging out Letti and Fez. We must get them to safety, but where can we hide them? Where is the one place they won't look? If only Micah was here. He'd know what to do.

Leonid and Jasmine come bursting through the front door then, out of breath. "Couldn't find the amulet," Leonid pants. "Searched everywhere."

"The coachman's dead," Jasmine says, "and one of the horses."

"Did you see Major Zungu?" I ask.

"He's gone," she says. "He and Mr. Frye both. They must have taken the other horse."

"They'll be going to the Shrine to tell the High Priest." I struggle to get up. "We have to hide the twins."

But Jasmine pushes me gently back onto the pillow. "You're injured. You need to rest. We can sort this out."

Aunty Figgy's medicine is starting to make me drowsy, and it's a relief to close my eyes and let the pain drift away.

It's late afternoon when Isi nudges me awake. My head aches, and my shoulder is throbbing. Isi nudges me again, and I push her away and groan as I roll over. I don't want to leave my soft bed—every inch of my body feels bruised and raw. She won't leave me alone, shoving herself against me and giving short, shrill barks until I'm forced to give in, and get up. I open the door for her and she runs out onto the stoep, barking at the sky.

The heat's more oppressive than usual. It feels as

though something is pushing down on me, on all of Greenhaven, and I can't get enough air in my lungs. Strange clouds hover above the forest. Isi runs back inside, nudging me away from the door, onto the stoep, and down the stairs onto the grass.

It feels like all the forces of the universe are gathering above Greenhaven, ready to explode into war. The horses whinny as they canter around the meadow, pawing at the grass and flicking their manes.

Isi runs along the edge of the forest, barking. She looks back at me, then at the path that leads to the Holy Well, then back to me. Hurry up, she seems to be saying. Come with me.

Every step makes my grazes burn, but I reach her at last, and she half jumps against me, licking my hand. Her muzzle presses into my hand again, pushing me down the path. I give in and do what she wants.

It's cooler in here, but the air is so still it feels solid. At last I reach the pond and sink down onto the wall, waiting for the serenity that usually hangs over this small clearing to calm my pounding heart.

"Please, Goddess, bring back my amulet," I pray. "Keep Micah safe." But there is no serenity here today. The usually clear water is muddy and churning. Frogs jump from the reeds, and the bees hover over the water, their buzzing so loud it sounds like people humming. A small buck comes running past, wild-eyed. It doesn't even notice me or Isi just meters away from it. The darkening sky is covered with a dense pattern of rippled clouds. I try and focus on the Goddess, on praying for safety, but she feels very far away. Isi must sense it, as she presses herself against me, not leaving me alone for an instant.

Suddenly she tenses and gives a low growl. The High Priest is walking through the trees, heading straight for me. My stomach clenches. I'm alone here. Too far to run to

the house, too far for Leonid or Aunty Figgy to hear me if
I shout. I'm injured, and without the amulet, the Goddess
can't protect me.

But he will not see I'm scared. Not after what he's done
to me. "Stay away," I shout. "This is Holy Ground."

"Ebba, Ebba, Ebba," he chuckles. "Don't be so dramatic."
He's tossing something from hand to hand.

What is it?

What is it?

No. No. It can't be.

It is.

It's my amulet.

He comes closer. Something weird is happening to the
water. It's not bubbling up into the well, it's draining out.
The bees have moved into a spiral formation, swirling and
rising then swooping down and rising again.

Isi's ridge of white fur stands up and she bares her
teeth in a snarl.

"Sit down, my girl," the High Priest commands, pointing to the wall. "Control your dog."

He's staring at me with his hooded eyes and much as
I want to, I can't look away, can't disobey him. I grab Isi's
collar but she slips out of it and runs off into the forest.

I twist the empty collar through my hands. Now I've
got nothing to protect me. No amulet, no Micah, no Isi.
And he's still focused on me, not blinking, not moving,
just sending waves of toxic energy that wrap around me
so I cannot disobey. I drop the collar and sit down, my eyes
still trained on his.

He leans towards me, so close I can see each indi-
vidual eyelash, the reflections in his irises. "Where is the
entrance to the bunker? Show me where you have hidden
my prisoners."

I can't look away, can't break the stare. I feel my limbs
moving, starting to get up, to take him to the house, show

THE FIERY SPIRAL TRILOGY

him the trapdoor under the bookcase.

The bees swoop across the water and begin to swirl around his head. He swats at them and at last, at last, his stare breaks. I look away, blinking, trying to shake him out of my head, to clear his energy from my mind. What was I doing? Did he hypnotize me?

"Help me, Theia," I pray. "Help me."

He takes a step towards me, pulling himself to his full height. The clouds rumble while flashes of yellow and blue light shoot across the sky. "Where are you hiding your friends?" he thunders.

"I don't know what you're talking about." My voice sounds very small. I press myself against the edge of the wall. Where is Isi? Her collar is in my hand, but she's gone. How can she have run off when I need her most?

"So you're not going to tell me? I have your boyfriend, you know."

Oh please, not Micah. "No, you haven't," I say. My mouth is dry with fear, and although I try to sound brave and defiant, my voice trembles.

"Indeed, I have. We caught him high up on the mountain. He's been talking—telling us all sorts of interesting things about you..." He leans towards me, his black eyes glinting as he stares into mine. "Major Zungu had to employ a few special tactics to persuade him, of course, but then he prattled like a girl. Like a snivelling, weepy girl."

He's lying. Micah wouldn't tell the High Priest anything. He would never put us in danger. He's just saying it to trick me into betraying my sabenzis.

At least, I think he's lying. What if they really have him? Did they torture him? Did Major Zungu recognize him as the boy he threw out of the ventilation shaft so long ago? I try to read the High Priest's face, but his pupils have locked onto mine and I can't look away. I can't grasp the thoughts that are flying out of my head, being replaced by ideas that feel so definite that they must be right.

He's an honorable man. He's an outstanding leader. He built the bunker in the mountain to keep us safe from the day of Purification. He is a hero....I must do what he says. Trust him. Tell him...

"You can have him back by suppertime, just tell me where to find your friends."

Who do I choose?

Micah, whom I love with all my heart? Or Fez and Letti, my best friends, my sabenzis?

"Why do you care so much about the twins?" I ask, trying to steady my voice.

"I don't," he sneers. "But I care that you think you can defy me. I know the stories in the Book of the Goddess. You think you're special. That you're going to save the world. And I'm going to show you that you're not more powerful than me. You aren't now, and you never will be."

He grabs my sore shoulder. "I haven't got all day," he snarls. "Tell me where they are or I'll haul you into the Shrine and have you executed."

The buzzing becomes frenzied as the bees circle above our heads like a cloud. They fly across my face, breaking up our eye contact.

"You need me alive. You know you do. You can't get the amulets without me."

His face darkens. "You stupid stupid girl," he says, shoving me backwards. I lose my balance and topple back into the well. I sprawl in the mud, groaning as pain shoots through me.

"Hurry up and make up your mind," he bellows. "Where are the twins?"

A lightning strike of anger surges across my head. My left hand has landed in the last puddle of water. My birthmark is burning as I scramble to my knees. "I'll never tell you!" I scream, and I bring my hand down hard on the wall.

Instant silence.

The bees stop buzzing and hang in mid-air. The water stops gurgling.

No rustling leaves or birdsong.

Nothing.

It starts softly, so softly I'm not sure it's real. But it is. The wall is shaking, rocks come loose as the rumble grows into a roar that shakes the ground and splits the wall in two. My head spins—or is it the ground that's moving?

I flinch as the Earth gashes open like a cleaver cutting through meat. The forest floor splits in jagged cracks and trees crash down, snapping like twigs.

The High Priest doesn't move.

"Who will it be, Ebba?" he booms. "Your sabenzis or Micah?"

Something flashes between the trees. Isi. He hasn't seen her running headlong at him.

She leaps at him and sinks her teeth into his wrist. He curses and tries to push her away. Her jaws are clenched and she shakes his arm until the amulet drops into the well.

This is my chance. It's to my left—somewhere in the mud near the yellow water lilies.

Gunfire! Was that gunshots?

Captain Zungu must be back. He'll shoot Isi.

"Isi! Leave him!" I yell, scrambling for the amulet. My feet slide in the sludge and I fall sideways onto my bandaged shoulder.

The High Priest leaps into the well. He's going straight for the amulet.

The big milkwood is splitting with a noise like gun shots. The bees swarm enraged above the High Priest and then descend in a black stinging mass onto his head.

Thunder crashes overhead as his screams rip the air.

Just three more steps. It's right there. Is that it glinting in the mud? But Isi has grabbed my robe and is pulling me back. "Leave me," I yell. "Leave me. I have to get it."

She tugs harder, dragging me backwards. With one last crack the milkwood falls forward, heading straight for me.

I throw myself into the reeds, but it's too late.

Darkness closes in.

The Rising Tide, Book 2,
The Fiery Spiral Trilogy
(Coming in 2020)

Time is running out for Ebba and all four amulets are missing. The General is now in control of the city and he is planning a genocide. Can she use her position as a member of the Council to stop him? Micah is heading the resistance with the gorgeous Samantha Lee. With nothing left to lose but his love, Ebba agrees to one final sacrifice.

The Fiery Spiral, Book 3,
The Fiery Spiral Trilogy
(Coming in 2021)

Ebba is in Celestia, the land of the gods, and the only way to return to earth is to journey across a barren, lifeless landscape until she reaches the Fiery Spiral. But the road is fraught with difficulties and danger. She must learn the meaning of love and courage before she can fulfill her true destiny. It seems like Lucas has to share her journey. But to save everyone she loves, she might have to give up her life—and her heart.

ABOUT THE AUTHOR

Helen Brain was born in Australia in 1960 and raised in Durban, South Africa. After school, she studied music at the University of Cape Town.

Before settling to a life writing and teaching writing online, she was a freelance journalist and editor, a screenprinter and crafter, and taught English, music and Ancient Greek.

Helen Brain lives in Muizenberg, a suburb of Cape Town, South Africa. She lives with her husband Ted and dogs. She has three sons and a grandson.

CPSIA information can be obtained
at www.ICGtesting.com
Printed in the USA
LVHW042033291019
635706LV00001B/1/P